Praise fo

"An engaging story that will leave mystery buffs satisfied and eagerly awaiting the author's next ski mystery."
—Reader's Favorite

"Filled with amorous relationships, political posturing, jealousy, ambition and, well, evil. It is a story that we know and love."
—Simply Saratoga Magazine

Praise for other Murder on Skis Mysteries

Loving Lucy

"A must read, hang on to your chairlift!"
—The Grateful Traveler

"Bayly draws on his experiences covering real crimes. A chilling mystery."
—Vail Daily

Murder on Skis

"Bayly's book is a real page turner, with more twists and turns than a slalom course."
—The Saratogian

"It's not just about skiing. More than you think."
—RCXcellent Adventures

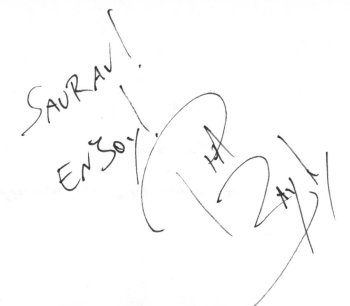

Back Dirt

A *Murder on Skis* Mystery

Also by Phil Bayly:

Murder on Skis

Loving Lucy: A Murder on Skis Mystery

Back Dirt

A *Murder on Skis* Mystery

Phil Bayly

SHIRES ❦ PRESS

4869 Main Street
Manchester Center, VT 05255
www.northshire.com

Back Dirt

A *Murder on Skis* Mystery

©2021 by **Phil Bayly**

WWW.MURDERONSKIS.COM

ISBN: 978-1-60571-599-5

Cover Design: Debbi Wraga & Carolyn Bayly
Igor Korets and Zhovba / Dreamstime.com
Author Photo: Carolyn Bayly

Building Community, One Book at a Time
*A family-owned, independent bookstore in
Manchester Ctr., VT since 1976 and Saratoga Springs, NY since 2013.
We are committed to excellence in bookselling.
The Northshire Bookstore's mission is to serve as a resource for
information, ideas, and entertainment while honoring the needs
of customers, staff, and community.*

Printed in the United States of America

To Carolyn, always my first and most valuable reviewer. And to Jimmy Carrow. We were only children when he told me that I was a good storyteller.

"Let me get the things I'm getting real easy. Then I'll go back to the things I'm not getting."

—Willie Nelson

1

He was neither sinking nor swimming. He wasn't floating on top of the water, but he also wasn't dragging along the rocks on the bed of the brook.

Rather, the body was suspended somewhere between the surface and the bottom, patiently being pushed downstream by the water's current.

Facedown, arms at his side, he was wearing a jacket with blue jeans and heavy boots. There was no struggling going on. There was no grabbing a lifeline as he passed.

He looked at ease in his element. Only, he wasn't breathing.

The body eventually would have caught on some brush or a fallen limb at a bend in the brook. But before that could happen, a man on his afternoon walk spotted the body as the current brought it closer to the old stone bridge.

The man walked to the parapet of the bridge for a closer look. Then he dialed 9-1-1.

"You've got somebody in LaChute Brook," he said, "and he doesn't look good."

By the time Joseph County Deputy Peter Colden arrived, the body had floated under the bridge and was slowly making its way out of view.

Deputy Tim Pattern was next on the scene. He exited his patrol car and joined Colden on the bank of the brook.

"Hang on to me," Deputy Colden said. "I'll try to get him."

Pattern grabbed Colden's belt and uniform trousers as the older deputy dropped to his knees in the snow along the stream bank and   reached out.

"Got him," Deputy Colden gasped triumphantly, grabbing the man's coat collar. But Colden's other hand, supporting his weight, slipped in the snow and nearly propelled him into the frigid water.

"Crap! I can't hold him," the deputy exclaimed. He released the corpse, and it resumed a gentle trajectory downstream.

"Oh God, no," Deputy Pattern mumbled to himself. He pulled his partner back to the safety of firmer ground. Pattern now knew his own destiny, even if he didn't desire it.

He dropped to the seat of his pants on the snow, inches from the water, and leaned forward. As his weight shifted, the deputy's legs slid into the bitterly cold liquid.

"No, no, no," he whimpered. He used one bare hand to steady himself against the bank and stood nearly crotch-deep in the brumal waters of LaChute Brook.

"Golly, golly, golly," Pattern sputtered as his eyes shut and his mouth became the shape of a little circle. "Golly" wasn't the word that first occurred to him, but cars were pulling over to the side of the road. Citizens of the town of Joseph were now lining the stone bridge to watch the law officers' recovery effort.

The crowd was within listening distance, and the deputy knew that Sheriff Williams wouldn't want obscenities heard coming from the lips of someone wearing one of his uniforms.

Deputy Pattern found that his submerged legs would support him, so he opened his eyes and spotted his target. With one hand still clutching the bank, he reached out his other hand and grabbed a pant leg belonging to the floating corpse. A small cheer erupted from the crowd as the body's momentum was harnessed by the law officer.

"What now?" Deputy Pattern looked up and asked Deputy Colden.

"We should wait for the coroner before moving the body," Deputy Colden said safely from shore. That meant Deputy Pattern was to remain in the water holding the victim.

Pattern winced at his partner, "You think so?"

"You know proper procedure," Deputy Colden responded. A smile appeared on his face. At some point, his friend's pain had become Colden's pleasure. "It won't be long. I'm cold, too. It's probably warmer in the water where you are. Brrr."

Rather than returning the smile, Tim Pattern aimed a disagreeable grimace at the dry deputy on shore.

"I'm starting to slip into hypothermia," Deputy Pattern said. He used a low voice, so the nearby crowd couldn't hear

3

him. "And the voice in my hallucination is suggesting ways I can inflict slow and lasting death on you."

Deputy Colden gave this some thought. He crouched down in the three or four inches of snow near the bank. "Gimme here," he said as he reached for the body.

Deputy Pattern lifted both of the corpse's wet legs out of the water. They were heavy and he barely got them onto the shore. Colden grabbed the legs and, with Pattern lifting the water-soaked upper torso, they dragged him onto land. The dead man remained facedown.

"Come on, then," the dry deputy said to the wet deputy as he extended his hand.

Deputy Colden was built like a short powerlifter. He pulled his soaking partner out of the water and watched as Pattern's legs collapsed, leaving him on his knees, taking a fetal tuck. The top of his head rested on the snow.

"You don't look well," Colden said with a hint of a giggle as he stood over his younger partner. Pattern slowly turned his stiff neck so he could make eye contact with the dry shoes of the dry uniform standing next to his head. Tim Pattern had murder in his eyes.

Deputy Peter Colden crouched down closer to Pattern's face. With a look of amusement and one hand on his knee, Colden held out his patrol car keys with the other hand. "Here, go warm up. I'll stay here with him."

Colden had to help the deputy to stand. Pattern took a moment to extend his legs and convince them to accept the weight of his 190 pounds. He walked to the patrol car, legs stiff like he was walking on stilts.

Deputy Colden turned to look over the crowd on the bridge. One of them, he thought, probably made the initial 9-

1-1 call. The law officer could not leave the body, but he'd need to figure out who that caller was and interview him.

Colden was distracted by the sound of car tires crushing snow beneath their rubber. He turned and saw Sheriff Smudge Williams' car pulling up.

The patrol cars in Joseph County were silver with red, white and blue letters printed on the side spelling "Sheriff." On the rear fenders, there was the county emblem, including the image of a First Native intended to be Mohawk Chief Joseph Brant. The Indigenous leader was presumed to be Joseph County's namesake, though no one was sure about the accuracy of that presumption.

Sheriff Smudge Williams was something of a local celebrity in the small county. As he extricated himself from behind the steering wheel of the patrol car and stood next to the open door, a few onlookers shouted, "Hi, Sheriff," from the stone bridge. He ignored them.

He surveyed the scene and saw Deputy Peter Colden standing next to a body on the bank of LaChute Brook. He looked for Deputy Pattern and saw him curled up in the passenger seat of the patrol car. The engine was running.

"What's with him?" Smudge asked as he jabbed his thumb in Pattern's direction and approached his senior deputy.

"He dove into the brook to retrieve the body. It was getting away from us," Colden informed his boss.

"Leave him be, then," Smudge responded. "Do we know who this is?"

"We didn't turn him over," the deputy answered as they stood over the remains.

"Do we know how he got in the water?" the sheriff asked.

"We'll probably have to wait until they get him to the wax museum," Colden said.

The sheriff raised his head so he could peer from beneath his baseball cap with the word "Sheriff" in big block letters. He looked Deputy Colden in the eyes.

"What's a wax museum?" the sheriff inquired.

"The morgue. That's what I call it," Colden replied with a smile. "Everyone there is lifelike, but none of them are moving."

"It's a morgue, Peter." Sheriff Williams wasn't smiling when he said it.

Deputy Colden cringed. He knew that when Smudge Williams got a bit angry with someone, he addressed them by their full first name.

"These are people," Smudge continued. "Someone loved them. This man gave and got hugs and Christmas presents. Have some respect."

"Yes, sir," Deputy Colden answered. He knew better than to banter with a pissed-off Smudge Williams.

"I'll stay here and wait for the coroner," the sheriff told him as he nodded toward the stone bridge. "Go see if you can find whoever made the 9-1-1 call.

"You bet, sheriff," Deputy Colden answered. After pausing a moment to see if there were any more orders, he turned and walked through the snow for the bridge.

Smudge Williams looked across the bridge and up LaChute Brook. He knew its path. He grew up here in Upstate New York. He fished and played in LaChute Brook's waters more times than he could count.

The brook poured from the top of the nearest mountain, called Le Trou Au Coeur. Early French settlers had given the mountain its name. It meant "The Hole in The Heart." There was a notch at the peak of the mountain. An Indian legend said the notch used to reach all the way into the heart of the mountain. That is where the spirits lived.

Le Trou Au Coeur was difficult to pronounce, especially because not many people living in Joseph County these days were French. A lot of them called the mountain by a nickname sounding similar to the French moniker. They called it The Joker. It was also called by the name of the ski resort perched on the side of the mountain, Battle Ax.

2

"I played with myself in 2020." The message was printed across a tee shirt being worn by a man presently sitting on the edge of JC Snow's desk.

"Shouldn't that read, 'I played *by* myself?'" JC asked the irreverent news photographer, Milt Lemon. "Because we were all sort of ordered to stay home because of Covid?"

"Who has better recall of how I spent 2020," Lemon asked, "you or me?"

Milt Lemon was capable of making JC and his colleagues laugh and groan at the same time. Milt crafted this talent like it was his calling in life.

"Do you like a good cold case?"

That question came from a new arrival at JC's desk in the newsroom at the television station in Denver, Colorado. The assignment editor, Rocky Baumann, was standing there.

"Do I like a cold case? If we're talking about beer, yes," JC responded with a grin.

"You're from Upstate New York, right?" Baumann asked.

"Yep, Saratoga," JC reminded him.

He'd been sent to Upstate New York by the TV station on assignment once before. It was slightly over a year ago, to report on a former New York state senator ultimately arrested in Colorado on murder charges.

"It worked out pretty well, last time," Rocky said. "Pat is thinking of sending you back. It might be an extended stay." Pat Perilla was the news director.

"Is there something new in the story about Senator Buford?" JC asked. "As far as I know, he's still in prison."

"He is. No, this is a new story," the assignment editor began. "There's an investigation into a county executive near Lake Placid."

Baumann was looking at his notes to make sure he was using the right term. Counties in Colorado were managed by county commissioners. "I guess counties in Upstate New York are run by a county executive?"

"They are indeed," JC confirmed. "Along with a county legislature."

"Anyway," Baumann continued, "this county executive might be involved in the disappearance of a man here in Colorado about forty-five years ago. State cops think the missing guy was murdered."

"It *does* sound like a good story," JC agreed. "Why the extended stay in New York?"

"Maybe it won't be," Rocky conceded. "But right now, the suspect says he didn't have anything to do with the disappearance. The Colorado Bureau of Investigation here thinks he did. So, this could drag out."

"And he's officially a suspect?" JC inquired.

"Publicly, he's more of a 'person of interest.' However, our source in the CBI tells us that they're sure he did it. We're thinking that you get to New York, interview the suspect, file a few stories and you're there when the CBI slaps the cuffs on him."

"Well, you're in luck. My social calendar was just scrubbed clean," JC declared. "I'm available. Did the newsroom just win the lottery?"

"You're right, it sounds expensive. But it's the start of a new budget year," Rocky noted. "We're flush with cash ... until we're not."

"I'm getting married, JC," Shara had told him.

JC's throat nearly nailed itself shut when he heard the words spill from Shara's mouth. She had flown to Denver, about a week ago, from Montana where she owned a bar. She thought that she needed to tell JC to his face.

"I still love you," Shara had said. "It may have been a mistake to come here to see you. Now, I'm confused."

She said that she flew in for only the day. She wasn't going to deliver the news over the phone. She would be flying back to Bozeman in a few hours.

"It's the distance," she told him as tears formed in her eyes. "You need to be here, and I need to be there."

JC was silent. It was not a bolt out of the blue. He thought it was like when an aging parent had been ill and finally died.

You knew it was going to happen, but it was still a shock when the day arrived.

"I don't blame you," Shara said. "Maybe I blame me. I just can't love you this much and only have you a few weeks in a year. By now, I don't even enjoy the day you arrive when you come for a week. All I think about is how much it's going to hurt when you leave."

They had lived together in Montana while he was unemployed, and it was magnificent. Then he had to return to work in Denver, where the money was. For the last year, they had endured getting by with week-long visits every four or five months.

Once Shara had kissed him goodbye and closed the door to his apartment behind her, he began to review all the things he had not said.

He could have said, "We'll just make sure we see each other more." But they both knew they had already tried that.

He could have said, "Marry me. We'll worry about where we live later." But they had already discussed that, too.

He could have said, "What if you sell the bar and move to Denver. We can buy another bar, together." But they had already failed at that one.

It was no use thinking about his moving to Montana. He loved it there, but it would be a steep pay cut. And while he respected the journalism there, it was a different level and pace than he was accustomed to. They both knew he would become frustrated.

JC had also recognized that he and Shara had been drifting apart. She seemed distracted. She wasn't as enthusiastic on the phone. Then, she told him not to come when he'd arranged some time off. She had blamed work.

Had he ignored the obvious signs? Maybe he did. Now, she was marrying someone else. Now, he had to survive this.

He thought about what he could have said and what he could have done, but none of it would have mattered.

"They'd been friends all through college," the news director told JC. The reporter had been asked by Rocky Baumann to join him in News Director Pat Perilla's office.

"Colin Cornheiser is the county executive in Joseph County in New York," the news director read off his notes. "Where the hell is that?"

"That's the North Country. It's getting pretty close to the Canadian border," JC told him. "It's actually just north of Lake Placid."

"Lake Placid. Home of the Olympics in 1980?" Perilla injected.

"1980 and 1932!" JC proudly added.

"So, you might get in some skiing," the news director remarked. "Maybe *you* should pay *us*."

JC smiled. "Actually," he added, "Whiteface is the mountain famous for the Winter Games in 1980. That's south, in Essex County. In Joseph County, north of there, there's a great ski resort called Battle Ax. It was built after 1980."

The news director gave JC an expressionless look, suggesting that he'd been told more than he cared to hear.

"Just a bit of a travelogue," JC remarked. "I'm letting you know that you've chosen the right guy."

The news director smiled knowingly and returned to his script.

"Anyway, Colin Cornheiser was a business major at college in Denver in the 1970s. So was Winston Reddish, a young man from a wealthy Denver family. Cornheiser and Reddish became roommates. They were both business majors. Everyone from back then describes them as best friends. Some say they were inseparable."

Perilla pushed some paper across the desk. JC picked it up and looked it over. It mostly stated what Perilla had just told him.

"Actually," JC remarked about something he saw on the bullet points, "that college stood out in those days as a rich kid's school. You said Reddish was from money. So Cornheiser was, too?"

"No," Perilla told him. "The CBI here says Cornheiser did not come from a wealthy family, or even an upper-middle-class family. It was an effort by the school to open their doors to some deserving poor kids."

"Where was Cornheiser from?" JC asked. "Could he have been friends with Reddish in high school and the Reddish family greased the wheels?"

"There's nothing like that noted here," the news director stated. "I'll give you the rest of this file when we're done. But it's odd. There's almost nothing about Cornheiser's background. It doesn't say where his hometown is or who his parents are."

"Just like all the history we learn," JC remarked. "The rich get their story told and the illiterate poor remain anonymous. Eventually, they are thrown in a pauper's grave without a proper marker. They disappear forever."

The news director stared at JC.

"Sorry, that's my aggrieved Scottish ancestors talking," JC apologized.

"Anyway," Perilla continued, "in their senior year at college, Reddish disappears. He's never seen or heard from again."

"Murdered?" JC asked.

"A cold-case unit with the Colorado Bureau of Investigation thinks so," Perilla told him. "But they've never found a body, a weapon or a witness. They just don't think a rich kid would walk away from all that money and a family he seemed to get along with. By now, the CBI thinks there would have been a trace of him, if he were alive."

"Those were times of turmoil," JC remembered from his history books. "People got drafted for the Vietnam War and made a run for Canada. Some people just wanted to be someone else and picked up and left. It was the Age of Aquarius, baby."

"Anything's possible," the news director said. "The cold-case outfit thinks Reddish may have been murdered, and they think Cornheiser may have done it."

"And that's why I'm going to Joseph," JC declared, summing up the tale.

"Yes," Perilla confirmed. "Cornheiser has already been questioned by investigators from Colorado. They visited him back East and it didn't quell their suspicions. It has all been quiet so far, but it's about to become public. And when it goes public, it is going to make a big bang."

"Am I going to break the story when I get out there," JC asked, "with what we know so far?"

"That's the plan. The information is all confirmed, as far as what I've told you and is written on the paperwork I'm giving you," Perilla said. "You pick it up from there."

"Just for my own edification, am I walking into an ambush?" JC asked.

"Is a powerful politician like Cornheiser going to be happy?" the news director framed JC's question with a question. "Will he be pleased that you've come to his backyard to break the news that he's being investigated for murder? Is that your question?"

"Yep," JC answered.

"Probably not," was Perilla's reply.

"Now, we've got to send a photographer with you," Rocky said. It was the first time Rocky had uttered a word in the meeting. "Milt is a single parent. He doesn't want to leave his daughter for that long a time. How about Bip Peters?"

"That's fine," JC said. "Bip is a good shooter."

Bip Peters was one of the younger news photographers, but talented. JC also knew him to be a fantastic snowboarder. That was a plus, in JC's gradebook.

"We might send out a producer to help you," Perilla told his reporter. "But not at the start. Let's see if you need one."

"Any consideration of lending me a bodyguard?" JC joked.

"New York has the strongest gun-safety laws this country has put to paper," Perilla noted.

"Yeah," JC agreed. "But in the North Country, they use that paper for target practice."

3

"He hadn't been in the water too long," the medical examiner told the sheriff. They were standing over the corpse of the man pulled out of LaChute Brook. He was illuminated by bright light in an otherwise dark room.

"It's kind of ironic," the M.E. noted. "He appears to have died from a hole in the heart." The medical examiner looked up at the sheriff. "And he was found at the base of a mountain called 'Hole in the Heart,' Le Trou Au Coeur."

The M.E. sensed that the irony wasn't as intriguing to the sheriff. It was a cue from Smudge to move things along.

The medical examiner was a doctor named David Ryan. He did his work for Joseph County inside facilities in Saranac Lake, belonging to the neighboring county of Franklin.

"His pockets were empty," Dr. Ryan stated, "except for one piece of paper."

"We looked in his pockets," the sheriff said. "We didn't find anything."

"It's a small piece of paper," the doctor told him. "It was crumpled up in the bottom of his jeans pocket. I thought you'd want to see it."

The medical examiner reached for a plastic evidence bag with a small piece of white paper inside. He handed it to the law officer, who examined both sides.

"Is it blank?" Smudge asked.

"Almost," the doctor replied. "The water got to it. In proper light, you can make out two Os. The letter O."

"The letter O, twice. Like in the word oops?" Smudge asked.

"Yes, but probably not that exact word," Dr. Ryan said. "I'd venture a guess that they did once belong with other letters. But, after the paper was soaked, all I can make out is two Os. Any idea what it means?"

"I haven't the faintest idea," the sheriff told him.

"Identify him yet?" Dr. Ryan asked.

"He wasn't carrying any identification," Smudge told him.

"Do you recognize him?" the M.E. asked the sheriff.

"No, I do not," Smudge replied.

"Then, he's not from around here," the medical examiner concluded. "You'd recognize him if he was local. It won't be long. We got a good fingerprint. And we'll back it up with dental records, once you get a name.

"We've got some contusions, too," the medical examiner said, "on his face and on his hands. Those are probably the places his body was exposed to the rock bed of the brook." The doctor was bending slightly and picking up the victim's hand. Dr. Ryan glanced at the sheriff to see if he was following.

"The scrapes on his head and hands could have come after he was dead," indicated the M.E. "But there's also some bruising. I'm not sure of the source. It doesn't look like a fist or being kicked by a shoe. But it's some sort of blunt-force trauma. It could be a fall."

The sheriff leaned in and looked closely at the wounds.

"It's easy to pick out a hematoma," the medical examiner explained. "He's light-skinned."

"Just to be sure we're on the same page," the sheriff said as he adjusted his ball cap. "The ironic hole in the victim's heart. That was caused by a bullet?"

"That's right," Doctor Ryan clarified. He was a little embarrassed that he hadn't come right out and said that a gun was the weapon. "He was shot in the heart."

"Shot twice?" Sheriff Williams inquired as he surveyed the naked corpse.

"Yes, shot twice. Very observant," the doctor said with approval. "But the one to the heart would do it all by itself. Maybe it was the second shot. The first shot might be the one that hit him in the stomach. He might have lived, if he got to a hospital quick enough. Maybe the gunman knew that he missed his mark the first time and took better aim the second time."

"That is very possible," the sheriff agreed.

Smudge Williams' real first name was Bobby. "Robert" wasn't written on his birth certificate, "Bobby" was. But everyone knew him as Smudge, the kid who always came home dirty because he was playing all day in the woods of Joseph County.

His parents had a ranch on the edge of those woods. It wasn't much of a ranch, but it was enough. There were some cattle, goats, a horse or two and plenty of fresh vegetables. The ranch house was only heated by burning wood. And there always seemed to be an addition under construction.

As a child, coming to become known as Smudge, he was growing up to be a big lad with a big chest, big hands and big arms.

To no surprise of townspeople, Smudge's parents were eventually ordered to send him to school. But to their great surprise, the child who always wore a baseball cap and torn pants turned out to be intelligent. Very intelligent. He was also a heck of a football player.

He went to college in the Midwest and was the team's star quarterback. He was also Academic All-Conference.

Sheriff Smudge Williams pulled onto a gravel pull-off on Bonnieview Road and parked his silver Chevy Tahoe with "Sheriff" printed on the side. Another silver Tahoe was already parked there. Deputy Tim Pattern was standing outside his vehicle waiting for the sheriff.

"Got yourself warmed up?" the sheriff asked him.

"Smudge, I don't know how water that cold can't freeze," the deputy said as he shook his head. He was wearing gloves today, and a black knit cap with the sheriff's insignia on it, and probably an extra pair of long johns.

Smudge had asked Pattern to join him. They would walk either side of LaChute Brook. They would look for some sort of identification to determine who their nameless victim was.

"Maybe the killer emptied his victim's pockets of anything that could identify him before rolling him into the brook," Smudge theorized.

"And maybe the killer just tossed the I.D. into the field, rather than be caught carrying it on him?" Deputy Pattern said, completing the sheriff's thoughts.

"Wouldn't that be considerate," Smudge added.

Tim Pattern was lanky and athletic-looking. He had brown hair and a new wedding ring. He and his bride had moved to Joseph for the deputy's job. Tim and his wife wanted a safe place to raise children.

Walking along the brook, up the side of the mountain, would be "old school," Deputy Pattern thought. But that's one of the things he admired about Smudge. Old school was usually a little more difficult, but it often worked.

He remembered a story Smudge told him when Pattern was interviewing to become a deputy. Smudge wanted to make sure the applicant understood how things were done in the Joseph County Sheriff's Office.

"We had this string of gas station robberies," Smudge had told Pattern during the interview, "not just here in Joseph County, but in the surrounding counties, too. The robber would pull up to the pump, pull a gun and take the cash.

"So, running out of alternatives," Smudge told him, "I drove my patrol car to every gas station within thirty miles. At each one, I'd stop and ask the attendant if he'd witnessed any behavior out of the ordinary. It didn't have to be criminal behavior, just someone doing something that people didn't usually do.

"So, one guy came out when I pulled up to his pumps," Smudge continued. "I asked him the same question. The guy thought a little bit. Then he said, 'No, the only thing different was when a car pulled up to the pump the other day and the driver just sat there in his car. I came out to see if I could help, but he rolled down the window and it was a neighbor of mine. He said hello, nice and all, and then pulled away.'"

"Did he buy gas?" Smudge said he asked the station attendant. "And he said 'No.' That was kind of funny.

"I knew then that guy in the car was the one robbing the gas stations," Smudge said. "He'd pulled up to rob that particular station, but he changed his mind when he saw that a friend of his was working. He didn't want to rob his friend."

Smudge and Deputy Tim Pattern had parked at one end of the old stone bridge, near where Pattern had secured the victim as he floated by.

They walked up opposite sides of LaChute Brook, quickly leaving buildings behind and entering into pastureland. Past the woods on the left would be the condos and stores belonging to the commercial village of the Battle Ax Ski Resort. The deputy could see a couple of ski runs toward the top of the mountain, below the notch.

Some of the snow underfoot was three or four inches deep. It was old snow. In other places, the snow had melted and there was just tall grass that had been matted down. When the law officers reached a fence, they climbed over it.

It was a cold cloudy day. The sun didn't shine a lot in January and February in the Adirondacks.

The brook was perhaps ten feet wide, but it would narrow as they climbed closer to the steep sides of Le Trou Au Coeur. The water was quiet enough that Smudge and Deputy Pattern could discuss things in a raised voice.

All the while, their eyes were on the ground, looking for identification, shell casings or any disturbance that would indicate the victim had been shot there.

"I should get a dog," Smudge thought out loud. And it wasn't only because he was alone in life. He had been alone since his wife died five years ago.

"A dog would already have found what we're looking for," Deputy Pattern said in an elevated voice across the brook.

"That's what I was just thinking," Smudge responded. This wasn't the first time he'd thought about getting a dog. But he hadn't done it yet.

They continued to walk up the banks of the brook. Their eyes were glued to the ground.

That is why they didn't notice the small cabin or the man standing in front of it with a shotgun cradled in his arm.

"That's far enough," the man announced, sounding like he meant business.

The interruption surprised Smudge, as well as his deputy on the other side of the brook. But Smudge had walked these fields before. He had just lost track of where he was. He recognized the old cabin with the faded paint.

He looked up and saw a man in a dirty gray jacket that maybe used to be blue. The man had an uneven gray beard and was wearing a red hat. Some shaggy gray hair hung down from under the hat. He was standing next to an old wheelbarrow.

The man was cradling a shotgun. Smudge recognized him as Bob "Stormy" Jordan, the owner of the fields presently being walked by the two law officers.

Smudge stood facing Stormy and thought about the term "Hayseed." Smudge wasn't exactly certain about the specifics of the term, but he thought that it probably fit Stormy.

"Robert," the sheriff declared, "what are you planning to do with that weapon?"

"Sheriff, I've got a right to use this gun to protect my property," Stormy announced.

"We're in full uniform, Robert," the sheriff informed the man. "Does that tell you anything?"

"I'm within my rights, sheriff," Stormy repeated. The sheriff gave that some thought as he squinted up at the gray clouds.

"Maybe you are and maybe you aren't, Robert," the sheriff said with an impatient edge to his voice. "But if you point that thing anywhere toward me, my deputy or my truck, I'll shoot you right through the head. You got that, Robert?"

Stormy's jaw loosened a little and his shoulders dropped. Next, he broke open the barrel of his shotgun and lowered it into the wheelbarrow beside him. Deputy Pattern looked at the ground and did his best not to erupt into laughter.

Smudge was smart and old school. Over the years, people had just stopped running against him when it was time for re-election.

4

"Some of those old stone walls have been sinking into the soil since George Washington was a boy," JC explained to Bip.

"Really?" Bip responded. This was Bip Peters' first trip to the East Coast. He made no effort to conceal his enthusiasm.

JC was pointing to the stone walls along the road, some covered in moss. If you looked for them, they were everywhere.

"They were stacked by hand by colonial men and women," the reporter told him. "They were clearing their fields for farming. A lot of those walls have lost their context. They often marked the boundary of the farm. It looks like they're meandering through the forest. But that forest used to be farmland."

The walls were old and historic and commonplace in the Northeast. During times of conflict, some of them provided protection for soldiers from France, Britain and the colonies who found reason to shoot at each other. And they found reason to do that for over a century.

Bip was going to be JC's photographer while they were working on their assignment in the North Country of New York.

JC thought that Bip was around twenty-eight years old. He had dark hair. It was spiked by using an application of gel. He had a face that every woman found appealing.

Flying into Albany, Bip had stared at ice boats sailing across the frozen Hudson River. Ice sailing was a two-hundred-year-old pastime, invented in Upstate New York, JC told him.

The 4x4 SUV they rented was now traveling up the Adirondack Northway, as Interstate 87 was called. It was called the Northway even when you were heading south.

They had already passed Exit 13, close to the home near Saratoga Springs where JC had grown up.

They had passed the famous horse racing track. They had driven by the Great Escape Amusement Park and Lake George. They passed a billboard saying, "You could be skiing by now!" It advertised the West Mountain Ski Area, much closer to the dense population centers of Glens Falls, Albany, Troy and Schenectady. There were five more exits before skiers and snowboarders could point toward the next and bigger ski resort: Gore Mountain.

There was paper perched on the dashboard of their car, as well as laid out across JC's lap. He was studying the subject matter bringing them to the North Country.

"It says here that Colin Cornheiser was born and raised in Kit Carson County in Colorado, sixty-five years ago," JC said.

"Burlington, to be exact." He was reading a new bio about the county executive of Joseph County, New York.

"I've never been there," Bip conceded. Bip had grown up in Telluride, Colorado. He said that his parents settled there when it resembled a ghost town, before it became a big ski destination.

"My dad still moans about it," Bip joked. "He says he could have bought the whole town, back then. And now he'd be a billionaire."

"Burlington, on the other hand," said JC, "is a big truck stop in a little town on I-70. It's on the Eastern Plains near the Kansas border. It has a radio station that everyone out there listens to, KNAB."

"What brought him here?" Bip asked.

"Good question," JC replied. "Maybe he was running from the law."

At Exit 30, they turned up Route 73 and drove through Chapel Pond Canyon. It was a popular spot for rock climbers in the summer and ice climbers in the winter.

The climbing faces were called The Beer Walls. Different routes up the rock had names like Frosted Mug and Seven Ounces.

They entered the Keene Valley, popular with climbers and hikers and shoppers looking for unique Adirondack furniture.

Stores began to appear along the road. Sloping Adirondack chairs sat outside the stores. The chairs had tall, slatted backs and wide armrests. Merchants lined them up on the lawn. A few stores tried to draw attention with a gigantic Adirondack chair placed by the road.

Inside the stores, there was the Adirondacks' famous twig furniture. There were desks, beds, rocking chairs, lamps, boxes, mirrors and picture frames. There were dining tables and matching seats. They were all built on the same principle of bending and varnishing branches to tame nature and provide us with places to sit or eat or sleep.

JC loved Adirondack furniture. He knew that it wasn't only found in the Adirondacks and Northeast anymore. But he still thought it was more abundant and built better in the Adirondacks.

Adirondack Park itself was a marvel of the 19th century. The land was set aside to protect it from ferocious timbering that was leveling forests near the greatest population densities in the United States.

The park was for people of all ages and earning brackets. The wealthiest Americans like the Vanderbilts, the Rockefellers and the Colgates built estates they called Great Camps. They were enormous mansions made of stone and twig architecture. They exuded rustic luxury.

The middle class was drawn to tent camps, lean-tos and log cabins in the Adirondacks. The park was a great congregation of social classes in the wilderness.

"Adirondack Park is the largest piece of protected public land in the country," JC told his gawking colleague. "Those huge national parks like Yellowstone, Yosemite and the Grand Canyon could all fit inside Adirondack Park with room to spare."

"Are we going in the back door?" Bip asked. "Because you know what I don't see here? Shiny new million-dollar homes like the ones erected all over the mountains in Colorado."

27

"There are some," JC answered. "But it's not the same wealth. The economy is a little stressed here. Adirondack Park is so big, there were already communities inside the new park boundary when it was drawn up. Those towns were allowed to stay, as well as all the houses. But it's impossible to build a factory or a smokestack industry here, inside the so-called 'Blue Line.' Most of the land has been declared 'Forever Wild' and it's not easy to make a living here."

"So, it's tourism or bust?" Bip asked.

"That's a pretty accurate statement," JC told him. "There are some colleges. But yeah, most people either live off of tourism, live off each other or they move here when they retire.

"We'll have to get you to Lake Placid one day," JC promised. "It's a really cool town. It's the grandfather of the winter sports movement in the United States."

With Bip at the wheel of their rental, JC pointed out the towering ski jumps on the outskirts of Lake Placid. Not far away, there were the bobsled and luge and skeleton tracks. Those among the public who dared could now pay to take a ride.

JC directed Bip to a shortcut to Joseph. They'd follow the East Branch of the Ausable River. They passed wood-frame homes with carved silhouettes on their lawn of moose and deer and curvy women. There were chainsaw carvings of bear.

There were maple syrup farms and roads with names like Lost-My Way and What-A-View Avenue. There was a sign as they entered the hamlet of Joseph saying, "Mountains Only."

The rented 4x4 turned onto Bonnieview Road and they drove north through a long corridor of trees. Traveling over the old stone bridge, the vehicle arrived in small downtown Joseph. A domed courthouse was in the center. It symbolized that Joseph was the County Seat of the sparsely populated area.

They pulled the car into a parking place and JC emerged taking a deep breath of the clean air. It felt good to stretch his legs.

JC had dark hair and a dark mustache. He'd come to Colorado to attend college in Fort Collins. He raced for the ski team there. That's where he met Shara.

He was in his mid-thirties now. His body was informing him in subtle ways that he wasn't a kid anymore. But he still had an athletic build.

He wished that he could carve about ten pounds off his midsection, but he wasn't willing to forfeit things he'd worked hard to get, like good food and the occasional fifteen-year-old, single-malt scotch whisky.

He'd been considering shaving his mustache lately. Outside of the Rocky Mountains, mustaches seemed to have been removed from the fashion menu. He was happy to find that was not so in New York's North Country.

"Where do we start?" Bip asked.

"I just wanted to get a look around," JC told him. "We have a couple of rooms at the Battle Ax ski village. We'll do our first live shot for our evening news, tomorrow. I've got to give our network affiliate in Plattsburgh a call. They'll be loaning us a live truck and an engineer."

JC walked across the road. There wasn't much traffic. He read the historical marker in front of the courthouse. It was the town's most prominent building, erected in 1923.

There was some snow on the grass, but it had melted on the road and sidewalks. There were not many people out walking. JC thought it looked like there just were not many people in Joseph.

Across the street from the courthouse was the storefront that housed the Joseph County Offices. JC thought the building looked like it was once a grocery store.

As he climbed onto the sidewalk, he locked eyes with a face that he recognized. The man looked like the pictures JC had been staring at since boarding his plane in Denver. It was County Executive Colin Cornheiser, the man suspected of murder in Colorado.

"Mr. Cornheiser," JC said to the smiling politician. JC recognized a politician's smile, especially when they couldn't place the face they had encountered.

"Hello," Cornheiser said as he extended a hand to shake. JC figured shaking hands was as natural to a politician as breathing. There might be a voter on the end of that hand.

Cornheiser didn't watch television news from Denver, and Bip wasn't carrying his camera, so the county executive had no cause to think that he was speaking to journalists.

But JC told the man who they were and that they worked for a television news station in Denver. Cornheiser put his hands in his pockets and studied the two men. The smile was fading.

"Well," the county executive finally said, "I can guess what brings you here. Why don't we go into my office?"

"Can we bring our camera?" JC asked.

"Let's get acquainted first," Cornheiser said. "There will be time for that."

Cornheiser led the pair through a glass door and marched toward a desk with an attractive brunette sitting there. She was stuffing envelopes.

"Patty, I'm going to be in my office with these two gentlemen for a while," the county executive told his administrative assistant.

"Ok, Colin," Patty responded.

"Have a seat, gentlemen," Cornheiser said as he moved behind his desk and sat. Patty closed the door, leaving the three men alone.

"Your last name is Snow?" Cornheiser asked amiably.

"That's right," JC answered.

"Well, you should like it here," Cornheiser smiled. "We get plenty of snow here."

It wasn't the first time someone felt obliged to remark about JC's name. It was something that had followed him since childhood. He heard his name included in riddles and in songs. It didn't bother him. He liked his name.

"When's the last time you were in Burlington, Colorado?" JC asked.

"I was last home when my dad died," Cornheiser replied. "That was five years ago. My mother passed a few years before that." JC wondered if Cornheiser was soliciting sympathy or just answering a simple question. The county executive was a difficult man to read.

He had a sturdy frame and thick gray hair. He had a strong face with a cleft chin. But his features were softened by wire-rimmed glasses. JC thought the glasses resembled the type hippies wore in the 1960s and '70s. Cornheiser's age was somewhere in his mid-sixties.

JC had read that Cornheiser would dress in vintage clothing a couple of times a year and give historic tours of Joseph. He was a history buff, apparently.

"So, your TV station sent you all the way out here," Cornheiser inquired, "because a couple of your state police officers sat in the same chairs you're sitting in and we talked for an hour? That's news now?"

"I promise you that I'll be fair, Mr. Cornheiser," JC answered. "But those CBI investigators are preparing to level some pretty serious accusations against you."

"I know they are," the county executive quickly said back. "But they're wrong. And your television station is going to be disappointed in their investment."

"For your sake," JC told him, "I hope that's true. Bip and I get paid the same, whether you're innocent or guilty."

"OK, go get your camera if you want," said Cornheiser with a frown. "I'm going to say the same thing I already told you. They're looking at the wrong guy."

Bip quickly returned with a camera, tripod and lights. It would take him a few minutes to set up his equipment. Bip had noticed when he carried his gear into the office that the county executive's administrative assistant was giving him an icy stare. She could apparently listen to conversations through the closed door.

"What was this building, prior to being the county offices?" JC asked. He told Cornheiser that they shared an interest in history. He thought some small talk might put the man at ease.

"It was empty for quite a while. Before that, it was a Loblaws," the county executive smiled. "They weren't out in Colorado. They were a Canadian grocery store chain. They had a lot of stores in Upstate New York, too. I swear, sometimes I can still smell fish."

Bip was ready and JC started the interview. Right from the start, Cornheiser admitted that he knew the missing man back in the mid-1970s. "Winston was my best friend," he said.

"Winston Reddish was in college with you in Denver?" JC asked.

"We were roommates. Best friend I ever had. He disappeared suddenly, just after we graduated. I have no idea what happened."

Cornheiser's elocution was steady and he never took his eyes off of the man interviewing him.

In his experience, JC had occasionally witnessed people fall to pieces during an interview on camera. Cornheiser was not one of those people. He spoke with confidence. His manner was likeable. Good politician, JC thought.

"Then, where did he go?" JC asked. "You were his best friend. You must have some insights." And JC saw it. For just a moment, Cornheiser's eyes turned away. It was only a flicker, but it suggested to the reporter that the county executive thought of something he definitely did not want to say.

JC gave him the silent treatment. The reporter was going to be sure that the next words spoken would be from Cornheiser. It was a technique JC used to get any subject of an interview to fill the silence. JC wanted them to say what was on their mind. Sometimes, those next words were benign. And sometimes, they blurted out the very thing they later wished they had not said.

"Winston's family was devastated," Cornheiser finally offered. "They were a prominent family in Denver and things like this didn't happen to people like them. His girlfriend was devastated, too—we all were."

"State investigators from Colorado have been here to speak with you?" JC asked.

"Yes, they have," Cornheiser responded without hesitation. This time, he was on camera.

"How do you expect the people of Joseph to react to the news when they hear about this?" JC asked.

"When *you* tell them about it?" Cornheiser replied with a bit of an edge in his voice. But then he softened. "I know, you're just doing your job. What will Joseph think? They've known me for thirty years. I hope they judge me on my merits."

The interview was over. JC and Bip were pretty pleased that they'd have it for their first live shots tomorrow. But JC also acknowledged to himself that Cornheiser had not done anything to damage his own position.

"I used to be in your business, you know," Cornheiser said as a grin returned to his face. Bip was packing his gear.

"How's that?" JC asked. He was relieved that the conversation wasn't headed for a tirade about fake news or yellow journalism.

"As a teenager," Cornheiser readily spoke, "I worked at the radio station in my hometown, Burlington. It was a small station, so I got to do a bit of everything. I had a regular shift as a disc jockey on Saturday. I'd do rip-and-read news on weekday afternoons after school. I even got my third-class engineering license to make sure the station stayed on their air when I was there alone."

Cornheiser laughed at the memory. JC thought that the county executive was the most relaxed murder suspect he'd ever met.

"Maybe he's a psychopath," JC suggested to Bip as they drove out of town. "Maybe he's told himself so many times that he didn't do it, that he really doesn't think he did it."

"He really seems like a nice guy," Bip inserted. "He's supposed to be a murderer?"

"Yeah," JC said without conviction.

"He doesn't seem like a guy who would murder someone," Bip said.

"Maybe," JC suggested, "he killed him with kindness."

5

"Do you think Stormy shot our victim?" The question came from Deputy Tim Pattern.

"He just considered shooting a sheriff and a deputy sheriff. What's that tell you?" Sheriff Smudge Williams responded.

Dead oak leaves blew across the snow as the two men approached their patrol cars, parked by the old stone bridge.

"Those oak leaves never stop falling," the sheriff muttered in frustration. "Raking leaves is a year-round undertaking here."

The two law officers had walked along the bank of LaChute Brook until the ground got too steep to continue. They had found no evidence that would enlighten them on the identity of the dead man found in the brook the other day, or the location where he was shot.

"Let's do this," the sheriff said to his deputy. "I want to know what's in Stormy's arsenal. We're going to learn what kind of gun killed that man, and I want to know if Stormy has that kind of gun."

"I'll take care of that, sheriff," Deputy Pattern said. He knew the sheriff was listening, even though Smudge was looking up Bonnieview Road.

The sheriff was looking at something too far away to see. He remembered seeing it, though.

"What's that land being cleared toward Battle Ax?" the sheriff asked.

"Oh, they're going to build a convenience store there. I think it will have some gas pumps, too," Deputy Pattern told him.

"Right next to the new Tomahawk development?" the sheriff asked.

"Yes, sir," said Pattern.

"Drive up there with me," the sheriff asked, or ordered. Smudge's asking and ordering were kind of the same thing, the deputy thought.

They both climbed into their patrol cars and drove for a handful of miles. They passed cleared pastureland and then miles of dense forest on both sides of the road. The trees were mostly paper birch, red spruce and balsam fir. There were plenty of rocks in the woods.

They pulled up to land that had been cleared of trees and rocks. It was leveled down to the sandy soil that dominated the landscape of Joseph County.

A couple of pieces of heavy equipment were parked along the side of the lot, but there was no activity going on. Smudge thought that was odd on a weekday afternoon.

The cleared land was in the shadow of the large Tomahawk Resort addition to Battle Ax. It was well on its way to completion. Soon, Tomahawk would provide new condos, townhouses, hotels, retail and restaurants for visitors drawn to the Battle Ax Ski Resort. It would also be put to use during the summer. There were future plans for a golf course, once more land could be secured.

But Sheriff Williams, followed by Deputy Pattern, had pulled onto the cleared spot just short of the development. The land was mostly swept bare of snow by the wind. There were just some sticks protruding from the ground and some plastic fencing around some shallow holes. There were also a handful of small tents, big enough to stand in but barely big enough to park a small car in.

"What's all this?" Smudge asked, as he walked the site.

"Not sure," the deputy told him.

Smudge removed his cap and scratched his head. It revealed a full head of hair, a little curly. Deputy Pattern thought that he could count the number of times on one hand that he'd seen the top of the sheriff's head.

"Well, I want to talk to somebody about this," the sheriff said.

"Yes, sir," Pattern replied. "I'll get right on that."

Smudge looked at his deputy and nodded his head. He liked Tim. He was smart, he was young and he was willing to do the grunt work. It was something that would serve the county well in the future, if Deputy Pattern chose to stay there. He might be sheriff someday, Smudge thought.

Sheriff Williams left the dirt site and drove north on Bonnieview Road. When there was no traffic coming from the other direction, he passed an Amish buggy.

There was a new Amish community near the hamlet of Joseph. The sheriff paid a visit to their farms, from time to time, to make certain they were alright. Otherwise, they kept to themselves. They didn't ask for his help. They administered their own justice, short of a serious felony.

One of their leaders, a man named Yoder, told Smudge that they came from an Amish community closer to Canada, about one hundred miles away. They were drawn by the affordable farmland.

Yoder said that those who decided to settle in Joseph shared a different philosophy about practicing their faith, compared to the community they departed from. Smudge thought the leader suggested that they were a little more liberal than the group they left.

But they were still Amish. They did not use electricity, their clothing did not have zippers, the men wore beards and they all drove horse-drawn buggies.

Smudge drove his patrol car over the stone bridge and to the parking lot in back of the Joseph County Courthouse. He pulled his Tahoe into his parking space at the jail. He saw County Executive Colin Cornheiser emerging through the door.

"Hi, Sheriff," Cornheiser saluted Smudge in jovial fashion.

"Hi, Colin," the sheriff returned.

Smudge knew that Cornheiser could have been coming out of that door for any number of reasons. While the door led to the addition in the back of the courthouse that maintained the Sheriff's Office and jail, it also led to the

County Clerk's Office, the Hall of Records, the District Attorney's Office, the Board of Elections and the courts themselves.

Joseph wasn't a big county, and if an office didn't fit into the courthouse, it fit in the County Office Building across the street, the former grocery store.

"Find out who belongs to that body?" the county executive asked as he stopped in front of the sheriff.

"I've probably got word waiting for me in the office," Smudge told him as he also stopped walking. "We've been running fingerprints. We don't think it's anyone local."

"Well, that's good. We'd probably have heard by now, if it was. Do you know who shot him?" Cornheiser asked.

"Not yet," Smudge said. He liked the county executive well enough, but Smudge was scratching at his face. It was another sign of impatience. He wanted to get into his office. He was anxious to find out who the dead man was.

The sheriff knew that investigators from Colorado had been in Joseph to visit Cornheiser. They had contacted the sheriff as a courtesy.

But the sheriff figured *that* was someone else's case, from someone else's part of the country. If Colorado wanted help, they would ask. Williams wasn't going to put it on his front burner until then.

"OK, Sheriff," said Cornheiser as he moved toward his car. "You'll get him."

"Take care, Colin," the sheriff said. What the sheriff did not know is that a television news crew from Colorado was now in town, preparing to broadcast news of the investigation into Cornheiser. And Cornheiser declined to mention it to the sheriff when he had the chance.

Smudge pushed through the glass door into the Sheriff's Office. His senior deputy, Peter Colden, was sitting at his own desk.

"We have the slug, Sheriff," Colden called out from his desk as Smudge entered his own office. The sheriff stopped in his doorway, waiting for more on the report to be shouted across the room. Nothing came.

"Why don't you join me," said the sheriff as he turned toward Colden.

"Right," murmured Colden to himself as he pushed out of his chair.

He took a seat in Smudge's office as the sheriff situated himself behind his desk. The sheriff didn't take off his cap.

Smudge thought that Colden's short powerful body looked a little like a fire hydrant. He had mostly dark hair, despite just turning fifty. He was putting on weight around his waist and the sheriff thought he could be a little thick between the ears. But he meant well and he did what was asked of him, though sometimes he had to be reminded.

"They're both 9mms, Sheriff," Deputy Colden reported. "One to the stomach and one to the heart."

"Likely weapon?" Smudge asked.

"It's on its way to the state police lab in Albany," the deputy said. "But it's likely a Glock 19."

"Great," the sheriff mused. "The single most-owned handgun in New York State."

"Yeah," Deputy Colden agreed.

The Glock 19 was basically a lighter and smaller edition of the handguns the sheriff and his deputies carried, a Glock 22. The 19 was light enough, even for a smaller person, perhaps a woman. And they were easier to conceal than a 22.

"You could have called my cell phone with that information about the slugs, you know," Sheriff Williams told his deputy.

"I should have. Sorry Sheriff," Colden replied.

"Got an I.D on the victim?" the sheriff asked.

"No, sir," Colden responded

"Got anything else?" Smudge asked.

"Not really," the deputy said.

"OK, keep me informed," the sheriff said, dismissing his senior deputy.

The sheriff did not have an undersheriff. Most sheriff's offices did. But Smudge thought it would just cause unnecessary discord in his ranks. They were a small department. Everyone was equal, meaning everyone had to share the grunt work and the glory. And they knew that the only one who outranked them was the sheriff.

Smudge looked out in the office to see who else was there. He saw his newest deputy, Elizabeth Grant. He was pleased with her, so far. She was strong and seemed capable of figuring things out.

"Liz," the sheriff called.

She appeared in the doorway of his office with surprising speed. She had short hair and was physically fit. The black uniform they all wore looked good on her.

They all wore the same uniform, even Smudge. It had a badge over the left breast and a patch with the county's emblem on the left upper sleeve. A U.S. flag was worn on the right sleeve. All the uniforms looked the same, black shirt on black pants, except the sheriff's uniform had a single star on his collar.

"Would you look over the gun registrations for our great county," the sheriff asked Deputy Grant. "See if Robert

Jordan of Bonnieview Road has a 9mm handgun, perhaps a Glock 19?"

"Is that Stormy?" the new deputy asked.

"That is Stormy," the sheriff showed that he was pleased. "You're new but you learn fast." That made the new deputy smile.

Smudge decided to pull out a map of Joseph County. He unfolded it and looked at the location of that site for the Tomahawk development and the new convenience store. He spread the map out on his desk.

Tomahawk and the site for the new convenience store were not that far from the brook where the body was found. There were a lot of construction workers on the Tomahawk site. Most were from out of town. That might be, he thought, where their victim came from.

"He may own one, Sheriff, but it is not registered."

Smudge looked up from the map and saw Deputy Liz Grant standing in his doorway.

"You already looked that up?" the sheriff asked, somewhat surprised.

"Computer," Deputy Grant revealed, looking at the creased paper map on the sheriff's desk. "And like I say, Sheriff, maybe it just isn't registered."

"You're right," the sheriff said. "Great." That last part was said sarcastically. The sheriff now seemed to be thinking about how to handle a delicate situation.

"OK, let's do this," he said to his new deputy. "Give Deputy Pattern a call with that information. I asked him to see if Stormy Jordan had one, once we found out what 'one' it was. Now we know it's a 9mm."

Smudge thought Deputy Tim Pattern dropping in on Stormy now might be a good idea. The landowner might still be a little weak at the knees from his run-in with the sheriff earlier that day.

On the other hand, Smudge thought, Stormy might be cantankerous and take a shot at his deputy.

"Let's do this," the sheriff told Deputy Grant. "Give Tim a call and catch up with him to be his backup at Stormy's. If Stormy indeed has an unregistered 9mm handgun, tell him that we want to 'borrow' it. And if he doesn't want to 'loan' us his handgun, tell him we'll get a subpoena and 'borrow' his entire collection of unregistered guns."

"Do you think Stormy shot that man found in the brook?" Deputy Grant asked.

"Maybe not," the sheriff guessed. "But if he's got a 9mm, let's send it to the lab and prove it's not him."

Deputy Elizabeth Grant left Smudge's office happy to have an interesting assignment in her young career.

"You've got a call, Sheriff," Deputy Colden shouted from his desk.

Smudge rolled his eyes. He'd have to get an intercom, he thought. He didn't like the "shouting intercom" Colden was using.

"Send it in," the sheriff shouted back.

"Sheriff Williams," he informed the listener on the other end of the phone.

"Sheriff, this is Cynthia Pfister," the voice on the phone said. "We've got someone missing."

"Who would that be?" the sheriff asked.

"Well, it's my partner. We're doing that archaeological dig for the new convenience store."

6

"In the village of Lake George, you can hardly turn over a shovel of dirt without finding the remains of a soldier. Revolutionary War, French and Indian War."

The source of that information was a woman wearing a worn but warm beige jacket with a corduroy collar. She was in her forties, the sheriff guessed.

"Who knows what you'd find under the soil here, unless you put a shovel in it," she told him.

Smudge Williams was getting a crash course on archaeology in New York's North Country. Cynthia Pfister was his tutor. She had short blond hair, a trim figure and an attractive face that was wind-burned as well as tanned from the sun.

Her hands appeared to be accustomed to manual labor, maybe digging. Her fingernails were short and looked like they got scrubbed a lot.

She was an archaeologist. She had called the sheriff yesterday afternoon to inform him that her partner in their small archaeological firm was missing.

She was asked to come to the courthouse and look at a picture of the man found in LaChute Brook. She choked a bit. The face was disfigured by spending time in the water, and occasional brushes with stones and debris in the stream bed. But she confirmed that the man in the photograph was her business partner.

That evening, she was taken to the morgue to make a positive identification. Sheriff Williams met her there, just to take a look at her reaction when she saw her friend on the stainless-steel table.

The dead archaeologist's name was Paul Campbell. Pfister told the sheriff that Campbell had grown up in Scotland. He'd come to the United States to study archaeology at Colorado College in Colorado Springs.

"We were partners," Pfister told Smudge as they stood on the site of the future convenience store. Smudge saw why Pfister had her hair cut short. When the wind blew, strands of hair reached just short of her eyes. He figured that she was in the wind a lot.

"What are all these sticks for?" the sheriff asked. "And the plastic fence?"

"They're test pits," she explained. "We were hired to do an archaeological survey of the site. A store is going to be built here. Just about all of Joseph County is considered a sensitive historic site because the French and Indian War, and to a lesser extent, the Revolutionary War were fought here. There was also a great deal of activity through here by the Iroquois Indians for thousands of years."

"Did the company building the convenience store hire you?" the sheriff asked.

"They're required to by the state Historic Preservation Law," Pfister told him. "We look over the site and tell them if there are any concerns about disturbing or destroying a significant site, like an Indian village or a place where French soldiers were buried.

"We didn't expect to find anything significant," she said. "An archaeological study had been done on Tomahawk, next door, and they didn't find anything."

"So, tell me about Paul Campbell," the sheriff requested. He zipped his jacket up a little higher. The wind was picking up.

"Paul was a sweetheart," Pfister said. "That Scottish accent got him in doors. Every woman seemed to swoon a little bit when they heard his accent."

"Including you?" the sheriff asked.

"No, no," Pfister said with a smile. "We tried that quite a while ago. It didn't work. Fun while it lasted, though," she said with a wink.

"You were better business partners?" Smudge asked.

"Yeah," she agreed. "We figured that out. But we were always good friends."

"Who gets the archaeological company now?" the sheriff asked her.

Cindy Pfister looked the sheriff in the eye. To her, the question sounded like he was trying to trap her. It suggested that she had a motive to kill Campbell. That pissed her off.

"I do," she said bluntly. "What are you suggesting? Why would I kill Paul?"

Sheriff Williams shrugged, "I don't know, I just met you."

Pfister's eyes started looking around the site. The smile that drained from her face was now miles away.

"You own a gun, Ms. Pfister?" the sheriff asked.

The archaeologist gave Smudge a disdainful look, "Yes, sheriff," she said. "A Glock 19."

The sheriff sort of smiled. He looked away and said, "Geez, who doesn't? Well, I'll ask you to bring it in, so we can take a look. I wouldn't worry about it too much."

He waited for a word that sounded like she would comply. It took its time arriving.

"Alright," she said.

"You going to be staying around for a while?" he asked.

"Yes, Sheriff," she said with frost hanging on her words. "I have work to do." Smudge figured that meant she'd continue surveying the convenience store site.

"Well," the sheriff informed her, "first, my people are going to have to give this site a going over. We have a murder investigation to conduct."

"Swell," Pfister responded, upon learning that her day just got worse. And she placed the blame squarely on the sheriff. "Have you ever investigated a murder? I thought two cases of cow-tipping might constitute a crime wave up here. Have you considered calling in some real police to help with this one?"

Smudge turned and walked back toward his Chevy Tahoe, thinking he had probably dashed any hope of making a new friend.

His phone rang.

"I just spoke with the family of Paul Campbell, Sheriff." It was the voice of Deputy Peter Colden on the phone. "It's the middle of the afternoon in Scotland."

"How'd that go?" Smudge asked.

"They're pretty shook up, of course," Colden informed his boss. "They don't know if they're coming here or if they're going to arrange for the body to be shipped back to Scotland."

"Do they have any insights as to what may have happened?" the sheriff inquired.

"No, sir," Colden replied.

"Alright," Smudge told him. "Do me a favor and give them another call in a couple of days. Maybe they'll be adjusting to their new awful reality and remember something that's important to us."

"OK, Sheriff."

Smudge had barely seated himself in his car when his phone rang again. It was Deputy Pattern.

"Hi, Sheriff," Pattern said. "So, Deputy Grant and I just left Stormy's house, since he didn't answer his door yesterday afternoon."

"Any luck?" Smudge asked.

"Yes, sir," Pattern replied. "Stormy gave us a 9mm handgun, unregistered. He wasn't too happy about it, but when I told him we'd come back with a subpoena and search for other unregistered guns, he complied."

"Well," Smudge directed, "let's send it to the lab in Albany. What kind of gun is it?"

"A Glock 19, sir," Pattern told him.

"Figures," Smudge said back.

"Hey, Sheriff."

"Yeah, Tim," Smudge responded.

"How did Stormy get a big piece of property like that?" the deputy asked. "I don't get the feeling he's ever put his nose to the grindstone, you know?"

"And I'd guess you'd be right," the sheriff answered. "He got it from his daddy."

"Inheritance, sure. Did he own the land Tomahawk is going up on?" Pattern inquired.

"No, he did not," said the sheriff. "His land stops where Tomahawk begins. They wanted to buy his land, for a golf course or something, but he wouldn't do it. He could have been a millionaire."

Smudge could hear his deputy, on the other end of the phone, expressing wonder at the story.

"What about the convenience store lot?" Deputy Pattern asked.

"Stormy was pretty much forced to sell that little parcel, to pay his taxes," Smudge said. "He doesn't like to move money in one direction or the other. He doesn't like to sell things and he doesn't like to pay for things. But they were going to take his land and his cabin away if he didn't pay up his taxes due for all that land."

"Wow," said the deputy. "I think I would have sold a little more of it."

"Me too, Tim. Me too."

7

" A Colorado cold case has brought investigators to the North Country of New York State," JC said as he looked into the camera.

His first live broadcast from downtown Joseph told evening news viewers back in Denver that the Colorado Bureau of Investigation was preparing to turn their findings over to a district attorney there.

"The focus of the investigation is currently the man serving as County Executive of Joseph County here in New York," JC continued. "But he used to live in Colorado. The CBI tells us that is where they think a murder took place. And the victim hasn't been seen since 1976."

JC's live report included the interview that he and Bip Peters had shot with County Executive Colin Cornheiser the day before. Cornheiser declared his innocence during the interview: "I wouldn't kill Winston," the politician said. "He was my best friend."

The rest of the story included an old photo of the missing man, Winston Reddish. A producer with the TV station back in Denver had located the picture in a 1976 yearbook from the college.

The producer's name was Robin Smith. She had been helpful to JC before. He was pleased when she was the producer who picked up the phone. He had to make daily calls to the newsroom in Denver, to report on his plans and progress in New York. He knew he'd be in good hands with Robin.

The live shot in downtown Joseph wrapped up the workday for JC and Bip. They had agreed to rise early the next morning to get in some skiing at Battle Ax.

"Is it colder here or something?" Bip asked. The sun had set hours ago. Bip was packing up his camera gear and said that he needed a warmer coat.

"Welcome to the Ice Coast," JC told him with a grin. "Colorado enjoys the southern sun. You're in the North Country now."

JC could remember the frigid formative years of his youth, skiing in the East. His first ski boots were too tight and felt as though they were built of ice. His dad had said, "You're lucky you're not wearing lace-up boots, like I did." That sounded like the truth.

When JC first learned to ski, the little hill relied on a relic from the past, a rope tow. As a little boy, he did not have the muscles to hold onto the rope when the hill got steep.

Despite holding it with all his might, the rope would begin to slip through JC's gloves. He'd slide backward until he felt the reassuring lap of the adult behind him. The child would ride to the top, resting against that lap.

Sometimes the lap belonged to his dad or mom, and sometimes it belonged to a perfect stranger. Whoever it was, they were happy to help a little boy trying to get to the top of the hill. He didn't need help skiing down. He was a gifted skier from the first day.

The next morning, JC and Bip grabbed some breakfast and got to the lift line. JC had never skied Battle Ax. It opened only a dozen years ago. He'd lived in Colorado all that time.

New York's newest ski resort still felt new. And it had all the amenities a modern ski area needed to offer.

The ski lodge was patently Adirondack. The exterior had large rough-timber posts and crossbeams. The walls were stone, except for portions that had birch bark siding.

It was a replica of a luxurious Great Camp from the past. There were sweeping porches on both upper floors. They faced the chairlifts. The porch railings were made of thick bentwood. There were turrets and steep pitched roofs.

In the winter, the porches were used only on a rare warm day until the last month of the season that was spring skiing. But the twig porches brought charm and served as a daily reminder to guests of where they were, the Adirondacks.

Inside the lodge were large fireplaces and big rooms with stone walls and thick log pillars. Photographs on the wall captured old black-and-white images of tents and campfires. Loggers or hunters or fishers sat or stood, side by side.

There were pictures of Great Camps. The families who belonged there lined up on the porch and stood still for the photographer.

And there were photographs of the pioneers of winter sport in the United States. They wore thick sweaters and thin leather gloves. Their smiles usually seemed to be on the verge of a laugh.

Behind the lodge, there were two main pedestrian streets lined with shops, hotels, condos, bars and restaurants. All the architecture reflected the same Adirondack Great Camp ambiance. Snowshoes and long varnished skis were mounted on the exterior walls.

Battle Ax was a more expensive ski resort than its neighbor to the south, Whiteface. But Whiteface would always be more famous, as home to the Olympic alpine ski races in 1980.

Whiteface was owned by the state of New York. For that reason, there was an effort to keep the price of lift tickets "within reach" for the taxpayers who helped pay the bills. And because Whiteface was on state forest land, it proved impossible to build a modern ski village at the site.

Battle Ax was private. Because it was on private land, Battle Ax could build a resort village at the base of its ski runs.

Skiers and snowboarders loved both mountains. But the state loved the tax revenues produced by Battle Ax.

During public hearings, proponents of building the new ski resort hoped it would be a game changer for the meager North Country economy. It would provide jobs and lure tourists carrying credit cards.

Opponents argued that this one development would lead to another, and another and another. They worried that the

Forever Wild status of the park, and its protective "Blue Line" would become forever blurred.

Now, the large Tomahawk Resort development next to Battle Ax was under construction. And those who fought for or against permission to build Battle Ax both voiced the same battle cry, "I told you so!"

Battle Ax got its name long before it was built. The founder of the ski resort, Averill Felix, told a story about his grandfather who, as a child, played on the hills that would later become ski runs.

The family story said that while running through tall grass on the side of the mountain called Le Trou Au Coeur, Grandfather Felix tripped and fell. When he investigated what he had tripped over, there was an old battle ax. It was presumably left there from the days the Iroquois called this area home.

The battle ax, now with a broken handle, had remained in the family and graced the wall, in a glass case, of the founder's office.

It was a rare day of sunshine in the East Coast winter. JC and Bip rode up a chairlift. It was about twenty-seven degrees with light wind.

"Twenty-seven and sunny," JC said. "My favorite!"

They had heard of a storm heading their way. It was already hitting Western New York and, with luck, would arrive later that night at Battle Ax and Whiteface.

"They're getting pounded near Buffalo," Bip said with enthusiasm. "Do they have ski mountains out there?"

"They have ski *hills*," JC corrected him. "But they get a ton of snow. That is the cruel curse New York endures for some long-forgotten slight. *We* have the mountains and *Western* New York gets twice as much snow. But the ski resorts out there do a nice job with what they have. And the snow can be amazing."

JC gave themselves two hours before they'd need to start their workday. Denver was two hours behind New York. Their live shots wouldn't begin until seven p.m. in Joseph County.

Bip was a snowboarder. This was the first time they had hit the slopes together. JC was impressed with Bip's ability, more than impressed.

"Do you race?" JC asked him.

"I do sometimes," Bip told him with a big smile on his face. "It's fun. It's all fun."

They skied down runs called Small Fang, Dean the Dream and Polly. The run called Montcalm was named for a French general. He won admiration in the North Country during the French and Indian War for his ability in battle and sensibility away from the battlefield.

They followed each other down a run called Dragonfly and found themselves at the top of the half-pipe.

"After you," JC laughed. "Then I'll sneak down the deck and pretend I did the half-pipe."

They shared a laugh. Bip said, "Give me a minute, I think I know a couple of guys over there."

By the reception Bip received from the snowboarders at the drop-in of the half-pipe, it seemed that he held a high rank among the group. He'd never set foot in New York, but he had friends there.

Bip returned and said, "Let's hang out a few minutes. These guys are sick. They're about to go."

The first rider dropped in and rode high up the opposing wall, gaining speed.

"Nice!" Bip and the others shouted as the rider soared above the near wall and grabbed the tail of his board with both hands.

"Whoa! Bloody Dracula!" Bip hollered. He explained the tricks to JC in between shouting encouragement, "Chicken Salad!"

The next rider dropped over the lip of the half-pipe and began with a 360-degree spin. He soared over the next wall but came down off balance. He slammed onto his back as he hit the flat bottom.

"Oooh, Back Dirt!" the riders on the sidelines cried out and laughed.

The fallen rider raised his arm and gave a thumbs-up as he coasted to a stop, still on his back. He had a smile on his face and that got the spectators laughing again, "Back Dirt!"

"Back Dirt?" JC asked Bip.

"Yeah," the snowboarder told him. "Like if he was riding a bike or a skateboard when he fell. His back would be all dirty."

And as the snowboarder rose from the snow, some of his colleagues laughed and brushed off his back, as though it had dirt on it.

"I've never heard that before," JC told the younger man.

"These guys tell me they made it up, like a week ago," Bip chuckled. "It's awesome, right? Guys like this make words up and five years later, they show up in the dictionary."

Bip and the others laughed some more as their fallen comrade rose and raised his arm in triumph.

"Back Dirt!" they shouted.

8

The snow was coming down the next morning. It fell on Battle Ax, Whiteface, Joseph and Lake Placid. Skiers and snowboarders were lined up at the chairlifts when they opened.

Smudge was thankful that three of his deputies had swept the convenience store site before the snow arrived. They had formed a grid and walked at a distance from each other. They were searching for evidence that a shooting had occurred, or anything else relevant.

"Not a thing," Senior Deputy Peter Colden had told the sheriff when asked what they had found.

"Was Cynthia Pfister at the site?" the sheriff had asked.

"She's kind of grumpy, isn't she?" was Colden's response. The sheriff took that to mean that she was there.

"I put her in a bad mood," the sheriff had said.

Deputy Colden's first priority during the snowstorm was to get the fender benders taken care of. There were two traffic lights in Joseph County, both situated at the Battle Ax ski area.

That is where a majority of the minor collisions took place. Drivers underestimated their speed and overestimated the space between their car and the car in front of them.

A third light also handled the Battle Ax traffic but was officially located in Essex County.

The next thing Deputy Colden had done that morning was make another call to Scotland, as the sheriff had asked.

"Nothing," Colden told Smudge, when asked if the victim's parents said anything useful to their investigation.

"Nothing was bothering Campbell when he last called home?" the sheriff asked. "He didn't complain to his parents about a problem or someone he wasn't getting along with?"

"They said that he sounded fine. I believe they said that he thought everything here was, quote, 'magic,'" the deputy informed his boss.

"In Scottish, that means everything is going well," said a voice, as a woman pushed through the glass door into the sheriff's office.

It was Cynthia Pfister. She was carrying a cardboard box. She made eye contact with the sheriff and she did not smile one bit.

"You said you wanted this," said Pfister. She maintained a stern look as she put the box on a counter that was between the door and the deputies' desks. She turned to leave.

"Will the sheriff know what this is about?" Colden asked. She stopped, turned, and looked at the deputy like he was stupid. The sheriff listened without rising from behind the desk in his office.

"He'll know what to do with it," Pfister said as she turned again and moved toward the exit. "Or he can call me, and I'll tell him what to do with it."

With raised eyebrows, Deputy Colden looked toward the sheriff. The deputy picked up the box and walked it into the sheriff's office and placed it on his desk.

"You've made a fan there," the deputy said.

"Women can't resist me," the sheriff replied as he pulled the lid off the box. In it, he saw a Glock 19.

JC and Bip Peters were just dropping their skis and snowboard back in their rooms after taking a few runs in the fresh powder. The TV station had booked them in affordable rooms at a log structure called The Thayendanegea.

That was the Mohawk name for Joseph Brant, the Indian chief Joseph County was presumably named after. Thayendanegea was unpronounceable to most visitors and residents alike, so the hotel was usually called "The T." It was in the Battle Ax resort village.

JC suggested getting breakfast in small downtown Joseph. They parked outside a café called "The Gill Grill." The sign was a likeness of a big fish. There was a busy fishing season that kept Joseph bustling during the warm weather. Hunting season was another busy time of year.

It was still snowing. A plow came by occasionally and pushed the snow against cars that had been parked on the street overnight.

JC scanned the little business district. It formed a square with the Joseph County Courthouse in the middle. In effect, every store could tell someone asking for directions, "We're across from the County Courthouse."

There were a couple of real estate companies and offices for some attorneys. There was a ski shop with long antique skis and poles mounted over the entrance.

There were two cafes, The Gill Grill and one that seemed capable of becoming a bar after lunch. That one was called "The Joker."

There were a couple of affordable motels. One had a sign with a skier, the other had a sign with a bear.

A store sold newspapers, books and a few groceries. There was a souvenir shop and there were the county offices.

At the end of the commercial district, around the corner and far down the side of the square, there was the Joseph County Museum. It was located in an old house.

It didn't appear that downtown Joseph had prospered that much, for a hamlet located near a big ski area. Battle Ax supplied its own shopping opportunities for visitors, in their own resort village. Tomahawk would offer even more chances to shop. Little Joseph would get the leftovers and the tax base.

They entered the café called The Gill Grill and chose a Formica-topped table. Before sitting, JC and Bip pulled down zippers and peeled off layers of wet ski clothing.

"Is the powder always this heavy in the East?" Bip asked as he fell into his seat. "It's kind of a workout."

"It's not always heavy," JC told him. "But most of the time, it is. There's a lot more water in the snow here."

Bip was examining his sweaty PolyPro undershirt and pulling it away from his skin.

"Powder is less frequent here, too," JC said. "The East doesn't get giant snowstorms nearly as often as we get out West."

"I'll bet it was easier on my snowboard than it was on your skis," Bip smiled with a grin. "I just ride across the top."

"I think you're right," JC conceded.

A pretty woman stopped at the table. She was clearly interested in Bip. She noticeably didn't look in JC's direction.

"I saw you at the half-pipe yesterday," she said.

"Really? Did I see you?" Bip responded with a smile on his handsome young face.

"I had a mask on. You were talking with some of the guys," she answered. "But I saw you go down the hill. You're really good."

"Thanks," said Bip with a charming smile. "Did you get out this morning?"

"Yeah," she said. "I just got back. Wasn't it awesome?"

JC realized that he was not going to be included in this conversation. While Bip and the young woman were busy flirting with each other, it gave JC time to think about where they had seen this attractive brunette before.

"We should go out some time," Bip said. That's my boy, JC thought.

"I mean, snowboarding," Bip said to her with an embarrassed grin. She was grinning, too.

"Hey, do you have a sec to help me with something, outside?" she asked the news photographer. Again, JC knew he was being purposely ignored.

"Yeah," Bip said with some enthusiasm. He told JC his breakfast order, got up and walked with Patty MacIntyre into the snowfall.

A waitress brought two black coffees to the table, took the order from JC and departed for the kitchen.

He absentmindedly reached for his phone. He caught himself when he realized he was about to call Shara.

It was a habit that he was trying to break. Seeing Bip with his new friend had triggered an old impulse.

Whatever Bip was summoned to assist with, it was a short task. He came back inside to take his seat at the table.

"Do you know who that was?" Bip asked.

"The administrative assistant to the county executive," JC answered. "It took me a moment to place her."

"Yeah," Bip concurred. "And she doesn't like you." Bip giggled a little. JC just smiled.

"Luckily," Bip continued, "she thinks you're to blame for the story about the investigation into her boss, and I just do what I'm told."

"You're an innocent victim," JC offered.

"Yeah," Bip agreed with a growing smile. "Sort of like you're bullying me."

"She likes you," JC told his colleague.

"I think I could get to like her, too." Bip agreed. "We're going to try to snowboard together tomorrow morning, if that's alright."

"I don't want to be a third wheel," JC said. "Go ahead, I'll find something to do."

"Anyway," Bip proceeded, "she didn't need my help with anything outside. She wanted to tell me something, a news tip."

"Do tell," JC responded.

"There was a guy's body found in a river here the other day," Bip began. "The sheriff thinks it's a murder, and the victim is from Colorado."

"That's interesting," JC said as he lowered his coffee cup. "A murder? Employees in vacation resorts do not usually just blurt that sort of thing out in front of the news media. Murders are bad business for resorts."

JC thought about that as the waitress brought their breakfast. Bip dug in.

"Why did she tell *you?*" JC asked Bip.

"Because I'm a stud," Bip responded with mischief, looking up from his fried eggs.

"No, that can't be it," JC responded with a deflating smile aimed at Bip. Actually, JC thought, the young man *was* kind of a stud.

"She didn't seem to like us much when we entered Cornheiser's office to interview him about a murder he may have committed," JC reflected.

"She didn't like *you,*" Bip said as he looked up again, still with a smile on his face before diving into some hash browns.

"A murder investigation would be a convenient distraction from her boss's problems," JC said.

"And she gets to go snowboarding with me," Bip said, grinning as he chewed a piece of bacon.

JC started working on his breakfast as he tried to arrive at some conclusions. He was still going to report on the investigation into Colin Cornheiser. But he was also going to look into the murder.

"Could he be the killer?" JC asked.

"Who?" Bip asked as he wiped toast over his plate where there used to be eggs.

"Cornheiser," JC snapped back, aware of Bip's lack of focus on anything beyond his food. "Am I disturbing your breakfast?"

"Sort of," Bip replied without looking up from his meal. Then, JC's point registered with him. "Oh, sorry. What were you saying?"

"Could Cornheiser have killed the man found in the river? Cornheiser is in quite a bind. Maybe the victim knew something damaging," JC theorized. "And both men were from Colorado. That's a heck of a coincidence. Maybe the victim knew something back in Colorado and then they happened to cross paths here."

"So, we're not going to report on the guy found in the water, unless it ties to the Cornheiser story?" Bip asked. "Because it might be a distraction?"

"Oh, brother," JC quickly answered. "Of course we're going to report on the guy found in the water. A good story is still a good story. Now, we have two good stories." They both smiled.

JC phoned the sheriff's office while he ate his omelet. He was patched to the sheriff and JC introduced himself.

"You're here in Joseph? That was fast," Smudge said, thinking that they'd only identified the shooting victim from Colorado the day before.

"We were already here," JC clarified. "We're doing a story about the investigation involving County Executive Colin Cornheiser and a murder in Colorado forty-five years ago."

Interesting, the sheriff thought. He provided benign details to the reporter. Paul Campbell had gone to Colorado College. He had come to New York to work as an archaeologist. He was shot in the chest. He was found in LaChute Brook.

"It would be great to get an interview on camera with you, Sheriff," JC said.

"About what?" Smudge asked. He wasn't about to get tangled up in the investigation into the county executive.

"About the murder," JC informed him.

"OK," the sheriff reluctantly sighed. "Come by this afternoon. We're still a little busy with cars sliding off the road and the like. The storm, you know."

"This afternoon is fine," JC said. "See you then."

Sheriff Williams was not required to do a lot of television interviews. He was a long winding road away from the nearest TV market, and news in Joseph usually was not about big crimes being committed. More like cow-tipping, the sheriff mused.

But there were a fair share of recreational accidents like drownings, skier deaths, hikers falling off cliffs and small wildfires. He did interviews about that, from time to time.

Upon completion of breakfast, JC wanted to see the sights pertinent to this new story, the death of a Colorado man in Joseph.

As the two journalists exited The Gill Grill, JC thought out loud: "So, what theories do we like?"

"That I'm a stud," Bip responded, grinning. JC had to laugh at that, too.

It was still snowing. They stopped their car at a pullover past the old stone bridge. Bip shot some footage of the bridge and LaChute Brook while JC got a feel for the scene. He followed the water's path toward the mountain called Le Trou Au Coeur. He was eager to learn more about the investigation.

They drove down Bonnieview Road. It was like a white cave when they drove into the forest. The sun hung low and snow stuck to the trees. There was a light gray sky overhead and snowplows hadn't reached the pavement below.

They were headed to the site where a convenience store would be built. They'd been told that the victim worked there. Some small tents marked the site. The weight of the new snow was causing them to sag.

JC got out of the car while Bip recorded some news footage of the lot. The reporter saw a woman emerge from a tent and he walked toward her.

Cynthia Pfister saw the camera. Bip was taking a low-angle shot. She then looked with a discriminating eye at the intruder approaching her.

"This is where the gentleman worked who they found in the water the other day?" JC asked.

"Yes, it is," Pfister answered impatiently.

"You knew him?" JC asked.

"We were business partners," the woman conceded, "and friends."

"I'm sorry for your loss," said the reporter. "We're a news crew from Colorado," JC told her. He handed her a business card and introduced himself.

"That was fast," the archaeologist said with a hint of disdain.

"We were already here," JC told her. "He went to Colorado College?"

"Colorado College?" she asked. "That's the hat he always wore."

"Yeah," JC said. "Good school."

"Yeah, we're not as stupid as we look," Pfister said without smiling. "We just like wearing blue jeans and getting dirty."

Grumpy. JC thought that was a good description for the archaeologist standing before him.

"What do you know about his death?" JC asked. He had not spoken long on the phone with the sheriff. That would come later in the day, on camera.

But JC had long ago learned that if you wanted to know about a police investigation, you may not be told as much by police as you will be told by the witnesses the police are talking to.

Cynthia Pfister decided to share the details that Sheriff Williams had shared with her. She didn't owe the sheriff a thing.

Her friend was shot twice, once in the heart, she said. He was found floating in LaChute Brook.

She told JC that the murder weapon was a 9mm, probably a Glock 19. When she said it, JC thought she looked a little angry. She pulled her gloves on and was looking around for something to do, other than talk to a reporter.

"Any idea why he was shot?" JC asked. The woman said nothing for a moment. But she thawed.

"No one had a good reason to shoot Paul," she responded with a quiet voice. "He moved to this country from Scotland. Everyone loved his accent."

The hard eyes of the woman seemed to soften as she looked down to the ground. She agreed when JC asked her for a short interview. He was sort of surprised that she did.

During the interview, Pfister said that Paul was a good guy and would be missed. She remembered that the interview would be viewed in Colorado and she said that Paul spoke fondly of the place he used to live.

"He may have played soccer in college. I think he was pretty good. But I just want people to know that he was a good guy," she said. "I don't want them to think he was mixed up in something because he was a bad person."

"That's kind of all we can ask for in the end, Ms. Pfister," JC told her after the interview was over, "that we deserve to be remembered with kindness."

"Call me Cindy," the archaeologist told the reporter. She still wasn't smiling.

"Hi, Harold," Pfister called out over JC's shoulder. She was looking at a man sweeping snow off his car near a sign for the Tomahawk Resort.

"Who's that?" JC asked.

"He's the archaeologist for the Tomahawk site. You come to know everyone if you're in this business and you're in the North Country," she said. "There are only so many of us."

"Did he know Paul?" JC asked.

"He knew Paul for a long time," she said. "You should interview him."

"Good idea," JC told her. "What's his name?"

"Harold DeWitt," she said.

"Big project," JC said as he looked over the nearly completed exteriors in the Tomahawk development.

"Huge project," Pfister agreed. "He works for a much bigger archaeology firm than ours. They get all the big projects. That development is going to double the tax revenue in this little county."

JC looked over the assortment of buildings on the Tomahawk property. Most of the work was being done indoors now, out of the cold. Tomahawk might be open for the summer, he thought.

"He may have gone to college with Paul," Pfister said. "Now look at him. He's getting rich, and I'm ... an archaeologist."

"Most archaeologists don't get rich?" JC asked.

Cynthia Pfister looked at the snow-covered ground and laughed. She patted JC on the arm and laughed some more as she walked away.

"See you later, JC," she said.

Bip secured his camera in the backseat of their car, using a seat belt. In the summer, the camera would go in the car trunk. But in cold weather, he said that it was better to let the camera ride up where it was warm.

The phone rang. It was Robin Smith, the producer back at the TV station.

"They want to know what you have today, JC," she said. The "they" would be the news director, assignment editor and all the producers of the evening news shows who would fight over who got JC's live shots from New York.

"I think we're going to get some testimonials on tape," he said, "from people in Joseph who really believe in the county executive. They don't believe he murdered anyone."

"Is there going to be enough story to keep you there?" Robin asked.

"It's too soon to tell, if you're asking about the Cornheiser story," JC told her. "But I've got a second entrée to offer: A new murder investigation here. The victim is an archaeologist from Colorado."

"Oooh," Robin responded with enthusiasm. "Archaeology? That's what I used to do, you know."

"That's right," JC responded. "I'd forgotten."

"Ten years," she told him.

"You were an archaeologist for ten years?" JC inquired. "Why'd you quit? Or were you fired?" he teased.

"Ha, ha," she mocked. "I was a great archaeologist. But it's hard to make a good living unless you own the company."

"Do you mind if I call and ask you archaeology questions," he requested, "if I'm going to add this story to my plate?"

"I'd love it," she told him.

JC asked Robin to look up some background on the archaeologist Paul Campbell, while he lived in Colorado. He also hoped she could find a picture of him. He asked her to tell the assignment editor that he'd do the reaction piece today regarding Colin Cornheiser.

"But tomorrow, I'll break the story about our dead archaeologist from Colorado," he told her.

"I'll tell them," Robin replied.

The snow was beginning to taper. There were spots of blue sky. Maybe the storm system had wrung itself out, JC thought. He decided it was time to swing by the sheriff's office.

They parked behind the courthouse and were ushered into Sheriff Williams' office. While Bip set up his tripod and lights, JC asked the sheriff some background questions and confirmed a few things.

"He went to Colorado College?" JC asked as he pulled out his long thin reporter's notebook.

"I think I told you that over the phone. He played soccer there. He had a soccer scholarship," Smudge added.

"He was originally from Scotland, right?" JC asked.

"Yes," the sheriff responded. "We've spoken to his family. They're pretty broken up about this, as you can imagine."

"I have a friend from Britain who played soccer," JC told Smudge. "He told me that he and his teammates were offered college soccer scholarships in the United States as soon as recruiters heard their accent over the phone." Smudge smiled at this.

Bip was set up and the interview got underway. They covered the basics of the investigation into the archaeologist's murder. The sheriff kept his answers short and generic as possible. He didn't anticipate the final question.

"You're looking for a 9mm handgun, a Glock 19?" JC asked.

"I'm not at liberty to discuss specifics of the investigation," the sheriff said. It was a stock answer, but Smudge looked annoyed. He wondered who had disclosed the murder weapon they were looking for.

The interview was over and Bip was packing up his gear. JC kept talking, now off-camera. He had noted that the sheriff wasn't happy about the murder weapon question. JC thought he might not be happy about that information getting to the public.

JC knew that police liked to keep secrets. Sometimes, a suspect would give himself away when he blurted out a fact about the crime that police had withheld from the public.

"How do you investigate a murder in a small town, Sheriff?" JC asked. "Everybody knows everybody's business in a small town."

"You're right," Smudge agreed. "A shooting like this would usually already have resulted in an arrest. A neighbor or relative would know that the victim and the perpetrator were bickering and someone's straw had finally broken."

"It becomes a small world, doesn't it?" JC asked. "We're here from Colorado, doing a story about your county executive who used to live in Colorado. Now, this new victim lived in Colorado. And I'm told that the archaeologist at Tomahawk Resort might have lived in Colorado, too?"

"Is that true?" the sheriff asked.

"The archaeologist of that site, Tomahawk?" JC replied. "I was told that he's an old friend of the victim, that they might have gone to college together."

"Well, that's interesting. I'll add him to the list," the sheriff said.

9

"What is happening to this world?" Those were the first words out of Harold DeWitt's mouth when JC introduced himself.

The reporter and his photographer had pulled their rental car onto the work site of the Tomahawk Resort. A sheriff's patrol car was just pulling out. The news crew parked their 4x4 and, on foot, commenced to search for the project's archaeologist.

They pushed through heavy temporary plastic sheeting in the doorways. It brought them inside the shells of what would become stores, restaurants and a couple of hotel lobbies. It was cold inside, but at least it was out of the wind.

Stairs were being framed that would take future guests up to their rented rooms. A long mahogany reception desk for check-ins was mostly covered by plastic and tape. There was sawdust everywhere and it was noisy with the sound of power saws and wood being dropped on the floor.

A construction worker pointed JC to a building on the other side of a new cobblestone walk. There was glass in the windows and the interior looked like completed office space. There was no sawdust.

That is where they found Harold DeWitt. He had a room with a table covered by survey maps. There were some pictures of dirt in cheap frames on the wall, and there were some thick reports bound in plastic on a bookshelf. Most importantly, the space was heated.

DeWitt was leaning against a relatively clean desk. He said that the murder of Paul Campbell was unnerving.

"He was my friend. We met in college. We were both studying to be archaeologists," DeWitt told JC. "I can't tell you how many digs we've done together. We'd volunteer for anything: digging up old bones when the phone company stumbled across them, looking for a burial ground near an old fort, finding old Indigenous campgrounds."

DeWitt's hair was prematurely gray. He was thin but handsome. He looked healthy enough, and exuded self-confidence. He smiled during most of the interview.

"Dinosaurs!" the archaeologist continued. "Colorado has a lot of dinosaurs buried beneath places that people walk every day. But, who am I telling? You guys are from Colorado. It's funny that you came all the way here."

"You stayed in touch, after college?" JC asked.

"Oh yeah," DeWitt told him. "You know, Paul already had some amazing experience when he came to the United States. In Scotland, he'd volunteered to work digs at castles.

"I really thought he had me outclassed. He was digging up eight-hundred-year old castles! How was I going to compete with that?" DeWitt asked with a smile.

"You two were competitive?" JC asked.

"No, no," DeWitt said, waving his hand as though waving that possibility away. "I just say that. We were good friends. He spent the holidays with me at my parents' house once."

"You're from Colorado?" JC asked.

"No, no, but I love it there," DeWitt said. "I grew up in Western New York, about four hours from here. That's where I met Paul, though, at Colorado College."

"And both you and Paul ended up here?" JC asked.

"Yes. Because I was from New York, I was in the pipeline. I'd hear about digs that we might find interesting. We worked together on the first couple. But then we found our own opportunities, I guess. We went in different directions. We always stayed in touch, though. I got him this job, you know, at the site next door."

"The convenience store site?" JC asked.

"Yeah," said DeWitt. "The guy developing that site asked me to do the survey, but I was too busy. So, I recommended Paul. I've steered him some business before. He always did a great job."

"Can we do a quick interview on camera, Mr. DeWitt?" asked JC.

"Yeah, I guess so," the man said in a more subdued tone.

Bip dashed out of the room to go get his camera. It gave JC a chance to ask questions that he knew wouldn't get answered when the camera was rolling.

"How did Paul get along with his partner, Ms. Pfister?" JC asked.

"Cindy? I think they got along well," DeWitt answered. Then he seemed to have something to add. "She doesn't get along with everyone, if you know what I mean. She's a little rough around the edges. She has a short temper. But I think she and Paul got along. It was impossible not to get along with Paul."

Bip returned with his camera and tripod and set up quickly.

"Why would someone want to kill Paul Campbell?" JC asked as the camera began to roll.

"I can't think of anyone less likely to be the target of a murder," DeWitt answered. "He was too nice a guy."

"When you say he wouldn't be the target of a murder," JC asked, "are you thinking that this may have been random, like a robbery?"

"I just can't see anyone who actually knows Paul *killing* him," said the victim's friend.

"I'm sure the police have spoken with you?" JC asked.

"A couple of sheriff's deputies just left," DeWitt acknowledged. "You just missed them."

"Did they find a wallet on the vic— Paul?" JC caught himself before using the term "victim.'" He tried to be sensitive around friends and loved ones who had suffered a loss of this proportion. He met a lot of people like that, in his business.

"They wondered if I'd seen it, or if he usually carried a wallet," DeWitt stated. "They asked if he carried a lot of money."

"Did he?" JC followed.

"He was away from home. You're away from home," DeWitt said. "Aren't you carrying more money than if you were at home?"

JC made a face admitting the fact. While he carried a company credit card, he also was carrying a lot more cash than he would if he were in Denver.

JC turned to Bip and signaled that he could stop filming. Bip hustled to pack up his gear. JC and the archaeologist shared small talk, but JC's eyes landed on a holster on a bookshelf. There was a handgun in the holster.

"Expecting trouble?" JC asked DeWitt. The archaeologist followed the reporter's eyes, landing on the holstered weapon. He laughed a small laugh.

"No," he said. "Unless you mean accidentally shooting my foot. I wear it when I'm doing work in the woods. There are a lot of tough characters out there, moose, coyote, bear."

"The bear should be hibernating in January," JC suggested. "And as for moose, there are about one hundred of them in this vast park. You'll be lucky to *see* one, let alone be attacked by one."

"You're probably right," DeWitt said. "But, I've heard some stories. I get some grief by the other fellas here when I show up at a site with a gun. But I don't flash it around. I just have it to protect myself."

The interview ended. JC and Bip headed for downtown Joseph. They needed to turn their attention to the story they would air that night, about how Joseph was reacting to hearing that their county executive was entangled in a forty-five-year-old murder investigation.

Driving up Bonnieview Road, after driving past the archaeology dig at the convenience store site, there were some pastures. Then both sides of the pavement were lined by thick forest. Occasionally, there was a break in the trees, cleared to place a home there.

Some of the homes were new and reflected affluence. Unplowed driveways revealed that many were vacation homes. After more trees, another opening would disclose a house trailer or a shack with faded paint and old sheds. Such was the economic disparity among neighbors on Bonnieview Road.

JC phoned his newsroom in Denver. Robin Smith was on the other end. JC told her the elements they would include in their story and the roll cues.

"Hey Robin," JC said before they ended their call. "Can you look for anything suggesting that the county executive here, Colin Cornheiser, ever crossed paths in Colorado with our murder victim out here, Paul Campbell?"

"Sure," she said happily. "I like a good mystery."

"Well," JC told her, "then you would love being out here."

"Have you ever cleaned this thing?" The sheriff's question was aimed at Cynthia Pfister. The sheriff extended his hand, holding a cardboard box.

Pfister took it and opened the box. In it was her Glock 19. She smelled grease. It had been cleaned and oiled. And he was giving it back to her.

"What's the matter," she grumbled as she looked at the law officer in the ball cap. "I'm not good enough to be a suspect?"

"You couldn't have killed anything with that," Smudge told her, "even if you'd hit them with the end of it."

The sheriff had found Pfister inside a tent at the convenience store site. The snowfall had ended. The sound of plows could be heard on Bonnieview Road as their shovels found pavement.

"I cleaned it up for you," Smudge told the woman. Her blond hair was hidden beneath a red knit cap.

"Thank you," she said, in a softer tone than he had become accustomed to hearing from her mouth.

"A dirty gun will foul, rust, the whole nine yards," he said. "Have you ever fired that thing?"

"At a target range?" she said in a questioning tone. "When I bought it?" she questioned again, as though she could not quite remember what year that was.

Smudge smiled. He said he would buy her lunch, to make up for thinking she was a murder suspect.

"I should probably have my murder-suspect radar checked," the sheriff said.

"I should probably have my asshole radar checked, too," she said with a smile. "Maybe you're not one."

10

"Who you going to piss off today?" The question came to JC from a uniformed officer sitting next to him at the breakfast counter at The Gill Grill.

JC was breakfasting alone because Bip was taking a couple of hours to snowboard with Patty MacIntyre. She happened to be the administrative assistant to the Joseph County executive. That was the same county executive who was on the verge of being indicted in Colorado for a murder dating back to 1976.

The previous night, the reporter had gone live from Joseph after asking people for their reaction to the investigation of their county executive. It was almost impossible, JC learned, to find anyone who had a bad thing to say about their elected leader.

They liked Colin Cornheiser and they didn't particularly care for some television reporter coming there to stir up trouble.

The journalist told his viewers in Colorado that the county executive was popular in Joseph. Most voters felt he would be good until they saw evidence that he was bad.

Now, JC found himself sitting on a neighboring stool with Senior Joseph County Sheriff's Deputy Peter Colden at the breakfast counter of The Gill Grill. They exchanged introductions.

"He was a college football star, you know," Colden said.

"The county executive? I wouldn't have guessed that," JC said.

"No, the sheriff," Deputy Colden told him.

"Where did he play?" JC asked.

"I don't know. In the Midwest, Ohio or Illinois," Colden said.

"I'll have to look him up," JC responded.

"So, who owns the new Tomahawk Resort?" JC asked the law officer.

"Same guy as Battle Ax," Colden answered. "Averill Felix. He's going to double his money, though, when Tomahawk doubles the size of his resort."

The deputy did not want to talk about the investigations. JC didn't think the deputy should do that, either, but it didn't stop a reporter from asking.

Once JC was confident that the deputy wasn't going to alter from doing the very thing he should be doing, the journalist wished him a good day and headed for the rental car.

Since he had the vehicle, it would be JC's job to pick up Bip at the base of Battle Ax after his morning of snowboarding. After driving the length of Bonnieview Road and taking a right into the ski village, he pulled up to Bip and Patty MacIntyre, waiting in the loading area. They both wore baggy snowboarding outfits and their boards were leaning against their shoulders.

"Hi kids, have fun?" JC tried to sound as much like a parent as he could.

"Hi, Dad," they both chimed and then giggled at each other.

"Do you need a ride, Patty?" JC asked, still behind the steering wheel.

"No, thank you," she said politely. "I brought my car."

With that, JC watched his news photographer and the county executive's administrative assistant exchange a warm glance and a smile.

JC thought for a moment that they were going to kiss. But they didn't. He surmised that it did not mean they wouldn't kiss later.

Bip loaded his gear in the rear hatch and hopped in the passenger seat. The radio was on. It was French-language rock and roll.

They had learned that at the elevation of the Battle Ax ski lodge, the frequency of a Montreal rock station overwhelmed the weak radio signals on the dial that could be picked up in Joseph.

As the crow flies, it was only about a hundred and twenty miles to Montreal from the ski area. Battle Ax was probably atop the tallest mountain between there and the Canadian border, so there was nothing to stop Battle Ax from hearing a French-language version of a hit song from the '90s.

"People here are grateful when they can pick up *anything* on the radio," JC told Bip. "The problem isn't the peaks, it's the valleys."

The New York native explained how difficult it was for local counties and towns even to build a communications tower so that an ambulance could talk to a hospital.

"They call them 'dead spots.'" JC said. "If your car goes off the road in the wrong place during a storm, your phone won't get a signal. You're on your own."

"Is that why they call them 'dead spots?'" Bip asked. "Because if you go off the road in the wrong spot, you're dead?"

JC smiled. It wasn't the first time that sentiment had been stated, but it didn't make it any less true.

"The state constitution doesn't allow motorized vehicles on much of this forest preserve," JC continued. "And without motorized vehicles, they can't build or maintain a tower to hang communications equipment on. First-responders from the Adirondacks file their complaints with the state capitol, but the problem seems next to impossible to resolve."

They maneuvered out of the maze of parking lots serving the ski resort. Bip was unzipping and peeling off layers of ski clothing.

"So," JC put on the best imitation of his own mother, "what did you kids talk about?"

"Nothing," Bip responded. "Seriously, she didn't say anything that would be useful to our story and I didn't exactly grill her. We were snowboarding. I wasn't doing a cross-examination."

"Wow," JC feigned betrayal. "Did she tell you that you can't play with me anymore?"

"She's fine," Bip told him. "She just really likes her boss. I told her what we said in our story last night and she probably hates you a little less now."

"Oh, I see," JC protested. "When she likes the coverage, it's *our* story. When she objects to it, it is *my* story?"

Bip gave JC a long look.

"Yes," the photographer said.

The radio broadcast from Montreal grew into static as their car proceeded to the lower altitude of Bonnieview Road. JC loved the sound of the French language. He was sorry it was now muzzled on his frequency.

He turned the car toward the hamlet of Joseph. Far from the boundary of the Battle Ax Ski Resort, he and Bip both noted ski tracks in the snow. The tracks came off the mountain and crossed pastures to reach the road.

"Backcountry skiers, I guess," JC said.

When he saw Cindy Pfister on the convenience store site, he pulled off the road and parked.

"We met Harold DeWitt," JC announced as he approached her.

"Hi, JC," she greeted him with a smile as she brushed her hair back under her knit cap. It was the first time he had seen her smile. It made him nervous. He didn't want to fall from grace again.

"You met him?" she asked. "How did that go?"

"He says that he got you and Paul this job?"

"There's probably some truth in that," she told him. "DeWitt has referred us before, if he's too busy to do a job."

"Friends help friends," JC offered.

"Exactly," she responded.

JC noticed a pin that Pfister was wearing on the breast of her dirty rugged jacket. The pin had a boar head on it.

"Is that Paul's?" he asked. He was pointing at the pin.

"Yes," she said. She looked at him as someone who knew her secret. "You recognize it?"

"The boar head of the Campbell Clan," JC told her.

She nodded her head. "You're Scottish?"

"More than a wee dram," he smiled. "My father's side."

"Paul gave this pin to me," she said as she handled it. "You know, some time is going to be set aside at the Burns Supper this weekend to remember Paul. Maybe you should come. You must know about the Burns Supper?"

"Oh, I'm quite familiar with the Burns Supper," JC informed her. "I've been to many of them."

"Well, Saturday is January 25th," Pfister reminded him. "It's Rabbie Burns' birthday."

JC explained the traditional Burns Supper to Bip. It was an event shared by the people of Scotland and those of Scottish blood across the world. It was a chance, each year, to celebrate being Scottish and celebrate the most popular poet in the country's history.

Robert Burns had been dead for over two hundred years. But at annual Burns Suppers, there were bagpipes, poetry readings and the serving of haggis.

"Paul took me to Burns Suppers," Pfister recalled. "There's going to be one at Battle Ax, in a back room at the bar there. Think about coming." Cindy gave him a smile as she walked back into her tent.

Yep, JC thought. That is one happy Cindy Pfister. He wondered why.

Bip took over driving chores from JC when they got back into the car. "I'm a creature of habit," Bip said.

"Nothing wrong with that," JC told him, and he pulled out his phone.

"Hey, Robin," JC said when she picked up. "If I make arrangements, could you go to my apartment and pick up my kilt?"

"Your kilt?" Robin asked as she started to laugh. "You mean that skirt that Scottish guys wear?"

"You know," JC said into the phone, "that may be an insensitive remark aimed at my culture. I'm not sure, I've got to think about it."

Robin laughed some more and agreed to run his errand.

"It's not an errand, it's work," he told her. "And I need you to ship it out here."

Approaching Joseph, where they would meet the live truck and prepare for the evening newscast, JC ended the call. He saw Sheriff Williams standing on the old stone bridge.

JC instructed Bip to pull over. The reporter exited the car and walked up the bridge to join the sheriff. Smudge was leaning on the bridge, looking up the brook at the mountain it flowed from. JC leaned against the bridge next to him.

"Do you have a dog?" the sheriff asked without turning his head toward the reporter.

"I did," JC responded. "She died about five years ago. It's tough to get over, when they die."

"Yeah, some people are like that, too," the sheriff told him. He seemed lost in his own thoughts. "But good dogs are easier to find than good people."

JC let a minute pass in silence. He needed to change the subject. The two men looked at the river.

"I hear you were a college football star," JC informed him.

Smudge turned to look at the reporter.

"You hear a lot of things," Smudge said to him. He was a little flattered. He did not mind being remembered for something he did well at one time.

"I looked you up," JC told the bigger man. "You were really good. You even played against that football star that has his own police drama on TV now."

"We were good for a middle-sized school," the sheriff recounted. "They were a major football power. Our school was paid a lot of money to travel out to their stadium in California and get the tar kicked out of us. He was the better quarterback, but I threw two touchdown passes that day and he only threw one. I still remind him of that."

"So, you still talk?" JC asked the sheriff.

"Oh yeah," the sheriff smiled. "We talk a couple of times a year. He usually calls to ask me something about police procedure, for his show."

"Good show," JC said.

"I agree," Smudge said. "Good show."

They both watched the brook run under the bridge. Then the sheriff said, "The reason he didn't throw more touchdown passes that day was because we couldn't tackle their running backs. They just kept running until they got tired. He could have thrown ten of them."

"Hey sheriff," JC said. He determined it was time to get what he came for.

It wasn't lost on Smudge, who had started scratching his face. He had been waiting for the reporter to get to the point.

"Could it have been a robbery?" JC asked. "Maybe even random?"

"Paul Campbell's murder? Why do you ask that?" the sheriff inquired. He was very interested in what was coming next.

"Have you found his wallet?" JC asked.

The sheriff said nothing. He figured this reporter would take that as a "I'm-not-at-liberty-to-discuss-it"-type of non-answer.

"So, it could have been a robbery," JC asserted.

"You don't want me to have *any* secrets, do you?" the sheriff said before walking away.

Smudge climbed into his Tahoe and shut the door. He watched as the reporter pulled out his phone.

"He's a pretty smart reporter," the sheriff said to himself. "Or am I just getting dumber?"

11

"**D**ig deeper!!"

JC was being lectured on how to do his job. The news director at his TV station in Denver wasn't happy with the progress JC was making on the story he'd been sent to Upstate New York to report on.

It was expensive to send a two-member crew to the North Country of New York to cover the looming arrest of a county executive for a murder forty-five years ago in Colorado.

"But you asked me to come here," JC reminded his news director, Pat Perilla.

"I sent you there to do a job," Perilla answered sternly on the other end of the phone.

"And I've doubled your money," JC insisted. "I'm reporting on the county executive *and* I've found the murder of an archaeologist from Colorado to report on. I've been here three full days and you've gotten three days of exclusive stories with meat still on the bones."

"So, what's your next story about the county executive going to cover?" the news director asked.

"I haven't a clue," JC admitted. "It's kind of a dry well until investigators from Colorado return and lead him from the county courthouse in handcuffs."

JC suspected that what really irritated his boss was that his boss was the one that thought it was such a great idea to send a reporter and photographer to Joseph in the first place.

"Do I have to put a crew on this Cornheiser story back here, too?" the news director barked. "Is that what it's going to take to keep this story moving?"

JC guessed that this question was supposed to stir JC's pride or conceit by suggesting someone else could dip their toe onto his turf. His turf supposedly being the Cornheiser story.

That's not what it stirred, however. Instead, it stirred doubts in JC's mind about Cornheiser's guilt.

"Maybe putting a crew on the story in Colorado isn't such a bad idea," JC told Perilla.

That seemed to make the news director only more irritable. JC thought he was making a lot of sense. He wondered if his news director's vexation was now an act, a misguided motivational technique.

JC had often read that fear was supposed to be a great motivator in the workplace. He did not see it that way. Over the years, he had been shot at, his skis had slammed him into hard surfaces at high speed, and he'd been beaten senseless by a guy with a baseball bat. Why would he fear an old guy sitting behind a desk?

JC was starting to feel himself digging a foxhole, ready to get into a fight with his superior. He cautioned himself not to do that.

But he was not going to give into pressure to say something about Cornheiser that police were suggesting privately but wouldn't say publicly, let alone prove. JC knew that if the allegations proved to be untrue, those law officers would be more than happy to let the news media take the fall.

JC was losing patience with the "gotcha" mentality that modern news programming seemed to find irresistible. He believed that "going negative" was usually a cheap trick.

Lately, he had observed a lot of people, not just journalists, who believed being negative was the same as being intelligent. JC believed that one did not always add up to the other.

"I'll keep looking," JC told his news director. That seemed to be what Perilla was searching for.

"The story about the archaeologist's murder is very interesting," Perilla said on the other end of the phone. "I'll grant you that."

It was mid-morning when his news director said he had a meeting to attend, hanging up the phone. JC slipped his phone back into his pocket and noticed there was an older gentleman staring at him.

The reporter had been taking in the view from the old stone bridge while discussing his shortcomings with his boss. The man was standing about ten feet away.

"He's not happy with you," the old man said to JC, who realized the stranger must have been listening to the conversation with Pat Perilla.

"You were listening for your own amusement?" JC asked him, a little surprised, rather than annoyed.

"Aye," the man said. "People usually say, 'I didn't mean to eavesdrop.' Well, they're not telling the truth. They heard you because they made every attempt to hear you. That's what I did, only I'm not going to tell a fib about it."

"An honest man," JC said and extended his hand. "I enjoy the rare occasion of meeting one."

"Patrick," the old man said while shaking with his thin hand.

"Do I hear a bit of a brogue?" JC asked.

"Ireland," Patrick said. "Born and raised in Cork."

"You were in Cork during the dangerous days there?" JC asked.

Patrick shook his head, "Aye."

"Did you come out this morning just to listen to my phone conversation?" JC asked. He showed a smile, hoping the man would understand that he was just joking, making conversation.

"I was on my walk," Patrick said. "You were in my way."

"Please accept my apologies," JC said after looking around him and seeing there was enough room to pass.

"No worry," Patrick responded. "Everything's grand."

It was a nice day. The skies were cloudy but there was not much wind. Patrick told JC that he took a walk every day.

"I walk from my house to that new development and back," Patrick said.

"Tomahawk?" JC asked.

"Aye," Patrick said. "I've been watching it go up. How old do you think I am?" Patrick asked.

JC knew he wouldn't win this game. It was a favorite game for some old people, and they played it well.

If JC guessed ninety, the man would be offended because he wasn't that old. If he guessed 70, the man would say "no" and make him guess more.

"Let's say 80," JC told him. A smile grew on Patrick's face.

"Ninety-five," the Irishman said, like a medal had just been pinned on his chest.

JC could not help but be a bit surprised. Patrick was skinny but stood up straight. His face had some red blotches, but his eyes were clear. He had a shock of white hair and a white mustache.

Rather than wear a jacket made from new high-tech materials to keep him warm, Patrick wore a thick wool coat reaching to his knees. It looked like it came from Ireland.

"What do you think of your county executive?" JC asked. He remembered that he told his news director he would look harder for local dirt on the county executive. It *was* the reason the reporter was sent to Upstate New York, after all.

However, JC had learned that when he ran a story telling his audience how popular a politician was, as he had two days ago, the next couple of days would normally bring calls and comments from people who despised that very same politician. That had not happened this time.

"Colin?" Patrick asked to the question JC had posed. "He's always done me right," the Irishman said. "I've no complaint. They say he might win a seat in the state assembly when that Tomahawk opens. He cleared the roadblocks like a bulldozer. He had to. The county is going to be rich in tax revenue from it. I hear they might lower our taxes."

"Everyone likes lower taxes. What kind of roadblocks?" JC inquired.

"Oh, the usual thing government does," replied Patrick. "Approval of the site plan, acquisition of the land, environmental review."

"Was everyone happy with the way he did it?" JC asked.

"I didn't hear any great complainers," Patrick told him.

"Do you hear anyone voicing complaints about his handling of anything else?" JC asked. "Any local scandals?"

Patrick thought about this and shook his head, no.

"You know," the old man finally said, "if I think *hard*, I remember achieving some great things in my own life. But without thinking hard at all, I remember every mistake I've ever made."

"I'm not half your age and I can say the same thing," JC responded, with complete sincerity.

"What I'm questioning, man," Patrick looked at JC. "Are those mistakes really so bad to lose all that sleep over them?"

"What if he killed a man?" JC asked.

"What if he didn't?" Patrick asked back. The old man smiled at the reporter, turned and resumed his daily walk.

"He has miles to go before he sleeps," JC said quietly to himself. He thought Patrick looked a little like the poet Robert Frost.

12

Ironic, JC thought, as he walked down the snow-lined sidewalk across from the County Courthouse. The TV station had just informed him they were sending a producer to assist him in Joseph.

JC had just gotten off the phone with his assignment editor in Denver. Rocky Baumann told him that they knew he was burdened by working on two big stories, instead of just the one they'd sent him to cover in Upstate New York.

He was told that Robin Smith would be flying to Albany. Joseph didn't have regular flights scheduled at the small airport. She'd get a rental car and drive to Joseph.

JC recalled that Robin was a former archaeologist, as well as being a go-getter. He could really use her input.

The reporter walked into the county offices and asked the administrative assistant if the county executive was available. Patty MacIntyre, unsmiling, rose from her desk, knocked on the door of Colin Cornheiser and entered, closing the door behind her.

When she emerged, JC was told Cornheiser would give him a few minutes before he had to leave for a meeting. JC tried to read MacIntyre's expression. He wanted to see if he was out of the doghouse now that she and his news photographer were becoming fond of each other. JC didn't pick up any encouraging signals.

"I understand that you met our resident author," Cornheiser said as he greeted JC and waved him to a chair in front of his desk.

"Resident author?" the reporter asked.

"Patrick! You didn't know?" the politician exuded. JC wasn't picking up any signals on Cornheiser's opinion of him, either. The county executive knew that JC had been sent to Joseph to report on a story that could be his ruin, a looming murder indictment in an old Colorado case. But Cornheiser exhibited no outward anger toward the journalist. For lack of a better term, JC had to describe his manner as "cordial."

"Patrick's an author?" JC reacted.

"Best seller," Cornheiser said. "It was years ago, but I think he's been living off the royalties ever since."

"What was it called?" JC inquired.

"*Dismembering Debbie*," Cornheiser recounted. "I remember reading it. It wasn't as gruesome as the title. It was a psychological dismembering. She wasn't even killed. It was a sordid tale, though, about a woman married to a member of the Irish Republican Army. Lots of intrigue. Patrick is from Ireland."

"He told me. He's a nice man," JC said, then changed the topic. "I understand you're thinking of running for the state assembly?"

"I've been approached," Cornheiser told him as he pulled off his glasses and began to wipe them clean. "But that kind of interest dries up when there are rumors that you murdered someone."

JC assumed that the county executive was referring to the reporter's own words, airing on the television back in Denver. Word spreads. The news media in New York was certain to pick up JC's story and report back to their own followers. It was possible, JC thought, that his words had spoiled Cornheiser's chance for higher office.

"Did you know the archaeologist who was murdered here?" JC asked.

"Are you going to accuse me of that, too?" Cornheiser asked with a lethal stare.

"I'm not out to get you, Mr. Cornheiser," JC said with a serious tone. "I do my job. The guilty are guilty and the innocent are innocent, regardless of what I do."

"Yeah," Cornheiser said. "I knew Mr. Campbell a little. He was a nice guy. We sort of hit it off when we learned that we both had lived in Colorado. I took him hiking once, when he first arrived here in the autumn. It's a shame, what happened to him."

"Any idea who would want him dead?" JC asked.

"No," he answered tersely.

"So, when did you move here to Joseph?" JC asked.

"Are you fishing now?" the county executive asked with a condescending tone.

"Not at all, Mr. Cornheiser," JC responded. "I feel like there's a gap in time in your biography, time between your college education and your arrival here."

"Maybe I traveled around a little," Cornheiser told the reporter. "I blew off some steam when I was finally finished with my education. Didn't you do a little of that?"

"I still am," JC told him with a smile. "Where did you travel to?"

"Still sounds like you're fishing," Cornheiser said in an accusing tone. "If you find out about other places I lived, you can dig up dirt on me there. Maybe I got a parking ticket in Winslow, Arizona? Maybe I got a speeding ticket in Salt Lake City? Then I'd be a multiple offender, right?"

"Is that where you went after college? Winslow and Salt Lake City?"

"Listen, I've got a meeting to go to," Cornheiser said as he rose from behind his desk. "Anything else?"

"How much money is the county going to collect in taxes from the Tomahawk Resort?" JC quickly asked.

Cornheiser did not have to look into a file or even reflect on the question for a moment. He knew the exact figure, and it made him smile. It would quickly add up to millions. It was the kind of money that could turn around a little place like Joseph.

JC found himself suddenly alone, with Cornheiser's departure. Cornheiser had rushed past, maybe on the way to the meeting he said was waiting for him. Maybe not. Patty MacIntyre appeared at the office door to show the journalist out.

Walking back into the fresh air, JC stared at the gold dome atop the courthouse. He was still thinking about Cornheiser. The reporter sensed he was hiding something.

JC felt Cornheiser was a politician with an inspiring story to tell about his personal life. It was a tale of rags to riches. He was a self-made man. Voters loved that stuff. Why was he so vague about his past, and his path to Joseph? JC thought that he definitely had a secret.

The reporter pulled out his phone. He called Bip and told him where to pick him up. Then, he made another call, to Robin Smith.

"I'm going to save you some postage," he said. "Don't mail me my kilt, just bring it. I've made arrangements with my landlord. He'll let you into my apartment and you can just grab the whole bag in my closet."

"Great," Robin said. "Can I see what's in the refrigerator?"

"Help yourself," JC told her. "I left a beer sandwich for you. I think there's some beer you can make into a beer salad, too."

"Sounds good," she said. "Do you have anything to drink?"

"I might have some beer," he told her, smiling.

"I hope you have some beer," she laughed.

"Are you doing anything Saturday night?" he asked. "I'll need a chaperone."

"I'm all yours, if you're buying," she told him.

He thought of about three punch lines to that remark. None of them, he thought, were appropriate between co-workers.

"Hey JC," Robin said. "I'm sorry about Shara and you. I thought you were a nice couple."

"Thanks," he responded. "She's a fine woman. Considering the distance, I should have known this was the only way it could end."

At the end of that phone conversation, JC watched a silver sheriff's patrol car pull up. Sheriff Williams got out of the driver's side and a deputy that JC didn't recognize got out of the passenger seat. She had a smile on her face and JC thought she was teasing her superior.

"Does this mean you're going to get a haircut and we might see you without your ball cap on once in a while?" asked Deputy Liz Grant.

"I just took her out to lunch," the sheriff responded, feigning annoyance. "I owed her an apology."

"Will you be taking her to prom?" the deputy teased.

"There is going to be a terrible task assigned to you in the near future," the sheriff gruffly teased back.

"Hi, JC," the sheriff said as he walked past without stopping.

At that moment, Bip Peters pulled into a space. He emerged from the rental car without turning off the engine. He assumed they were going somewhere, but he had his own news to deliver.

"You'll never guess what I just saw," Bip exclaimed.

"Reruns of your favorite TV show?" JC guessed.

"An Amish buggy!" Bip explained that he had never seen one before. "Very retro," he said.

13

"I hope you brought some magic bullets, because I'm starting to shoot blanks," JC told Robin Smith.

"I brought your kilt," she announced. "That thing is heavy!"

"I know," JC apologized. "Sorry."

They were sharing breakfast at The Gill Grill. Robin had arrived late last night. She checked into her room and slept off the jet lag. Over coffee and waiting for their food, JC was getting her caught up on the two stories they were reporting.

Bip was given a couple of hours at the start of the morning to go snowboarding with Patty MacIntyre at Battle Ax, again.

"What a cool place!" Robin marveled. "I love everything about it." She was spinning in her seat to look at things hanging on the walls of the diner.

"It is a unique area," JC conceded. "I don't think there's anywhere in the country just like the Lake Placid Region." A waitress came and placed plates of omelets and hash browns in front of them and refilled their coffee.

"I've never been here. It was dark when I drove up," Robin said. "But it was a bright moon. People have old gondola lifts hanging in their front yards," she laughed. "And I saw the ski jumps. They're huge! Lake Placid looks like a fun town," she said. "I missed the shortcut here and came through Lake Placid."

"Lake Placid is an immensely fun town," JC concurred.

"So, let me get this straight," Robin said as she put her fork down. "Lake Placid is not on Lake Placid?"

"Some of the village of Lake Placid is on the body of water called Lake Placid," JC smiled. "But the best-known part of the village of Lake Placid is on Mirror Lake."

"And where's the alligator?" she laughed.

"He's in Florida," JC laughed, too. Robin wasn't the only one who had asked that question, ever since a disaster movie with the same name as the village.

"So, there are only two ski resorts in world-famous Lake Placid?" Robin asked.

"Yeah," JC told her. "In Colorado, there would be half a dozen. There have been a lot of little ones, over the years. There was Dream Hill behind the Mirror Lake Inn, there was Marble Mountain near where Whiteface is today. There was Scott's Cobble, Fawn Ridge and some others. Only Whiteface survived, until they built Battle Ax."

"This is my first time to New York," Robin told him, giggling. "Where are all the skyscrapers?"

"Right," said JC. "That's what everyone thinks New York is, skyscrapers from border to border. I think the North Country in New York is a lot like Colorado."

"There are so many trees," she said.

"That's a big difference between the Adirondacks and the Rockies," JC said, comparing it to arid Colorado. "Mother Nature waters this garden a lot."

"And the fishing and hunting gets them through the warmer months?" she asked.

"Believe it or not," JC told her, "Lake Placid is busier in the summer than it is in the winter. "Hiking is so popular in the High Peaks that it's becoming a problem. The trails are getting crowded and the parking lots are overstuffed. State police and forest rangers have to come resolve the traffic jams. You've got more than twenty million people in New York and another eight million in Quebec. A lot of them come here to go for a walk. That's a lot of feet walking across the grass."

"So, it's all stressing out Mother Nature," Robin said.

"The poor woman probably can't wait until it's winter again," JC grinned.

They both accepted one more refill on their coffee while JC looked over the bill for their breakfast.

An old man walked in the door of the café. JC recognized him as the Irishman, Patrick Ross, and invited him to sit at their table. He introduced Robin.

"So, you were hiding something from me," JC told the 95-year-old.

"What's that?" Patrick asked.

"You're a great author." JC said he had been informed.

"What did you write?" Robin inquired.

"*Dismembering Debbie*," JC informed her after Patrick responded only with humble silence.

"I read that book!" Robin exclaimed. "It's about a woman in Ireland, tortured by the hatred around her. Everyone was kind of suffering from the same anxiety, but they all blamed each other for it."

"Aye. That's the short version," Patrick smiled.

"What else did you write?" Robin asked.

"That was it," Patrick told her with a smile. "Just the one. Are you a touch Irish?"

"I am!" Robin told him with enthusiasm. "But only a fraction. I look more Irish than I am."

Patrick was smitten with Robin. She had red hair and a great figure. She was bubbly and very pretty. JC wondered if he'd ever noticed just how pretty she was.

"So, why not?" JC asked. He was looking at Patrick now.

"Why not what?" Patrick asked, as he was studying JC.

"Why didn't you write another book?" JC asked. "You were famous, and I'd guess you had offers to make even more money."

"Aye, I did," Patrick said. The old man took a while to weigh further response.

"I had something to say," Patrick told them. "You say it and then you're done."

JC looked at the time on his phone. He apologized for being rude, but they had to leave Patrick to finish his breakfast alone. They had work to do.

"What a sweet man," Robin said in the car.

"I hope I'm that smart someday," JC added.

JC pointed out LaChute Brook as they crossed the old stone bridge, telling Robin about the discovery of Paul

Campbell's body. Then, he pulled off the road at the site of the archaeology dig at the future convenience store location.

Getting out of the car and walking the grounds, they saw no sign of Cindy Pfister. But Robin took great interest in the site, her background being in archaeology. She peeked inside a tent.

"They've done test pits," Robin said. "It's not easy in the cold, but it looks like they got things started before the ground got hard. They must have a deadline to meet."

There was an ATV parked next to a tent. It had a plow on the front.

"So," Robin explained as she looked around the site, "they use the plow to clear the snow off. It looks like they're using gas heaters to soften the ground inside the tents. I see an electric jackhammer, but it's not dirty. I'm not sure that they've actually used it. This is hard work, all of it by hand."

"And that?" JC asked, pointing to piles of dirt at the edge of the site.

"That's back dirt," Robin said.

"Back dirt," repeated JC. "Like snowboarders when they fall?"

Robin gave him a blank stare.

"Back dirt is what snowboarders call a fall on their back," JC said. "I just learned it. They say that if they were on bikes or skateboards, their back would be all dirty."

"Archaeologists had it first," Robin said, defending her turf. "Back dirt is the soil they've been digging out of the holes. They sifted the soil through a screen. If they determined it didn't hold any artifacts, they chucked it aside. It's clean, so they may just throw it back in the holes when they're done."

"What do you mean 'they?'" a voice from behind them asked. JC and Robin turned and discovered Cindy Pfister standing there. She looked like she had just captured two trespassers.

"Sorry you caught us nosing around your site," JC apologized. "But my tour guide is one of *your* people."

"*Your* people?" she said with a puzzled look. "Are you an archaeologist?" Pfister gruffly asked Robin.

Robin acknowledged that she used to be. She told Pfister the archaeology firms she worked for and listed a few better-known sites she had worked on. That led to discovering mutual friends they had in the field.

"Why is the soil so sandy here?" Robin asked.

"It's relatively young soil," Pfister said, speaking to Robin as she might to a colleague, "about ten thousand years."

"The last glacial age," Robin shared.

"Right," Pfister confirmed.

"Are those erratics?" Robin asked her, pointing at two large boulders sitting nearby on the Tomahawk site.

"They are," Pfister remarked. "The bulldozers worked around them. You're not faking it, sister." The two women laughed.

"Are you using an electric jackhammer?" Robin asked.

"Paul brought that with him. Do you know about Paul?" Pfister looked at JC and Robin said that she was aware of Paul Campbell's death.

"I'm sorry for your loss," Robin said. Pfister returned a look of acknowledgement.

"Yeah, we have an electric jackhammer. But we haven't used it," Pfister said. "We got real late notice of this job. But we had the foresight to dig some test pits, see what might be promising and erected tents around them. I've got gas heaters in the tents. It keeps the holes workable. It's going alright."

"Does she pass?" JC asked when Pfister's test of Robin's credentials appeared to be completed.

"With flying colors," Pfister declared. "The 'they' you described as the archaeologists working on this site, though, is a bit exaggerated. Since my partner's passing, that just leaves me here."

"You're working on this site alone?" Robin exclaimed.

"I am now," Pfister told Robin. "It's not a big site, and the abutting property just did a survey and they didn't find anything. We expected to work hard and make some fast money."

Robin looked toward the Tomahawk Resort site.

"They shared their report with you?" Robin asked.

"They did," Pfister acknowledged. "Most of the contact was between their archaeologist and my partner. They were old friends. But we still planned to do a competent analysis of our own, in addition to their report. We dug the test pits we thought we'd need before the ground froze. We were really just getting started when Paul died."

"I'm really sorry," Robin said.

"Thank you," responded Pfister. "Come on in."

The archaeologist led them inside a tent. A test pit was in the center of the protected area, with enough room to move around its sides.

There was a trench dug from the pit. It led to a sump pump.

"You have to pump out the pit to keep it dry?" Robin asked.

"Sometimes," Pfister responded. "You know, I could use someone like you on this site. Would you like to quit working with him and come work with me? I'm sure it would pay less!"

"Boy, that's a tempting offer," Robin laughed as she pulled off her mittens and looked at her hands.

"Yeah, you don't have claws for hands anymore," Pfister observed with a smile. "You've escaped our sentence to the rock pile."

"Sorry," Robin said.

"Don't be," Pfister replied, still smiling. "I've got some people who might be able to come up and help. So, Irish? Scottish?"

Robin laughed, "Both!"

"Bring her," Pfister said, looking at JC.

14

"Sheriff, the state police lab in Albany says that Stormy's gun is not the murder weapon."

Deputy Pattern stood in the doorway of the sheriff's office.

"But," the deputy added, "were you aware that Stormy did time for negligent homicide? And it involved a handgun."

"You are telling me something that is new to me," Smudge responded. He put his pen down and pushed away the report he was working on. Deputy Pattern had his full attention.

"It was in Ohio in the early 1980s," Pattern continued. "Stormy said it was an accident. Police said it was murder. The judge called it a tie."

"So, manslaughter," the sheriff speculated.

"He served three years in an Ohio state penitentiary," Deputy Pattern said, to conclude his report.

"If he was living in Ohio then," the sheriff thought, "they probably didn't get word of it here. Stormy grew up here but he must have moved away. I was familiar with Stormy's father when I was young. He was smarter than his son, but not really so different. He wouldn't have let it be known that his son was doing time in prison."

"That means Stormy isn't allowed to own a gun," the deputy said. "He did three years for a felony."

"It would appear so. That's one issue we have to deal with," the sheriff agreed. "The other issue is the possibility that Stormy has another 9mm."

"Anything is possible," the deputy answered.

"Did you ask him?" the sheriff asked.

"No, I didn't," the deputy answered, obviously embarrassed.

"I just thought of it myself," the sheriff said, letting his deputy off the hook.

"Let's do this," Smudge advised. "I'll go with you and we'll have Peter and Liz meet us out there. We'll explain to Stormy that he can't have his handgun back because he's a convicted felon. We'll ask him if he owns any other 9mm handguns. He's also going to have to turn over his guns. I don't want this to blow up, but the law is the law."

"And what if he's as belligerent as he usually is?" Deputy Pattern asked.

"If he goes along with all this, I'm fine with ending it there. Give us the guns, own it up to a misunderstanding and call it a day," the sheriff said. "If he doesn't confess to his felonious background, we'll have to go to court for some paperwork and force him to relinquish his guns. That's what I'm trying to avoid."

"Is he still a suspect?" Deputy Pattern asked.

"Of course he's a suspect," the sheriff said. "He thought about shooting *us*."

"Hey, Sheriff," Deputy Pattern said. He'd paused before leaving to carry out the sheriff's instructions. "I was thinking about that little note the medical examiner found in the victim's pocket after he was dragged from the creek."

"What about it, Tim?"

"Ohio has two O's," the deputy stated.

"So it does, Deputy." The sheriff responded.

JC and Bip drove toward Joseph. Robin stayed at the hotel. She was going to research Cornheiser's "Missing Years" after college and before coming to Joseph. They wondered if he had an arrest record or something else he was hiding.

The visit to the archaeology site also sparked Robin's interest in what sort of artifacts would be found in Joseph, if there were any to find.

"That's a good way to get your bike stolen," Bip said as he drove down Bonnieview Road. Both men looked at the bike as their car passed it. The bike was unattended, leaning against a fence. It stood in about five inches of snow, but the seat and frame were snow-free. It looked like it had been recently used.

"It's not locked. Did you see it this morning?" Bip asked.

"It wasn't there this morning," JC assured him. "And that isn't even a Fat Tire bike," he said curiously.

"No," Bip snickered. "That's a road bike with thin road tires."

"The roads are clear," JC observed. "I guess someone rode their bike there."

"And went where?" Bip asked. It was a fair question. The bike was leaning against a fence that bordered a pasture. There wasn't a single building in close proximity.

JC and Bip continued down the road to gather footage they needed to provide updates regarding both of the stories they were covering for the evening news. They could report that there's a possibility Campbell was killed during an armed robbery, because his wallet still hadn't been located.

They could also report, after talking on the phone with state Republican Headquarters in Albany, that Cornheiser's budding candidacy for the state legislature was dying a slow death because of the investigation in Colorado connecting him to the death of a college friend.

JC's phone rang. It was Robin, telling him that she had compiled a fairly complete bio of the murder victim, Paul Campbell, including some pictures of him as a teenager in Scotland.

He was born in Fife, about an hour from Edinburgh. His brother died during the Coronavirus Pandemic, so his family had suffered two terrible tragedies in close proximity.

Campbell lived in Colorado for about eight years, Robin said, moving from Colorado Springs to Denver after he graduated from college. Then he moved East, receiving a postgraduate degree in New York City.

It was good material, JC thought, including neighborhoods where Campbell lived while in Colorado. JC knew that viewers of his story that night would relate more closely to the victim, learning that he probably ate at the same restaurants as they did or shopped at the same grocery stores.

"Great job, Robin," JC told her. Bip pulled their car up to the live truck where he would edit the video for their stories.

"You're going to make me look a lot smarter than I am," JC told Robin over the phone. "I could have used you here sooner." He could tell that she was pleased to be appreciated.

The call ended and JC followed Bip up three stairs on a metal ladder and into the back of the satellite truck. That's where the crude edit bay was. It had everything necessary to edit a story for the news. But the space, barely fitting two adult men, would fall short of a two-star rating for comfort.

"What are you doing tonight?" Bip asked JC. It was Friday. They had the weekend off.

"I was going to go out to dinner with an old high school friend," JC said as he pocketed his phone. "He was going to come up from Saratoga, but he had to cancel."

"Are you racing tomorrow?" Bip probed.

"I think so," JC told him. "I'll work on my skis tonight and see how I feel about it. I haven't been getting much training in. Stop by my room and have a beer."

Bip was silent. It didn't take JC long to figure that out.

"What's that I smell?" JC asked.

"What, do you smell smoke?" Bip asked in alarm. It wasn't out of the ordinary for wires in TV trucks to smoke or short. Bip was searching the racks holding the editing equipment.

"No," JC told him, trying to identify the aroma. "I think it's love in the air."

"Funny," Bip said with a sarcastic sneer as he relaxed.

JC had figured out that Bip was going on a date with Patty MacIntyre, the administrative assistant to the county executive who was under investigation.

"Would you mind wearing a wire?" JC asked with mock seriousness. "Maybe let me give you a list of questions that could incriminate Cornheiser? I could be on headphones in a car down the street, and when I hear the code word, I can come in and arrest her."

Bip stopped editing and looked at JC.

"Funny," he said, "but it ain't gonna happen." Bip returned to editing, but the smile remained on his face. He was looking forward to his night.

After the live shots, the two journalists returned to The T and went their separate ways. JC told Bip that he hoped they would have a great time.

"Do you think I'm growing on Patty?" JC asked.

"Yeah," Bip responded. "Like a wart."

JC now had the rest of the night to himself. In his hotel room, he pulled two chairs from a small table in the corner and spread the chairs about three feet apart. He covered them in towels.

He spread newspapers on the carpeted floor beneath the chairs and reached into a bag sitting on the bed.

Next to a six-pack of Saranac, there was a steel file, a diamond file, two brushes, an iron and some wax. He balanced his skis across the top of the chairs and plugged the iron in.

There was a knock at his door. One hand was holding a beer, so he opened the door with the other. Robin Smith was standing there.

"What are you doing?" she asked with a smile.

"Working on my skis," he told her, still standing in the door.

"Where'd you get the beer?" she asked. "And do I hear music?"

"The music is just the hotel's clock-radio," JC answered.

"You didn't tell me you were throwing a party," Robin said as she pushed her way into the room.

"Yep," he said. "All my friends are here."

"Where's Bip?" she asked as she spotted the six-pack and pulled out a beer for herself.

JC told Robin about Bip's new friend, Patty. Bip said that she was going to give him a tour of downtown Lake Placid.

"And what about you?" Robin asked.

"This is how I planned to spend my night," JC gestured to the iron, wax and his skis. "That's how I got the name 'Mr. Excitement.'"

"I've never heard anyone call you that," she teased.

"OK, you're right," JC announced as he looked over his sorry surroundings. "Just let me get this layer of wax down. While it dries, we'll go get a beer at the lodge. K?"

"Kay!" she said with a smile.

The waxing done, they pulled on jackets and marched up the hill in the cold air. The stone columns and rough timber crossbeams loomed overhead as they entered a side door to the lodge and followed the music upstairs.

The bar's name, Poo Ice, made JC laugh.

"Poo Ice?" Robin asked.

"It's a nickname for snow here that gets dirty and then freezes," JC told her, elevating his voice over the music.

"It looks like poo?" she asked with a grimace.

"I'm afraid so," he laughed.

There were large propane-fueled torches outside on the porches. But it was too cold. No one was sitting at those tables.

JC and Robin climbed onto a pair of stools at the bar and ordered. They got craft beers from the Big Slide Brewery, located near the ski jumps in Lake Placid.

They were seated in a room that reflected the same bentwood architecture as the porches. There was peeled bark and the low lighting almost cast the illusion that they were in a dark forest.

High on the walls, there were old shields and banners boasting the names of venerable ski clubs from across the country. There was Sitzmark from Milwaukee, the Schussers from New Hampshire and the National Brotherhood of Skiers.

There were also clubs from New York State, like the large Out of Control Ski Club, Nubian, Albany and Schenectady.

"Come to collect your second-place medal?" asked a voice next to Robin. But he was looking at JC.

"Russell!" exclaimed JC after looking down the bar. His face broke into a big grin. "Did you come here to race, or are you a display in the antique-skier wax museum?"

Russell Driver laughed at that. JC introduced him to Robin.

"Russell," JC explained, "is one of the oldest racers here and one of the fastest. He only skis so fast because he knows how angry we get when we see an old man beat us."

"So, you usually beat him?" Robin asked Russell while pointing at JC.

"I always beat him," Russell told her with a smile, "unless he cheats."

"He cheats?" she laughed.

"He must," Russell told her, "if he beats *me*."

Russell was a man that JC both liked and admired. Some people said, back in the day, he could have been the first Black member of the U.S. Ski Racing Team.

"It's no one's fault," Russell said. "Opportunity eludes us in many mysterious ways. But there is a child of color at this

114

very moment who is working hard and will win a medal in alpine skiing for the United States."

JC said that he looked forward to the day.

"It will just be one more man finishing ahead of you in a race," Russell laughed. "Things are slowly changing for the better. People of color are finding the mountains. They come with skis and snowboards and they are welcomed."

"Overdue," JC said.

"Overdue indeed," Russell agreed.

"What does that pin mean?" Robin asked. She was pointing at a pin on Russell's jacket.

"That tells you that I fought in Vietnam. The last year or so."

"The Vietnam War?" Robin said. She was startled and impressed.

"Another burden the Black man was happy to carry for his white brothers," Russell said. "Eleven percent of the United States was Black. Twenty-three percent of the combat troops in Vietnam were Black."

"Wow," Robin responded. "Thank you for your service."

"You are welcome," he said. "And how did you come to sit with a man who will lose to me in the race tomorrow?" He was grinning and pointing at JC. "It must involve charity."

"Where is your beautiful wife who makes being with you so much more tolerable?" JC asked.

"Loni is in your fair hometown, Saratoga Springs," Russell answered. "She is being toasted as a great person. So, I thought that I would allow her to have the limelight all to herself and come here to race."

"Does this have to do with her book?"

"It does. It turns out that *Squeaky the Squirrel* has struck a chord."

JC explained to Robin that Loni Driver had written a children's book about a year ago called *Squeaky the Squirrel*. And it had been finding an audience.

"It's a big hit, right?" JC asked.

"It is," Russell responded proudly.

"So, now she's rich and doesn't need you," JC jabbed.

"You are a cold-hearted man," Russell responded. "However, publishers write their contracts in fine print and with invisible ink. You don't get as rich as you think. Happily, she still needs me."

They ordered more beer and some bar food for dinner.

"If Loni is in Saratoga, who is going to dress you in the morning?" JC joked.

"I will await her call and follow her instructions to perfection," Russell laughed. So did Robin.

"That sounds like true love," Robin said.

"It is, for Russell," JC said. "For Loni, it's sympathy." They all laughed some more.

"How did you meet your wife?" Robin asked Russell.

"My wife tricked me," Russell began. He had a glint in his eye. "She would park her little new car in front of my house each night.

"Now, I knew that she didn't live in my house, nor across the street. She lived down the hill," Russell said. "She told me, when I asked why she parks in front of my house, that her car would get scratched or broken into if she parked it by where she lived.

"But do you know why I think she parked in front of my house?" Russell leaned in and asked Robin. "Because she wanted to meet me. She thought I was cute!"

Russell laughed, as did Robin and JC.

"Now, if you will excuse me," Russell said as he pushed himself away from the bar, "I must return to my room and telephone my beautiful wife to hear of her triumph."

"See you tomorrow, my friend," said JC.

"Good luck tomorrow," Robin said. "I hope you win." Russell grinned at her and JC stared.

"You realize," JC said to her, "if he wins, that means *I'll* lose."

"Oh, I was at your apartment to pick up your kilt," she told him. "I saw all your medals hanging in your den. You have enough."

"Yes, you have enough," Russell said, laughing.

"It's my bedtime, I think," Robin said and stifled a yawn. "I'm still jet-lagged. I think I'm going to hit the hay."

JC offered to walk her back to their hotel.

"I can walk you back," said Russell. "JC, finish your beer."

JC looked at Robin for a sign that she was fine with the arrangement. She stood and poured the rest of her beer into JC's glass.

"Finish mine, too," she said. "I want to go to bed and you still have to finish your skis."

"You did a great job today," JC told her. "I think you kept me out of trouble."

"It was fun," Robin said with a smile. She turned and walked down the stairs with Russell Driver.

Alone now, JC turned and scanned the sports being played on TV sets above the bar. One television was showing Haley O'Brien on *The Snow Report.*

"She is hilarious," a man on the next barstool said. He glanced at JC and pointed at O'Brien on TV. "I don't even ski and I watch her show."

"I like it, too," JC acknowledged.

"You got a ski race tomorrow?" the man asked.

"That's right. I guess you won't be racing," JC replied.

"Naw," the man said. "But I could help a bobsled get down the mountain a little faster." He laughed as the big man patted the considerable bulge above his belt.

"I helped build the new course you're going to race on, though," the man added. "Over the summer. I drive heavy equipment. They wanted to pull down some trees to make it wider. Safer, I guess."

"So, do you have any tips that would help me tomorrow? Did you leave a tree in the middle of the course that I should avoid?" JC joked.

"Naw. You guys are crazy to go that fast," the man said.

"You live here and you don't ski?" JC asked.

The man had a camouflage baseball hat on his head and he was wearing jeans. He wore a blaze-orange down jacket despite the comfortable temperature inside the bar and he was drinking a Genesee.

"I hunt and fish," the man said. "If you add them up, our season is longer than yours."

JC thought about that. He had not realized it before, but the guy was right. JC introduced himself.

"Frank Roy," the man said. "It's French, but we pronounce it the English way now. We've been here for a while."

"So, what do you do in the winter, Frank?" JC asked.

"I work," the man said. "I've been working out at Tomahawk. You know, the new development?"

"I do," JC told him. "Did that bring a lot of jobs here?"

"It sure did," Frank said. "And when we're done building it, there'll be a lot of people hired to keep it running."

"So, what are you doing at Tomahawk," JC asked.

"I drive a dump truck," the man said. "You can't believe how much stuff has to be dragged away from there. Dirt, boxes, construction debris. My first load was dirt, while they were still checking to see if there were any old skeletons there."

"You mean the archaeologist?" JC asked.

"Yeah," Frank responded. "He said that he had more dirt than he needed, so he pointed at some piles and asked me to take them away. That was my first day on the site."

"Where do you take dirt?" JC asked, now just making conversation and pulling on his jacket. His beer was empty and he had to finish working on his skis.

"He gave me directions to some clearing in the woods. It was eleven miles from here," Frank said. Then he leaned closer and dropped his voice, "I don't know if he was paying anyone to dump there, if you know what I mean. But, I'm just paid to drive the truck. Any trouble? The guys with the deep pockets take care of that. Mr. Felix, I guess."

"Averill Felix," JC clarified. "The owner of Battle Ax?"

"Yeah," Frank Roy confirmed. "He's the man with the most money. So, he's kind of the law around here."

JC bought Frank Roy another Genesee and headed back outside.

I'll have to pay Mr. Felix a visit, JC thought to himself.

15

"Pretty!"

JC turned to locate the familiar voice. He saw Robin and Bip standing on the other side of a plastic mesh fence that was separating the general skiing population from the racers and the start area. Bip was on his snowboard, Robin was on frontside skis.

"I like all the colors," Robin said. "What are you skiing on?" She was pointing at JC's skis, lying in the snow next to him.

"They are orange skis," he said sarcastically. "I'm a little worried about beating the yellow skis and the silver skis."

"Ha-ha," she responded, returning his sarcasm with more sarcasm. "Why do you have a boring helmet?" She was looking at JC.

"My black helmet?" he asked. "It fit my head when I tried it on."

"Boring," she repeated.

Aside from JC's black helmet, the splash of color from other helmets in the start area contrasted with the thick gray clouds overhead. There was no hope of the sun breaking through over the ski run called The Joker.

Competitors also wore colorful racing suits. There were mixtures of red, blue, green and yellow. The skin-tight material was made from layers of polyester. The surface of the suits was slick, so the wind would slip over it.

This was a race for adults. It was called "masters-level" racing, for those past the age to compete in college and below the skill level to compete with world-class racers.

There were age groups of both genders. The first racers out of the gate would be the oldest, perhaps in their 70s. Then, the age groups gradually dropped to eventually include racers who were still in their 20s.

The racers at Battle Ax that morning warmed up their muscles near the starting gate, as they awaited the start. Some would run in place, lifting their knees high. Some employed a routine of stretching. Some ran a short way down the hill, turned and ran back up.

The conversation among the racers was more subdued than at other races. They were nervous. This event was a Super-G. It was one run, all-out, everything on the line.

Speeds would exceed those in a giant slalom or slalom. Crashes would pose greater risk of injury

"When do you go?" Robin asked. "We came to cheer you on."

"Thank you," JC told them with sincerity. "You probably have time to take another run. If you miss the first few racers, you'll only miss the slow old men."

JC deliberately made the remark at a slightly higher volume, so Russell Driver would hear him. Russell was older than most of the racers, so he had an earlier start.

"I suppose you believe that your psychological shenanigans will weaken my resolve," Russell said with a smile as he approached. He said hello to Robin and JC introduced him to Bip.

"Thank you for walking me home last night," Robin said. He nodded and told her the joy was all his.

"Russell is older than most of us," JC told Bip. "Hence, we slow down so he can win, once in a while."

"Don't let him tell you that these people are nice enough to do that," Russell said to Bip. "They're not."

"Bip took me over to the half-pipe and showed me a couple of tricks," Robin said. "He's really good! He did a flip!" JC and Russell were both genuinely impressed.

"Hey, guess who we ran into," Bip said to JC. "Harold DeWitt, the archaeologist at Tomahawk. He was skiing. We took a run together."

"He's not bad," Robin added. "He's a pretty nice guy. We rode the chair lift up together."

They were interrupted by the call, "Racers to the start!"

Russell was already stripped of his outer layer of clothing. He tossed off a jacket he had been wearing over the shoulders of his thin racing suit.

"These race suits aren't very warm," JC told Robin.

"Good luck!" Robin and Bip called out as the racers moved toward the start house. "We're going down lower so we can see more of the race."

The snow surface was hard with a thin layer of man-made snow over the top. It was typical of the snow found in the East. It would carve and it was fast.

"Dust and crust!" an enthusiastic racer shouted.

"The light's flat, so let's scat!" another racer bellowed. That got a lot of chuckles. The light *was* flat. It was not a strange occurrence to skiers in the East. Cloudy skies were the norm from the months of mid-December to mid-February.

But many skiers who grew up in the East and Midwest learned to ski at night, under lights. So, they learned as children to ski when it was hard to see.

JC thought that flat light might be the greatest difference of all, between skiing in the East and the West. Skiers in the East kept their knees bent, stayed over their skis and learned to "see" the snow in their feet.

When it was his turn to race, JC shook off the jacket hanging on his shoulders, revealing a green and gold racing suit left over from his days on the team at Colorado State University.

There were a few small holes torn in his suit. He thought of the holes as hard-fought medals, won by bashing the gates with such fury that the contact ripped the fabric.

After the starter began the countdown, JC kicked through the starting wand, propelling himself downhill. The Super-G course was steep and threatening. It did not have many turns to slow the racers down. JC loved this kind of course.

Racers found that some courses suited them better than others. Some racers excelled on a tight course with a lot of turns. In Super-G, some racers were intimidated by the speed.

But JC loved the speed and loved to bend his skis in the turn to generate even more acceleration.

He held his tuck across the finish line and threw his skis sideways. Snow sailed as he dug his edges in, to slow down and stop before becoming tangled in the plastic fence. He was breathing hard. It was difficult to steady his head as he turned to read the clock and the order of the finishers, so far.

He saw his time and it was above Russell Driver's. That meant JC had beaten him, so he knew he had a good time. He pushed out of the finish corral before the next racer, from Jiminy Peak, arrived with a full head of steam.

"You were really fast!" Robin greeted him.

"Nice run, man," Bip said.

"Thanks, but I don't think it beats a backflip," JC said to Bip. JC was still panting.

"Treasure this moment in rare air," Russell said as he extended his hand to congratulate JC. "You won't beat me again."

They all laughed at Russell's bravado. He was asked how his run went.

"I skied like a bag of hammers," Russell said.

"This is your first time skiing in the East, right?" JC asked Robin. "What do you think?"

"It's good," Robin said with enthusiasm. "I was told the East is all ice. But the snow is good. It's really groomed well."

"I did find a Chatter Box," Bip noted. Robin looked at him for a translation.

"The chute that was all ice," Bip explained.

"Oh, yeah," Robin said. "I went around that. I stayed on the groomed stuff. But I hit some little round pieces of ice," and she looked at Bip for assistance.

"Ball Bearings," Bip said.

"Yeah," Robin laughed, "ball bearings."

"But she's a good skier," Bip told his friends. Robin was happy with that compliment.

"Did you race in high school?" JC asked her. She shook her head, no.

"Moguls," Robin declared proudly.

"Wow, Respect!" Bip proclaimed. JC and the others nodded and showed their esteem for the bump skier.

"If you can get an edge here, you can get an edge anywhere," JC told her. "If the best racers in the country don't grow up in the East, most of them choose to come here for their ski academy.

"Bode grew up in the East," he offered as an example. "Mikaela grew up in Colorado but she came to school in the East. Colorado has some of the best snow in the world but racing in Europe is more like racing in the East."

The awards ceremony commenced, and the racers all gathered in the finish area. A race organizer stepped up on a box and announced the age-group winners, distributing the medals. Fellow racers applauded and, at times, offered good-natured jeering at their friends who climbed the podium.

JC was the fastest racer of the day. He walked to the front of the crowd and bowed to allow a ribbon to be slipped over his head, a gold medal hanging from it. He smiled as some of his friends accused him of skipping part of the course to achieve that fast time.

JC walked back to join Russell, Bip and Robin. Russell wore a medal for winning his age group. They congratulated JC and he instinctively glanced down at his medal, smiling.

"Look at you," Robin said. "You're beaming."

"What do you mean?" JC asked her, pretending to be defensive.

"Your little medal," she said with a grin.

"It's not *that* little," he protested.

"I know, you're proud of it," she said. "Don't worry, I think it's cute."

They exchanged a glance. It was the kind of glance that JC wasn't certain they should be sharing.

16

JC eyed his reflection in the mirror of his hotel room. He straightened his green and maroon kilt. He checked the flashes holding up his thick, wool, knee-high socks. The Scots called the socks "hose." Everything looked straight.

He still had time before leaving. He opened his laptop with the intention of posting something on social media for his television station. He was not as regular a contributor to social media as his management wished he would be.

He scanned the posts on Facebook and his eyes settled on one. It was the post of a happy couple announcing their wedding date. The woman in the post was Shara.

JC slowly closed the laptop, like closing a door on part of his life. The image on his computer was a shock. He thought he was prepared for that inevitable moment. It turns out that he wasn't.

There was a knock at his door. He stood and peered into his sporran to check if he brought an adequate amount of cash, his driver's license, his phone, a pen and paper and some business cards.

He opened the door. Robin was standing there. She was wearing an emerald green dress that fit tightly and reached the floor. JC breathed deeply and tried to make his admiration less obvious than the truth.

"You clean up well," he told his producer. She smiled. She knew what he meant.

"I like your skirt," she said.

"It's a kilt," he replied with a grin.

"And your purse is cute," she giggled.

"It's a sporran," he informed her.

"You're wearing garters?"

"They're called flashes," was his response.

"To hold up your socks?"

"Hose." He was sorry the moment he said it.

"Oh! I'm wearing hose, too!" She laughed.

"Have we had our fun now?" he asked.

"Not all of it, I hope," she told him with a smile.

They made the short walk to the lodge. The Burns Supper would be held in a room adjoining the bar.

"You didn't wear your gold medal," Robin needled him.

"I forgot. I intended to," JC fibbed.

They walked through the dark bar with the posts that looked like tree trunks, the bentwood picture frames and furniture.

They passed through two heavy wooden doors and entered a large room designed to look like a forest. There were trees along the walls, reaching to the ceiling. There were string lights hanging above.

The tables were lined up in a large horseshoe with chairs on both sides.

"Your cute skirt," Robin asked him, "does it mean anything?"

"The maroon and green tartan means my family belongs to the Lindsay and Crawford clan," he told her. "My great-grandfather was the last one to live in Scotland."

He paid for two glasses of wine at the bar and they scanned the crowd arriving for cocktail hour.

"Have you ever eaten haggis?" JC asked her. She stared at him, like he'd asked her if she ate live mice.

"It's good," he assured her. "I love it, though if you order it ten times in Scotland, you'll be served ten different versions. I must say, I like it with some sauce."

"But the same yucky ingredients?" she asked.

"Pretty much," he told her. "But don't worry, some of the ingredients are illegal in the United States, so they have to make adjustments here."

"Do they add chocolate here?" she laughed.

"No," he said. "Not a bad idea, though."

They spotted Cindy Pfister, the archaeologist. She was wearing Paul Campbell's boar head pin.

"You brought her!" Pfister said, grinning at them both.

"You didn't leave me much choice," JC told her.

Cindy Pfister informed them of plans to remember Campbell. It was on the program for the night. Then she was pulled away by someone who was tending to that matter.

Pfister had taken a clear liking to Robin, JC noticed. Robin was a good addition to the team, he thought. He had also noticed that he wasn't thinking about Shara.

"Look," Robin said, "there's Patrick!" The old Irishman entered the room alone and Robin led JC to join him.

"Patrick!" JC greeted him. "What's an Irishman doing at a Scottish gathering?"

"A room full of Scots isn't as good as a room full of Irishmen," Patrick conceded. "But it's the best I'm going to do." A broad smile spread across his face.

He stated that he came for the short memorial for Paul Campbell. Patrick had spoken with him, on occasion, during his walks past the convenience store dig site.

"They're sending his body home tomorrow," JC told Robin and Patrick. "The sheriff said there was no more evidence that they were going to get by keeping him, so he can go home to Scotland for burial."

The sound of bagpipes interrupted their conversation. A piper entered the room and the crowd fell in behind him. They followed him around the room twice.

"Join us for dinner, Patrick," said Robin. They found three seats and poured single-malt scotch whisky from a bottle placed in the middle of each table.

"I tried bagpipes," JC told Robin and Patrick. "I was lousy at it. I could never get past the chanter."

The chanter, he explained, was like the pipe on a bagpipe, but without a bag. It was a woodwind instrument.

"There are eight notes on a chanter," JC laughed. "I can play six."

"So, you can't play the bagpipes and you can't cook," Robin said. "Is there anything you're good at?"

"Why did I forget my medal?" JC asked.

"Oh, that little thing," she joked.

The formal portion of the night included a keynote speaker and the short remembrance for Paul Campbell. Then the haggis was paraded into the hall with bagpipes blaring.

Over dinner, JC asked Patrick about circumstances bringing him to the United States.

"I remember a handsome young Scot telling me that a big move is always about a woman," JC told him.

"Aye," said Patrick. "It's always about a girl." Patrick winked at Robin.

"So, you came to the U.S. to follow a woman?" Robin asked.

"No!" Patrick exclaimed. "I came here because they were going to kill me in Ireland!" They all laughed.

"Is there a true story that comes with that?" JC then asked.

"Aye, there is," Patrick told them. And he settled in to tell it.

"I was only about ten years old," he started. "I was living in County Cork. I had a job driving a horse-drawn milk wagon out from a country farm into town.

"Sometime later, I learned that a vice-admiral in the British Royal Navy, a man named Somerville, had just been assassinated by the Irish Republican Army near Cork. I didn't know it at the time, but it put the IRA in a bad light with both Catholics and Protestants."

"One day," he continued, "some soldiers waved me down and asked me to give them a ride, since I was going their way. I really didn't have a choice and stopped to let them climb on.

"Well, I rode them into town and they were nice to me the whole way," he said. "They joked with me and told me stories about what they did to Catholics who they caught smuggling guns to the Irish Republican Army.

"We reached town and they hopped off my wagon. They all waved and laughed and wished me well," Patrick told them. "But I exhaled for the first time since I'd picked them up. You see, my wagon had a double floor. Beneath the floor that the milk cans sat on, was a compartment full of guns for the IRA."

"I knew," Patrick said as his eyes appeared to go back to that time, "they were giving me a warning. They knew I was smuggling guns. But I was a wee lad and they knew that the adults had loaded that wagon. It was my warning never to do it again."

"Wow," Robin said. JC looked at Patrick in wonder.

"Not long after that," the old man concluded, "some soldiers grabbed a school friend of mine. He'd been doing something similar. Maybe they thought he had something to do with Somerville's death. But we never saw my friend again. He disappeared off the face of the earth. I chose to come to America and live with an aunt."

Following dinner, guests at the Burns Supper were asked to come forward and read a favorite poem written by the "Ploughman Poet."

JC rose and read his favorite, called "Such a Parcel of Rogues." Robert Burns wrote it about Scotland's parliament, centuries ago, who chose peace with England, but forfeited independence.

"It is time for me to go," Patrick announced. "I have a car waiting for me downstairs."

"May we walk you out?" Robin asked.

"Certainly," Patrick said, "after a wee dram to salute a wonderful evening." That was agreed to and accomplished with fifteen-year-old Glenfiddich.

The three of them descended the stairs and entered the cold winter air. JC and Robin helped Patrick into his ride, Robin giving him a kiss on the cheek.

"What now?" JC asked as Patrick's car pulled away into the darkness.

"I wouldn't refuse another wee dram," she said. "Is there anywhere we can get some at this time of night?" They saw that they were surrounded by closed storefronts in the village.

"I've got some," he said, not sure that he should have said it.

"Where is it?" she asked with a smile.

"I've got it in my room," he said, not sure that he should have said that, either.

"Good," she said.

They exchanged a glance. JC was uncertain in the wisdom of that, too. They were co-workers, he thought to himself. This could become a big mess. But they strolled back toward their hotel.

She asked him about his descendants in Scotland.

"Enough about JC tonight, alright?" he said to Robin, smiling. "Let's talk about you. Tell me about growing up."

"I was born in Denver, I went to high school in Denver and I went to college in Denver," she said.

"You know," JC offered, "Denver is thought of as an exotic destination to the rest of the world. You don't have to seek paradise if you already live there." He opened the door into their hotel, allowing Robin to enter first.

"I loved history." She continued the thumbnail of her life. "Archaeology was perfect for me. I was always getting dirty as a child. I liked doing things that got me dirty. I'd do jumps on my bike, I'd roll on the ground with my dogs, I'd play football with the boys."

"Are you sure you want to do this?" JC asked. They were at his hotel room door. That's where the scotch whisky was.

She wrapped her arms around his neck and gave him a kiss. His heart raced.

"Officially, I'm your superior," he said quietly. "I don't want you to do anything that you don't want to do. You don't have to do this."

"I've wanted to do this for a year," she whispered in his ear and pushed in the door to his hotel room.

The door closed behind them as she asked him, "Do you wear this skirt proper?"

"It's a kilt," he said.

17

Are you done apologizing?" Robin asked. "You didn't seduce me. You didn't take advantage of me because I kind of work under you."

"You did fine work under me," he smiled. She smiled back.

They reclined in his bed, holding each other close. They watched the rising sun pour newborn beams of light through the window.

"You're a good guy," she told him. "You have respect for women. You're a sweet man."

"I just don't want you to get hurt ..." he began. She pressed her finger against his lips.

"We're fine," she said. "We'll figure out what to do next, in good time, OK?" He gave her an admiring smile and kissed her.

"What do your initials stand for?"

"Jean Claude," he told her. She elevated her head and looked at him.

"When we're alone," she asked, "can I call you Jean Claude?"

"Sometimes," he grinned. Her head slowly fell back to his chest. Long periods of silence passed in their conversation. They were content and comfortable under warm covers.

"Russell is such a nice man," Robin said. "He walked me home and told me such lovely things about his wife."

"Loni," JC offered the name of Russell's wife. "He left last night to join her in Saratoga."

"Did you stay at the bar much longer after I left Friday night?" Robin asked.

"Not really," JC told her. "I had to finish tuning my skis, to win that big medal." She giggled.

"But I got in a conversation with a dump truck driver," he said. "Nice guy. He's working at the Tomahawk site. He said that he's been hauling a lot of dirt from there. He also suspected that some of the dirt isn't going to legal dump sites."

More silence passed. They had their eyes closed.

"I've got to make an appointment with Averill Felix," JC said.

"The owner of Battle Ax?" Robin asked.

"Yeah, I just wonder what he has to say about all this," JC stated. "He must have worked closely with Cornheiser to get Tomahawk approved."

"What about the illegal dumping?" she inquired.

"That could be a good story for the local newspaper," he thought. "But it's not something our viewers in Colorado would care about."

"I'll set Averill Felix up for you," she said. "I'm your producer, after all. I'll take care of it tomorrow."

"Today is Sunday, isn't it?" JC asked.

"Yes, it is, Jean Claude," she said smiling. "You have today off. And your pillow talk needs some refinement. It shouldn't include discussion about work."

"You don't find the discussion of dump trucks and business owners arousing?" he asked.

"You'd better get me very drunk," she said, "before you rely on those particular words to get in my knickers."

"Then what is on the schedule for today?" he asked.

"I think you should tell me something that has nothing to do with work," she said, "and then we should go skiing."

"That's a fair suggestion," he replied. Then, he began to think about what he could tell her that was not work-related.

"Did you know," he inquired, "that the term 'vacation' was invented to describe wealthy New Yorkers coming to the Adirondacks? They were vacating the city for their great camps, and just began to call it 'vacation.'"

"Is that true?" she asked, somewhat impressed.

"There are a number of magazine articles that say it's true," he told her.

They rose from bed, dressed and made their way to the mountain. Outside, the sheet metal on cars reflected the early morning sun. Vehicles were lining up to get into the parking lots at Battle Ax.

The forecast called for early sun and then a day of clouds. That weather forecast could be stamped on the calendar for the entire month of January in the Northeast.

In the lodge, sweaters and helmets were being pulled on. The sound of zippers could be heard as warm jackets were secured. The conversation was enthusiastic and brave. The thumping sound of ski boots was heard hitting the floor, heading for the doors leading to the lifts.

The breeze made a whistling sound in the tall chairlift towers as JC and Robin rode to the top of the mountain. They were headed for a mogul run called Chowder Fest. Robin had watched JC race. Now *she* was going to show off a little, bashing bumps.

They stole glances at each other as they rode the lift.

"I'm not positive that we should let that happen again," he said.

"You don't want it to happen again?" she asked.

"Honestly?" he said, "I *do* want it to happen again. I just ..." She put her leather mitten over his mouth.

"Then, Jean Claude," she said as she smiled at him, "it probably will."

18

"Sheriff, we got a problem," Deputy Colden shouted from his desk as he hung up the phone.

"In here, Peter," Smudge hollered back, summoning the deputy to his office, rather than use their loud-voice intercom.

"Oh, right," Deputy Colden said at a much lower volume, and he headed for the door of the sheriff's office.

"What's up?" Smudge asked.

"A plow-service driver just drove onto Stormy's property to see if he could talk him into a contract for the winter."

"He apparently hasn't met Stormy," the sheriff surmised.

"It doesn't sound like it," the deputy agreed. "So, Stormy pointed his rifle at the man in the plow and told him to get off his land."

"And did the man leave?" the sheriff asked.

"He did," Colden replied.

"Did anyone get shot?" the sheriff asked.

"No, sir," said the deputy. "But the plow driver didn't like having a gun pointed at him. He wants to file a complaint."

The sheriff thought for a moment. He had a feeling that this was going to become more than just taking a snowplow driver's complaint.

"Oh, hell," the sheriff said as he rose from behind his desk.

"What are we going to do, Sheriff?" Colden asked.

"We're going to do what we're sworn to do, uphold the law," the sheriff said as he grabbed the keys to his patrol car.

"You take the complaint," he told Deputy Colden. "I'm going out to have a talk with Stormy."

"Do you want me to go with you?" the deputy asked. It would be protocol to have some backup when going to talk to someone about taking away his guns.

"Nope," the sheriff responded.

Sheriff Smudge Williams believed that enforcing the law in a small county required him to apply the rules as you would have the rules applied to you. It wasn't the Golden Rule, but it was at least a shiny *Brass* Rule.

Until recently, most everybody in Joseph grew up in Joseph. They all knew each other, or at least their brother went to school with somebody else's sister.

If he was breaking up a bar fight on a Saturday night, Smudge knew who was likely to pull a knife and use it. If there was an argument in the town park, he knew who was likely to throw the first punch.

The law was still the law in Joseph. But Smudge Williams thought he had a better-than-even chance of preventing a small thing from erupting into a big thing.

"Stormy," the sheriff told the grizzled rancher upon arrival, "I'm going to have to ask you for your whole collection of guns."

"I got a constitutional right to have 'em, Sheriff," Stormy said, standing outside his cabin.

"No, you don't," Smudge told him. "And it would help if you didn't point them at people."

"He was trespassing," Stormy insisted.

"Besides," the sheriff continued, "you did prison time in Ohio. You can't own those guns."

"That was Ohio," Stormy said.

"It's a *federal* law," the sheriff replied.

"I lived in Ohio then," Stormy responded.

"Robert, I used to live in Illinois," Smudge said. "But if I left Illinois owing money for my cable TV, I still had to pay it when I returned to New York."

Smudge didn't think it was the best analogy, but it had Stormy thinking.

"This is the 21st century, Robert," the sheriff said. "You can't just run for the border and the posse will stop chasing you if you get there first."

This news seemed to come as a complete surprise to Stormy. The sheriff, on the other hand, was re-thinking his neighborly approach. He thought that a piece of paper from the court might be a good idea.

"Robert," the sheriff said, "I can't come in your house if I don't have a court order."

"Well, then you can't come in my house," Stormy said, as though it was his idea.

"But," the sheriff told him, "I plan to get a court order. So, gather up your firearms and expect to see me back here tomorrow. Today is Sunday, and I'm not going to bother a judge about this today."

Stormy didn't say a word. He gave the sheriff one more look, turned and walked through the door into his cabin, closing it behind him.

"Both are redheads, both are knockouts, and both ski," Bip told JC. They were having a discussion that Bip had initiated as they ate breakfast. It was now Monday morning.

The conversation began with JC asking his news photographer how his date went Saturday night with Patty MacIntyre, the snowboarder and administrative assistant to County Executive Colin Cornheiser.

"We went to dinner at a place called The Mirror Lake Inn. It was fantastic. What a cool place," Bip told him. "Then we went to some bars. That's a great town. The stores were open, I bought some Olympic souvenirs."

Then Bip asked JC how Saturday night went with Robin at the Burns Supper.

"Fine," JC told him. "We had fun." Bip waited for more, but it did not come.

"Did you do anything Sunday?" Bip asked.

"Skiing," JC shrugged as he ate a bagel with cream cheese. Bip waited for more, but it did not come.

"I knocked on Robin's door Sunday morning," Bip said with nonchalance. "I wanted to see if she would join me for breakfast."

JC said nothing.

"She didn't answer her door," Bip said. "I don't think she was home." He feigned surprise.

Bip stared at JC, waiting for more. More did not come. Bip stared longer, until JC reluctantly made eye contact.

"You seem to have a type," Bip smiled. "Redhead, beautiful, skier. Plus, as a producer, she makes you look smarter than you are."

"I can't disagree with that," JC said with a little smile.

"And she doesn't live seven hundred miles away," Bip added. JC gave him a look. Bip was actually making him feel better about the confusing turn of events. JC smiled at him, as a gesture of thanks, and pushed himself away from the table.

"We have work to do," the reporter said. Bip rose and followed JC out the door of The Gill Grill.

With Bip behind the wheel, their car headed for the Battle Ax ski village. Coming out of the forest into pastureland, they both looked in wonderment at a man on a bicycle.

He pedaled along the side of the road. His legs were strong, driving the bike forward at a quick pace. Strapped to his broad back was a pair of snow skis.

The bearded young man had just rolled to a stop and was pushing his bike over the snow to lean against a fence post. Bip pulled the car over and stopped.

"Hi," JC greeted the man while climbing out of the car.

"Hello," the man responded in a friendly manner. He was wearing well-used, dark ski bibs and a thick, well-used, dark-blue down jacket. Buttons had been sewn on them to replace the zippers.

"Where are you going skiing?" JC asked him. The young man pointed toward the mountain, with a smile.

"I will cross the pasture. It belongs to a friend of mine," the man said. "Then I will hike up the LaChute Brook Fork Trail. At the top, I hike north along a ridge and then I have about four chutes to choose from to ski down." JC looked up the beaten path in the snow that the man was set to follow.

"Are those your tracks?" JC asked.

"Yes, they are," the man told him.

"You couldn't just take a chairlift, could you?" JC stated.

"No," the man said with a smile. JC smiled back.

"I've never heard that the Amish ski," JC told him.

"More of us are starting," the young man responded. "I read an article in *Powder Magazine* about Amish who ski in Montana. Very good article. I thought that I would try it."

JC and Bip introduced themselves. They told the man that they had seen his bicycle and wondered who would park their bike in a pasture. And they wondered where he went from there. The man laughed and pointed up the mountain.

"I am Inus Miller," the young man said. He was twenty-two years old and said that he had been skiing for about three years. He had a beard that was becoming bushy and no mustache. There was also a sparkle in his eye. It looked like joy, and confidence, JC thought.

"Do you ski?" Inus asked. JC said that he did. Bip said that he was a snowboarder.

"I do not think that I could snowboard," Inus told them. "I also use skins when I hike to get to my ski runs. I do not think I could do that on a snowboard." The Amish man smiled during the entire conversation. He seemed happy to talk skiing with skiers.

"There are not many of us that ski, right now," Inus said about his community of ten Amish families. "But the young ones see what I am doing and want to come. They are too young, but they will come when they are old enough."

The Amish man suggested that they should join him one day. Bip pointed at his snowboard, opting out. JC looked up the mountain at the chutes that Inus would climb to and expressed his doubts.

"I think you're tougher than we are," JC told him.

"But you are probably better skiers than I am," Inus responded with a smile.

JC and Bip allowed Inus Miller to continue with his trek to the chutes that he would ski. They watched as he hiked toward the mountain, with skis, poles and a backpack. He looked happy.

The journalists had an appointment with the multi-millionaire whose grandfather stumbled over a Mohawk battle ax decades ago. They pulled into the ski village and parked outside the corporate headquarters.

They were shown into a second-floor office that was unlike any the journalists had ever seen. They had been in the offices of governors, senators and billionaire businessmen. This office, they both thought, was better.

It was designed to look like the interior of a log cabin. There was even chinking between the logs in the walls. There was a large light fixture overhead that was inside an overturned canoe.

The room had a stone fireplace that extended through the ceiling. The walls were decorated with old oil paintings of snow-covered mountains, men fishing in wooden boats, moose, and hunters walking through the woods with their dogs.

The furniture was all made with bentwood and twigs. It might have been the best single room in the Adirondacks.

"I designed it to look like a cabin I rented at the Lake Placid Lodge," Averill Felix told them. "I stayed there while this ski area was being constructed.

"All that's missing," he said with a grin, "is a view out my window of a loon paddling on Lake Placid."

Averill Felix was a tall man, looking younger than his seventy-something age. He had a full head of gray hair with a wave in the front. He was lanky, with long arms and legs. He looked like he had lived a charmed life.

"He seems to be a stand-up guy," Felix said, when JC asked him what he thought of Colin Cornheiser. "He did everything he could to help get Battle Ax built, and now Tomahawk. Voters should be grateful to him. The high taxes in this county will be a thing of the past. We're putting Joseph County on the map!"

"And Tomahawk will be a big payday for you?" JC asked.

"Of course," Felix said. He looked at JC like that was a foregone conclusion.

"I didn't know him," said Felix when JC asked the ski resort owner if he was acquainted with the murder victim, Paul Campbell.

"It is a terrible shame," Felix said. "But I doubt it's related to Battle Ax or Tomahawk."

JC knew of the opposition launched against Battle Ax. There were those who felt it violated the "Forever Wild" concept inside the Blue Line of Adirondack Park.

A lot of important strings had to be pulled to get Battle Ax built, and laws were blurred. Once Battle Ax was approved, Tomahawk was almost a sure thing.

But JC wondered who else might have strong feelings about the development. Someone's feelings may have been so strong, on either side, that Paul Campbell's life was collateral damage.

"Aside from the environmental and ecological concerns," JC formed his question, "was there other opposition to building Battle Ax or Tomahawk?"

"There were concerns among the Mohawks," Felix acknowledged. "Not opposition, but concerns." And he raised his hand, with an index finger extended, to emphasize the difference.

"And we really wanted to respect their culture and hear them out," he continued. "That's why we went the extra mile with our archaeology survey. The Mohawks thought that there might be a significant old village around here. We looked, but Harold DeWitt found nothing. If he had found something, it might have been a different story."

After shooting their interview, Bip packed up his cameras and lights as they prepared to exit the impressive office of Averill Felix.

"If you don't have time now, come back and take a look around," Mr. Felix told them as they were leaving. "Go up the hill. Have you seen the homes we're building up there?"

Walking back outside, JC helped Bip load his gear in the car.

"When's the last time you went for a run?" JC asked him.

"With all this snow on the side of the road?" Bip asked. "I'd be too easy a target for the first truck that slid off the pavement. I wouldn't mind, though."

"I think I know just the place," JC told him.

So, the reporter and photographer returned to their hotel just long enough to change into their running gear. Then, they drove back to Tomahawk and parked their car at the bottom of a hill.

They ran past a stone sign indicating they were entering a Tomahawk subdivision for luxury homes. They climbed the hill and began to see large houses under construction on five-acre lots.

The homes had spacious porches on the upper level. Large windows faced in all directions, offering a brilliant view of Battle Ax. Each lot was cordoned off from the next by an abundance of white birch trees.

The contemporary post-and-beam construction included multi-car garages and a small building out back. Some of those structures became a pool house, some a guest cabin, and some a shed for gardening tools and a lawn mower. Most of these expensive homes would be vacation retreats.

It was another assurance that when Tomahawk Resort opened, Averill Felix was going to make a fortune.

JC reflected on their interview with Averill Felix. It was usable but not spectacular. It included another glowing appraisal of Colin Cornheiser and nothing on Paul Campbell, who Felix said he didn't know.

"What are we missing?" JC asked Bip as they ran up and down the rolling hills. "We have a development that's going to make everybody money. There's no law against that. We have a politician who's about to be accused of killing somebody, and yet everybody loves him. And we have a dead guy whose murder makes no sense at all."

"Since when did murder make sense?" Bip replied.

The longer they ran, the less they talked. They were breathing hard. But it was good to suck in the cold mountain air and feel the breeze against their faces. They reversed their direction when it was time to return to the car. JC was anticipating a scheduled meeting over the phone.

He was dreading the daily conversation with his superiors in Denver. He didn't think he had much progress to report.

"Do you want a story about an Amish skier?" JC asked his assignment editor, Rocky Baumann, over the phone.

"A what?" Rocky asked.

"An Amish skier," JC repeated.

"What do the Amish mean, when they use the word 'skier?'" Rocky asked.

"Um, it means 'one who skis,'" JC told him.

"Really?" Rocky asked. "The Amish ski out there?"

"At least one does," JC answered.

"And we can get a TV story out of this?" Rocky asked. "I don't think the Amish like to be photographed, do they?"

"That's my understanding," JC said. "I thought I was being facetious. I guess we could get a story, but it would take a lot of time."

"Oh, brother," Rocky answered quickly. "No, we don't need any more stories that require time. Are we making any progress on this Cornheiser story?"

JC explained that "progress" was a subjective term. Yes, they were making progress. No, their audience would not gasp or cling to the edges of their seats when hearing what they had to report that evening.

"JC," Rocky said with a sigh, "we're beginning to think we made a mistake sending you out there. If and when Cornheiser is arrested, we can cover it from here. And the murder of the archaeologist from Colorado is interesting, but we're spending good money on stories that are beginning to sound thin."

JC's problem with the scenario described by Rocky Baumann was that it was accurate. The reporter privately agreed that his employer was not getting their money's worth from him.

"Give us a couple of days," JC asked. "We got off to a good start. We have viewers interested. We just have to find something that keeps them from going to the refrigerator. If we still don't have any new developments in a couple of days, I can't blame you for pulling the plug."

"Wow," Rocky said. "That's an unexpectedly reasonable response."

Yeah, that's me, the good loser, JC thought.

JC asked Bip to drive him to the sheriff's office and wait for him outside.

JC closed the door to Sheriff Williams' office behind him and sat down. Smudge, sitting behind his desk, watched the arrival of his unannounced guest. He didn't remember asking for the door to be closed, so this annoyed him a little.

"May I ask your honest opinion, Sheriff?" JC asked.

"I didn't know I'd been giving you dishonest ones, up to now," the sheriff responded.

"I mean," JC continued, "I don't usually ask this kind of question if I'm speaking with a politician."

"That's what I am, I am sorry to say," Smudge told him. "I don't get to be sheriff if I don't get people to vote for me. So, what's this about?"

"Colin Cornheiser," the reporter told him.

The sheriff frowned. It was not that he did not want to discuss Colin Cornheiser's problems in Colorado with a reporter. It was that he didn't want to discuss them with *anybody*.

"If we must discuss this, are we off the record?" the sheriff asked.

"Yes, I can live with that," JC said.

"You realize that I carry a gun?" Smudge asked. He was insinuating that he'd been burned by reporters who violated "off the record" before, and he didn't intend to let the next one who did it live.

"Yes," JC responded, knowing exactly what the sheriff was telling him.

"Go ahead," Sheriff Williams reluctantly told him.

"Do you know of anything that you can think of that Colin Cornheiser is guilty of?" JC asked.

"No," the sheriff told the reporter, after pausing to think. "I wasn't in Colorado and I didn't know Cornheiser in, what are we talking, 1976, 1977?"

"And you think that he's as pure as the driven snow?" JC pursued.

"Geesh," the sheriff exclaimed. "No one is that pure. I'll bet you're not. But I'll say this about Cornheiser: since he's arrived in Joseph County, I've only known him to walk a straight line. He's kind of a nerdy hippie, but he's never been convicted of so much as jaywalking. And I don't hear much to the contrary."

"Does he pass the smell test?" JC asked the sheriff.

"Since he arrived in Joseph County, he has," Smudge told him. JC studied the sheriff.

"You're not showing all your cards, are you?" the journalist asked.

"And why would I start doing that?" the sheriff asked.

19

"When did you decide that I didn't kill Paul?"

Cindy Pfister was at her second lunch with Sheriff Smudge Williams when she asked the question. They were at The Gill Grill, across from the county courthouse and the jail.

"I never really believed it," the sheriff told her. "Your reaction to seeing him, when you went with us to the morgue, didn't strike me as someone responsible for putting him in that position."

"I'm accustomed to seeing the dead," Pfister told him. "Only, they've normally been dead for two or three hundred years."

The sheriff smiled and worked on his bacon, lettuce and tomato sandwich, thinking about what to discuss next. He hadn't been on anything even resembling a date in many years.

"Did you ever have a nickname?" he asked.

"Punch," she told him. She saw his questioning expression, so she provided an answer. "I was on the girls soccer team in high school. We all had nicknames. First, mine was 'Fist.' You know, short for Pfister. But 'Fist' transformed into 'Punch.' That one stuck. Some of my friends suggested that I played rough."

"I've heard that," Smudge said with a smile.

"I can't believe I just told you my nickname derived from my past violent tendencies," she said with a grin. "Does that make me a suspect again?"

"You weren't much of a suspect to begin with," he told her. "And don't forget, I've seen your weapon."

"Maybe someday," she said as she looked at him, "I'll get to see yours." Smudge smiled, caught by surprise. He thought for a moment about if he'd misunderstood. He didn't think so.

"How did your wife die?" Pfister asked after an appropriate length of silence. Smudge appreciated the way Cindy could ask a personal question bluntly and seem sensitive at the same time.

"Kayak accident," the sheriff told her. "The kind I respond to once or twice every summer."

The sheriff and the archaeologist took a few more bites of their lunch, walking softly around a delicate subject.

"She loved the Adirondacks," Smudge said. "I met her when I lived in Illinois. She followed me to New York with some trepidation. But in the end, if I said that I wanted to move back to Illinois, she would have stayed in the Adirondacks. She would have chosen them over me."

"I doubt that," Pfister said. She gave him a compassionate smile. No more needed to be said about why Smudge Williams lived alone.

"I need your help," the sheriff said. "I need to know more about archaeology. Somehow, it's going to tell me why Paul Campbell was killed. Right now, I don't have a suspect and I don't have a motive."

Pfister told him that she was available to answer his questions, any time. At that particular time, though, the sheriff's phone rang.

Cindy Pfister observed as the sheriff listened to the caller. Then he said to the caller, "That's just great." But the tone of his voice didn't sound like it was great.

"I've got to go," the sheriff told Pfister. "That was work." He still hadn't moved from his chair at the table.

"Wasn't this work?" Pfister asked about their lunch.

"Not really," he smiled.

Leaving the restaurant, the sheriff opened the door for Cindy Pfister and she climbed into the passenger seat. He drove her to the convenience store site and dropped her off. She gave his lips a quick kiss before exiting the patrol car.

The sheriff pulled away from the convenience store site momentarily forgetting where it was that he was in such a hurry to be. The memory of that kiss lingered as he headed for Stormy Jordan's place.

And then it vanished.

Smudge saw protesters at the entrance to Stormy's property. He counted less than ten of them, but they looked intent on getting attention.

Deputies Colden and Grant were already there, waiting in their patrol cars. They got out of their cars when the sheriff arrived. They moved his way.

The protesters held signs saying things like, "Leave his guns alone," and "Read the 2nd Amendment."

"A talk-radio show host has made Stormy a celebrity cause," Deputy Elizabeth Grant told the sheriff.

"I wonder who called him," Deputy Peter Colden said, eyeing Stormy's cabin at the end of the gravel driveway.

"You've got the paperwork?" Smudge asked Colden.

"Yes, sir," the deputy responded, holding a search warrant signed by a county judge. The sheriff then approached the protesters. He knew a few of them.

"Hello, Philip. Hello, Maggie," Smudge said to a pair of demonstrators. They were husband and wife. Smudge had seen them at a lot of protests. They seemed to be organizing this one.

"Hi, Sheriff," Philip said, "We have a legal right to be here."

"I agree, Philip," Smudge said. "And you could have picked a worse day for it." The skies were cloudy and there was always some wind blowing off the mountain across Stormy's open pasture. But at least it isn't raining, the sheriff thought.

"It's getting a little chilly, Sheriff," Maggie said. "We have someone running into town to get us hot chocolate."

"Good idea, Maggie," the sheriff said. He saw an SUV pull up. It was a TV news crew out of Plattsburgh.

"Well," the sheriff said as he made eye contact with all the demonstrators, "it's showtime. We need to go do our duty, just as you need to do yours. Just make sure you give us some room when we pull our cars in, so we don't run you over."

"Alright, Sheriff," said Philip in a quiet voice. Smudge almost felt like he was scripting a show with the protesters. In a way, he was. Smudge just didn't want things to get out of control. Get your protest on television but don't get your toes run over.

The sheriff and the other two patrol cars pulled into Stormy's driveway and proceeded to his cabin. The protesters and the TV camera stayed at the entrance, where bright yellow signs were posted. They said "No Trespassing."

The news photographer videotaped the protesters and used her long lens to capture the sheriff and his deputies pull up at the cabin. Deputy Colden handed Stormy the court order. Stormy gave the sheriff a look.

"Am I under arrest, Sheriff?" Stormy asked.

"Not if we clear up this misunderstanding without any trouble, Robert," the sheriff told him.

Stormy had spoken with a lawyer offering free advice on a radio show. He had been told that he could face a year in jail for possessing firearms as a convicted felon.

Stormy backed up and allowed the law officers through the door. A half dozen rifles and handguns were set out on a thoroughly worn couch that used to be red. Smudge looked for another 9mm. He didn't see one.

The room itself was dark and could use some dusting. But it was neat and Smudge noticed that washed dishes were lined up next to an empty sink.

Stormy, standing beneath a dusty mounted deer head and some old photographs in picture frames, kept an eye on the sheriff. The sheriff kept his eyes on Stormy.

Smudge had asked his deputies to take a look around. Maybe Stormy had forgotten that a rifle was hanging on the wall or something.

With nothing better to do, Smudge moved in to take a closer look at the picture frames under the dusty deer head.

One of them was of a young man holding a baby. The photograph was a polaroid and there was a crease across the corner, as if it was the only photograph like it that Stormy had. It would have to do, Smudge thought.

The young man in the picture looked a lot like Stormy, a long time ago. The baby he was holding was wearing a pink hat, so it was presumably a girl.

Both the young man and the baby girl squinted into the sun as they posed for the photograph. Stormy was smiling. Smudge wondered when the last time that happened.

Deputies Colden and Grant arrived back in the room, having performed a sweep through the small house, and gave the sheriff a positive nod.

"Find any others?" the sheriff asked his deputies.

"No, sir," they responded.

"That all of them?" the sheriff asked Stormy.

"That's all of them, Sheriff," Stormy said. It was the verbal confirmation that Smudge was waiting for.

"Then," the sheriff said, "we'll be going. Stay out of trouble, Robert." Stormy was handed a receipt.

The sheriff and his deputies walked out of the cabin and loaded the firearms into the rear hatch of Colden's car.

"Wow," Deputy Grant said to her colleagues. "That could have gone a lot worse."

"Stormy rarely puts his best foot forward," the sheriff said. "But he really doesn't mean to kick you with either of them."

The patrol cars pulled out of Stormy's driveway, following a path the protesters opened for them. The TV crew videotaped the law enforcement presence as it disappeared down the road. Then the photographer stowed her camera in the backseat of their car and also left. A few minutes later, the protesters left, too.

JC was thinking that he wanted to visit the archaeologist, Cindy Pfister. His phone rang as Bip drove them in that direction.

"Hi JC," it was Robin's voice on the other end. She was working on her laptop in her room at The T.

"Do we know why Paul Campbell visited a national park in Saratoga County? It's called Saratoga National Historical Park," Robin asked.

"It's a battlefield," JC told her. "The site of the Battle of Saratoga during the Revolutionary War. A lot of Scots fought there. I'm not surprised that a history buff from Scotland would make the trip on his day off."

"But I'm looking over his company expenses," Robin said. "Cindy Pfister gave me a bunch of papers to look through. He charged the visit to his company credit card. That would suggest he was there for business reasons."

"We're heading in Cindy's direction right now," JC told his producer. "We'll stop and ask her what she knows."

"I think I'll hop in my car and meet you at Cindy's," Robin said, knowing she might be needed to interpret archaeology jargon.

JC and Bip arrived first, but Robin arrived at the convenience store site a few minutes later.

"If Paul charged it to the company, then it was company business," Pfister told them. "He was completely honest."

"Why was it company business?" JC asked.

"I don't have any idea," Pfister told them.

"I can look through more of his notes," the archaeologist said. She looked at Robin and asked, "What did you see in the papers I gave you?"

"I found a credit card receipt for gas and a receipt for entry into the national park," Robin told her. "I found a couple of brochures and a map of the park. On the map, he had circled a feature called 'The Great Redoubt.' Any clue what that is?"

"I know a little about the battlefield," Pfister told them. "The Great Redoubt was a fortification the British built, mostly out of dirt, during the two Battles of Saratoga."

"What does it have to do with Battle Ax and Tomahawk?" JC asked. Pfister gave him a look indicating that she didn't have an answer.

"Let's go look," Pfister said, leading them to the biggest tent on the dig site. "I haven't really gone over his notes. I need to. I just didn't want to be reminded of … what happened."

JC and Robin followed the archaeologist into the tent. Pfister explained that this particular tent was used as their office. It had a table with folding legs and a stack of plastic storage containers. Some of the containers had papers in them, others were empty.

Bip had returned to the car to get his camera. He trailed behind the trio as they walked to the tent, shooting footage that might prove useful at any time.

"That's odd," Pfister said as she bent over a cardboard box that she had opened. "His notes should be in here."

The box had "Paul" in large letters scrawled on the side in permanent marker. It belonged to Paul Campbell and it was all but empty. There were a few pieces of paper describing the task they were assigned to do, but anything indicating what he was working on was nowhere to be found.

"You didn't work the site together? Side by side?" JC asked.

"Normally, yes," Pfister said. "But the last couple of days that Paul ... was alive, I had other matters to attend to, so he was working on the site alone."

"And you have no record of what he was working on?" Robin asked. "His findings?"

"All his notes should be here," Pfister sighed as she pointed to the empty box. She looked for another box that looked like it, but there was nothing similar in the tent.

"I was out of town," Pfister told them. "I didn't talk to him before ... before he was found in the brook."

JC noticed Pfister wiping away a tear as she stared at the box, like another piece of Paul Campbell had been taken away from her.

"I'll look at the rest of the stuff you gave me," Robin told the archaeologist. "I haven't looked through everything. Then, I'll get it back to you."

They emerged from the tent. JC was wondering where Campbell's paperwork would go. And he wondered if Pfister was as surprised by their disappearance as she said. He remembered that *she* would now be the sole owner of the business.

"Hi, Harold," Pfister called across the lot, waving politely at Harold DeWitt as he walked to his car. It was parked at the edge of the Tomahawk Resort site. It was the closest parking spot to the convenience store lot.

"Find anything?" DeWitt smiled and walked toward them. "Hi guys," he said. "JC and Bip, right?"

"I'm impressed," JC responded, noting that DeWitt had remembered their names. "And you met Robin Smith, our producer. I think you took a ski run together?"

"Yes! How could I forget? That was fun," DeWitt said as he shook hands all around.

"You seem to be interested in Cindy's dig here," JC said.

"We're all in the same business," DeWitt responded. "It's a labor of love, for all of us. We're not in it for the money. There is none!"

DeWitt and Pfister laughed, but the woman added, "Don't give me that, Harold. You've landed in a bed of feathers." She was pointing at the Tomahawk Resort.

"Your ship will come, Cindy," DeWitt countered. "You're too good an archaeologist to go unrewarded."

"Paul has been very supportive of our little project," Cindy told the journalists. "He keeps an eye on us. I think he's afraid we'll kick dust on his coliseum." The two archaeologists shared a chuckle.

"So, you two. You're scientists," said JC. "Do you know what Back Dirt is?"

Pfister and DeWitt looked at each other and then looked at JC suspiciously.

"This sounds like a trick question, but I'll give it a try," Cindy said. "It is dirt removed from a dig hole by archaeologists and deemed to be absent of any relics or artifacts or useful information," she told them. "It is set aside and usually used to fill the holes when we're done with the dig."

"Nope," JC told her with a smile. "Bip?"

Bip now had a big smile on his face as he lowered his camera and informed her that it was what local snowboarders were now calling a fall on their back.

"Like we got dirty," Bip informed her. Pfister and DeWitt laughed at that.

"Well," they said at the same time, "we had it first."

"That's what I said," Robin declared.

Pfister excused herself, saying that she had work to do.

"Take care, guys. Let me know if you need anything," DeWitt said as he headed back to his car.

"Let me know what you find, Robin," Pfister said as she disappeared into another tent.

"I want to see what you already found," JC said to Robin.

"You can come back to my room," she said. "It's all laid out there."

"Cool," said Bip. "I'll take lunch."

"Bring us something," Robin told him. Bip looked at her, wondering if she and JC would want to be interrupted. She gave the photographer a look. "I'm hungry!"

At Robin's room, inside The Thayendanegea Hotel, there was paperwork spread across one of two double beds in the room. The notes, receipts, photos, books and forms were from another box belonging to Paul Campbell.

JC sat on the cleared bed and fingered through the materials, not knowing what he was looking for.

Robin showed him the glossy map each visitor to Saratoga National Historical Park received upon their arrival. She pointed out the circle made in pen of The Great Redoubt on the battlefield.

JC picked up one of the books. It was a British history of the Battle of Saratoga in 1777. There were three sticky notes used as bookmarks. They'd been placed there by Paul Campbell.

JC opened the three marked pages. He read each of them and placed the open book down on the bed.

"Hey Robin," JC asked, "have you ever heard about the mystery of General Simon Fraser?"

20

"He was shot off his horse while leading his troops during the second Battle of Saratoga."

"There were two?" Robin Smith asked.

"Yeah," JC told her. "There were two days of combat in the Battle of Saratoga, nearly a month apart."

JC was providing Robin with a brief biography of Simon Fraser after finding that Paul Campbell, the murder victim found in LaChute Brook, had marked three pages in a history book. All three of those pages referred to Simon Fraser.

"Simon Fraser was a British general who fought at the Battle of Saratoga," JC told Robin. "He was from a wealthy Scottish family. The commanding general, John Burgoyne, was fond of him and Fraser was popular with the other officers and troops."

"You seem to know something about this general," Robin noted.

"The Saratoga Battlefield was one of those trips we made in school, when I lived here," JC told her. "Then, you returned to the battlefield with your parents every few years. Saratoga is called the turning point in the Revolutionary War. It's pretty important to the history of the Capital Region. It's a great park."

"Did the general die?" Robin asked.

"Yep. General Fraser was taken to a home near the battlefield after he was shot by a rebel sharpshooter. He died the next morning."

"So, what does this have to do with Paul Campbell?" she asked.

"Haven't a clue," JC said, shaking his head and putting the book back on the bed.

"But it was important to him," Robin said. "And whatever reasons he had for thinking it was important are probably missing from that cardboard box. Do you think someone stole his papers?"

"Maybe Cindy Pfister did," JC responded.

"What?" Robin said, giving him a look as though he had said something repugnant.

"Look, who is in a better position of knowing what he was up to and to dispose of his papers without arousing suspicion?" JC asked. "She just inherited the entire business. The money all belongs to her now."

"I was an archaeologist," Robin reminded him. "Her business probably isn't worth that much money."

"That we know of," JC answered. "But Paul Campbell was either a random victim or he was murdered for a reason. Maybe Cindy Pfister had a reason."

Bip showed up with lunch just as Robin's phone rang. While the food was spread over a small table in the corner of the room, Robin looked at JC and silently mouthed that she was speaking with Cindy Pfister.

"Can we come over and see it?" Robin asked into the phone. "OK, we're just going to have a sandwich and we'll be there in about forty-five minutes."

"She says she found something we might be interested in," Robin told JC as she put away her phone.

"That's convenient," JC muttered.

"Is it possible?" Robin asked, resisting the thought that Cindy Pfister might be implicated.

They ate their lunch and climbed into two cars, heading to the convenience store dig site. They found Pfister inside one of the small tents. She said that she was working on a hole that began as a smaller test pit.

Pfister had her red knit cap pulled down over her ears to stay warm. Her sturdy beige jacket was open and revealed a heavy sweater. She was accustomed to working in cold weather.

But her hands were bare. She'd been working in the dirt with her fingers and small tools.

A dirty toothbrush and some small wooden picks were on a table holding artifacts with labels.

"So, this is what I thought you'd find interesting," the archaeologist said to the three journalists.

"That's wampum," she said, holding out her smudged hand to reveal a few beads made out of shells.

"And that's wampum made by the English or French," Pfister said as she picked up some other items from a large cloth on the table next to her. "The Europeans made it out of glass. They'd use it to barter with the Indians."

"This is a piece of pottery," she said, reaching to pick up more items. "And this is a point, probably an arrowhead."

"There are also flakes and stone tools," the archaeologist said as she waved her hand across items sorted on the dark green cloth.

"Really cool," Robin said.

"Are they valuable?" JC asked.

"Historically, they are," Pfister told him. "They tell a story."

"How about money-valuable," JC inquired.

"Some of these stone tools might be a thousand years old," she said. "But you wouldn't get much money for them. They're not that hard to find, if you know where to look."

"So, it's the story that's valuable," JC interpreted. "That's why you thought we should come out and look."

"Right," Pfister said. "Paul and I should have known this stuff was here. There's a lot of it, judging from just the test pits. This was a Mohawk settlement that they probably used repeatedly. And it was probably pretty big."

Pfister looked at the three journalists, gauging if they understood what she was getting at. They didn't.

"Look, we *should* have known we'd find artifacts at this site, but we didn't," Pfister told them. "One of the indicators that we use to survey an archaeological site is to read reports of any archaeological digs that have gone on nearby. In this case, there was a dig right next door. We were digging, at different times, twenty or thirty yards from each other!"

Pfister was looking toward the site of the Tomahawk Resort as though she could see through the canvas side of the tent. And JC could see her temperature was rising.

"There was nothing in their report," Pfister said, exasperated. She was looking up at JC and Robin. "Paul and I both read their report. They said they found absolutely nothing to indicate there was a human settlement here."

"But if you found it here," JC pointed to the ground, "then you think DeWitt had to have found it there, on the Tomahawk site?"

"He must have," Pfister told him. "I'm finding a rather rich site. There are a lot of artifacts."

"Did Harold DeWitt decide to look the other way?" JC asked. "Would the discovery of an old Mohawk camp stop a development like Tomahawk?"

Pfister shook her head.

"No!" she said vehemently. "It could delay things while a more complete archaeological dig was done," she speculated, "but it wouldn't kill the project."

"Could they be forced to change their plans? Build around the site?" JC asked. "That would cost them money."

"Money is one thing Averill Felix doesn't have to worry about," she said bitterly. "They might have to move things around if something colossal like a burial ground was found.

"Could they be forced to build a museum?" JC asked. "That could get expensive."

"I wish, but no," she told him. "In situations like this, developers have felt the need to spend a few dollars to build glass display cases in nearby buildings, or a wall of glass shelves, to exhibit what was found. It's a little public relations gesture to remember who was here before them."

The three journalists stared in silence at the artifacts, the open hole and Cindy Pfister's burning fuse.

"It's selfish," she said, dropping back to her knees in the dirt near the pit. "I hate archaeologists who behave like shit. I need to talk to Harold about this."

She was fuming. They were reminded of her reputation for having a short temper.

"If Paul found something that would maybe not stop, but delay Tomahawk," JC asked her, "would it be reason to kill him?"

"I don't know," Pfister said with a surrendering look. It *was* a pretty momentous leap to a motive, JC thought.

"Who would be hurt by a delay of Tomahawk?" he asked her.

"This isn't as hypothetical as you might think," Pfister admitted. "Dig results have been faked for love and money. Who would lose money if Tomahawk was delayed by, say, a season? Maybe it would cause them to miss opening for the next winter of skiing. *That* would cost a lot of money."

"The developer, Averill Felix?" JC began. Pfister nodded her head affirmatively.

"I've seen a developer bribe an archaeologist to look the other way," she said.

"The archaeologist, then," JC offered. "If he was caught taking a bribe, he'd be ruined forever, right?"

"Right," Pfister said.

"And how about the politician who fought off opposition to the development by promising jobs and lower taxes?" JC suggested. "And hoped to parlay this into a seat in the state legislature?"

"I hadn't thought of that one," Pfister agreed. "I heard how Colin Cornheiser fought for Tomahawk. It's probably no coincidence that the newspaper said Mr. Felix was going to be Cornheiser's primary campaign contributor."

"And if Cornheiser has killed before, what does he have to lose?" Robin added, reminding all of them that Colin Cornheiser was expected to be indicted on murder charges in Colorado.

JC, Robin and Bip walked out of the tent and through the cold air to their cars.

"Now what do you think about Cindy?" Robin asked.

"She makes a good victim. But she still is in the best position to be in the middle of this," JC said. "Maybe she and Paul took a bribe and Paul got cold feet. Maybe she was in on it with DeWitt, or Averill Felix. Maybe she called us here to orchestrate her appearance of innocence."

"She sure was ready to throw Cornheiser under the bus," Bip added.

"Well, Cornheiser had the motive," JC said, "and maybe the experience."

JC wanted to touch base with the sheriff. Robin headed back to her computer at The T.

When the reporter and photographer walked into the sheriff's office, there was a boy sitting in a chair behind the counter who looked like he was about fifteen years old.

"His brother broke his leg skiing this morning," Deputy Colden told them. "But when dad went to get his car to take the boy to the hospital, the car was gone!"

The fifteen-year-old behind the counter now looked like he had fallen asleep in the chair.

"The car, it turns out," Deputy Colden said, barely above a whisper and with an amused look, "had been stolen by *this* kid, the brother. He had taken it into town to buy a case of beer! He's fifteen years old! And when he finally showed up back at the condo, he was drunk!" The deputy couldn't help but show a small smile.

"How's the brother?" JC inquired.

"With the broken leg?" Colden asked. "He'll be fine. Kids are like reptiles, they grow their parts back. Anyway, that's the kind of cases we usually get around here, not murders."

Then, the deputy saw Sheriff Williams look up from his office.

"I think the sheriff will see you now," Colden told JC, and went to raise the teenager from his slumber.

"Cornheiser? Pfister?" The sheriff expressed his surprise when JC asked if the county executive and the archaeologist were suspects in Campbell's murder. The reporter also asked about Averill Felix and Harold DeWitt.

"We just spoke to Cindy Pfister," JC told the sheriff. "She is convinced that the archaeology report for Tomahawk was faked. There's no misunderstanding that a lot of money is riding on Tomahawk, is there? And that could benefit all of them. Cornheiser has political ambitions. Plus, it's a heck of a coincidence that Cornheiser is from Colorado and the guy floating in the brook turns out to be from Colorado. What are the odds?"

"No, you are right about that," the sheriff said. "But Averill Felix has more money than he could spend in a lifetime. And you said yourself, archaeology wouldn't stop Tomahawk, just delay it a little."

"Unless there's something we still don't know," JC responded.

"Averill Felix has a Glock 19, Sheriff," bellowed Deputy Colden from his desk. The sheriff dropped his head a little and shook it with subtlety.

"Peter!" the sheriff bellowed, trying to stop his deputy from using the "loud-voice intercom."

"He registered it with us a couple of years ago," Colden said as he appeared in the doorway to the sheriff's office.

"And I was thinking about that piece of paper found in the victim's pocket, with the two Os on it. Colorado has two Os, I was thinking. Could he have known something damaging about Mr. Cornheiser?"

"Peter!" the sheriff said in a sharp tone, silencing his deputy. "Is there anything else you'd like to share with the news media?"

Deputy Colden looked at the reporter and photographer and recognized his mistake. He shrank back to his desk.

"If nothing," the sheriff shared a pained smile with the two journalists, "we're transparent."

21

"He should be here."

JC was walking across a high bluff on the old battlefield in Saratoga. His producer and photographer were in tow.

The bluff was perched above the Hudson River and protected by two British cannons.

There was signage so visitors to the battlefield knew the significance of this spot. One sign offered a sketch of The Great Redoubt during the battle, with wooden fortifications and sentries posted. The other sign offered an artist's rendering of General Fraser's funeral service.

"His body was supposed to be here," JC told them. "But historians using modern methods can't find him."

The ground was a mixture of dead grass and patches of snow. Bip began busying himself with his camera. He loved assignments that offered him good visuals.

The battlefield offered cannons, granite monuments, pasture, groves of trees and sweeping views. Bip was happily going about his work, toying with rack focus, slow zooms and starbursts.

Robin caught JC brushing his hand through some soft needles on a pine tree.

"Do you know that these pine needles have more vitamin C than citrus fruit, like an orange?" JC asked, looking over his shoulder toward Robin.

"Really?"

"Yep, this is an Eastern White Pine," he told her. "When some early French explorers were suffering life-threatening scurvy, the Iroquois led them to Eastern White Pines. They made tea and it saved the Frenchmen's lives."

"Were you a Boy Scout?" she asked.

"I was a Cub Scout," he said. "The Boy Scouts didn't think I was made of the right stuff."

"That's kind of sad," she said with a little smile.

"I have a lot of emotional scars like that," he said, smiling back.

"Can we make some?" she asked. "Not the scars, the tea."

"Sure. And I'm not ruling out the scars." They exchanged a look, the kind he had misgivings about. Then, he reached into a pocket of his coat and pulled out an empty plastic bag.

"It's a good thing that you happen to be carrying a plastic bag," she stated, giving him a quizzical look. "Do you always do that?"

"I always carry one or two of them, in case I see something that I should pick up."

"You mean, like dog poop?" she asked, smirking.

"I was thinking of evidence," he told her. "But, sure, dog poop, too."

She began pulling pine needles off the tree and placing them in the bag.

"How many?" she asked.

"You're asking me? I nearly burned down a luxury hotel trying to warm up a Pop Tart. You're asking me how to recreate an ancient Native recipe?"

She gave him a look that said, "You are hopeless" and kept dropping pine needles into the bag.

"Let me know if you see a ghost," JC said as he walked across the clearing.

"Really? Do they think this is haunted?" she asked.

"Before I moved to Colorado, I interviewed an author here named David Pitkin," JC told her. "He said to me that people have seen an officer on horseback and another soldier firing his musket."

"Was the officer General Fraser?" she asked. JC shrugged.

"If it is," she added, "we can just ask him where his body made off to." She laughed at her insight. JC had to laugh, too.

"So, where is he?" Robin asked her reporter.

"That's the mystery. No one really knows," JC told her with a smile. "One theory says that wild animals got to the grave and dragged him off. Another theory suggests that he's still here, they just haven't found him. There's also some who say he was taken back to Scotland for burial. There's even a TV show that dramatized that theory a couple of years ago. But the show was dramatic fiction. That particular explanation happened to be useful to their story line."

"What do you think?" she asked.

"He was from a well-connected family and a war hero," JC said. "If he was returned to Great Britain for burial, there would be some record of it. There are witness accounts that say he was buried here, at The Great Redoubt on the battlefield. That part isn't disputed. That was his request. Rebel snipers were even shooting at the funeral party during the brief memorial service."

"Then, where did he go?" inquired Robin.

"That's the unsolved mystery of General Simon Fraser," JC said as he walked about The Great Redoubt, scanning the scene.

"Somehow," JC told her, "this has to do with Paul Campbell."

"Was Simon Fraser ever in the area now known as Joseph County?" Robin asked.

"It's possible he was there more than once," JC responded after thinking about that. "You may be looking at this the right way."

"I try," Robin told him, proud to contribute.

"General Fraser fought in this area in *two* wars, the Revolution and the French and Indian War before that," JC told her. "In both wars, he was stationed for a while due north in Canada. He almost certainly had to pass through Joseph County to get from Canada to many of his battlefields on American soil."

"He knew people in Canada?" Robin asked him.

"He spent some winters there, when the military was waiting out the bad weather," JC replied.

JC walked the rolling terrain that was once The Great Redoubt. He was turning things over in his mind.

"Maybe that's where his body went," he finally said.

"Where?" Robin asked.

"Canada," JC told her. "Or at least someone *tried* to get him to Canada."

There would be no live shots from Upstate New York that evening. JC and his crew had been given two days to come up with a compelling story to warrant staying in New York instead of returning home to Colorado.

The sky was dark when they returned from the Saratoga Battlefield. They knew they were on the verge of something, but they'd run out of daylight.

Before heading back to Paul Campbell's history books, the journalists thought that dinner and a drink at the Poo Ice Bar in the lodge was a good idea.

"There are two Os in Poo," Robin said, remembering the piece of paper found in Campbell's pocket. JC opened the door for her, entering the Poo Ice Bar.

"There are two Os in moo," JC responded.

"Maybe," Bip added, "Paul Campbell was killed by Colonel Mustard with a frozen piece of poo in a cow pasture. Moo!"

"Maybe," JC said, "he died when someone snuck up on him and yelled 'boo!' Or maybe they're just booing our poor taste in humor."

They sat next to a table where a family was eating. The children looked bathed and scrubbed after a day of skiing. The parents looked like they could use a good night's rest. They had sweaters and shirts from Utah.

The bar was better lit than it would be when the dinner rush was over. It was easier to see the banners and shields belonging to ski clubs from across the country. JC thought they were a nice touch.

Their table was beneath two shields and a photograph. One shield belonged to the Wedeln Ski Club from New Hampshire. And there was a Nord Strand Ski Club from Evanston, Illinois.

The photograph was a head-and-shoulders shot of a legend in the Lake Placid Region, "Dew Drop" Morgan. He was a world-champion bobsledder and a World War Two flyer. He then became a popular bartender in Lake Placid. JC had been told about Dew Drop by a customer whom Dew Drop liked to call "Crash."

One of the children at the next table was staring at JC. JC stared back, amused.

"How was skiing today?" he finally asked the boy.

"Fine," the little voice responded in a little voice.

"Did you see any snow sharks?" JC asked. The boy's eyes showed uncertainty.

"Are there sharks in the snow?" the boy asked. JC looked at the boy's parents for approval. They didn't seem to object.

"Don't worry," JC told him, "they're friendly sharks. They're not like the ones in the ocean. They like to play." The child's eyes began to glue themselves to his storyteller.

"You don't have them in Utah. But in the East, we have snow sharks," JC said as he lowered his eyes to the boy's level, "They swim out of the woods and when they play, they like to grab the tips of our skis."

The boy looked in wonder at his parents.

"Did you fall today?" JC asked the child. The boy said that he had.

"It was probably a snow shark," JC told him. "But don't worry, they don't eat children. They just like to play with them. To a snow shark, children are 'Catch and Release.'" That amused the parents.

"Is that you, JC?" asked a voice at a table behind him. JC turned and saw a face he knew. It was a ski racer from Jiminy Peak who started behind him in the super-G at Battle Ax.

"Hi, Bert," JC said. He couldn't remember Bert's last name. Bert was sitting at a big round table with seven women. They were probably in their fifties and seemed to be well acquainted. Bert introduced all of them.

"These are the Magnificent Seven," he said as we waved to the women, who didn't seem to need much of an excuse to share a laugh.

"This one's my wife," Bert said when he pointed to a blonde with a big grin.

"Wait a minute!" another woman cried, "I thought I was your wife!" That got them all laughing, including Bert.

"These girls have known each other since high school," Bert explained as the women jeered at each other about that era. "They all get together each year and go off somewhere. This time, they let me tag along because they needed a designated driver." The women laughed some more.

"They have gone to Mexico together," Bert continued. "And they spent a week on a dude ranch together."

"The horses still complain about that weekend!" said one of the Magnificent Seven. They all laughed some more.

"We call these weekends our 'Diaper Dash,'" another woman giggled. "Because we're trying to get everything in that we can, before we're all wearing diapers!"

Now the ladies were laughing so hard that they nearly fell off their chairs. Bert just shook his head and smiled. Then, he rose from his chair and shook JC's hand.

"Good seeing you, JC," Bert said. "Maybe we'll see each other at the next race. These girls are only staying a few doors down. They can walk home." And he headed for the door, leaving the Magnificent Seven to order more drinks and share another funny memory from the past.

"Who was that?" Robin asked as she sipped from a beer called Bamboo Basher. It had an image on the can of a ski racer bashing through slalom gates.

JC leaned in toward his friends and lowered his voice so he wouldn't be heard at the next table.

"He's a nice guy named Bert," JC began. "But I can never remember his last name because we always call him 'Bodily Function Bert.'"

JC explained that at big ski races spread over three days, a bunch of racers would routinely share a condo to save money. Some got beds and some slept on the floor.

"The standing rule was that if you had a spouse or a date, you got a bed," JC explained. "If you were single, you slept on the floor or maybe a couch." JC looked over his shoulder to make sure he wasn't overheard.

"Bert always came alone, so he slept on the floor," JC said. "I spent time on the floor, too, usually with Bert nearby."

"Poor JC," Robin faked sympathy. "You couldn't find a date?" JC shook his head sadly.

"But Bodily Function Bert is a legend," JC told them with a grin. "All night, he snores, coughs, farts, wheezes, sneezes, and makes some other sound that is unidentifiable. None of us have been able to figure that one out. Anyway, that's why we call him Bodily Function Bert."

The three journalists shared dinner, more stories and more drinks. The Poo Ice Bar had a good vibe that night.

"It's going to rain tomorrow," one of the Magnificent Seven said to the trio.

"Seriously?" Bip asked.

"Yes, hon," one of the women replied. "Ooo, he's a handsome one," another said. All the girls laughed. One of them pulled a dollar from her purse, offering it to Bip, and that just set them all off in hysterics.

"It's really going to rain? It's late January!" Bip said to JC. As the only one at the table born in the East, this had become JC's fault.

"I told you we should have gone to that lake in Georgia," groused one of the seven women. Having learned that JC grew up in the East, she gave him a mock grimace, followed by a smile.

"My snow melts and becomes your lake," JC countered. "So, you're welcome." He smiled.

"Oooo, that's a good one," one of the women said.

"That's your beach," JC followed. "This is my beach."

Bip's head had slowly landed in his hand, which was propped up on his elbow. He looked tired and excused himself for the night.

Almost as soon as Bip had surrendered his chair, it was filled by a man bearing three fresh Bamboo Bashers.

"I think this was your chosen poison, right?" said Harold DeWitt as he pushed a can to each of them.

"Thank you," Robin said. "I love the name. The bamboo alludes to old slalom racing poles, right?"

"Pretty *and* smart," JC said.

"Agreed!" DeWitt chimed in, raising his can in a toast to the two journalists.

"Have you spoken to Cindy?" JC asked DeWitt.

"Since the three of us spoke?" he asked. "No, I haven't seen her."

"She's finding artifacts on her site," Robin said. "She wonders why *you* didn't." JC was glad Robin was directing this line of questioning. She was the archaeologist, not him.

"What's she finding?" DeWitt asked.

"Wampum, European and Indigenous," Robin told him. "Pottery shards, some points."

"That's a pretty small sample she's working with," DeWitt answered. "She may have hit a lucky lode. A Mohawk party could have spent a weekend there. It doesn't mean it's anything significant."

"Did you and Paul Campbell talk about findings on the convenience store site?" JC asked.

"There was nothing to talk about," DeWitt said after sipping from his beer. "They hadn't found anything before Paul ... died."

"Could Cindy be mistaken?" JC asked.

"Well, she knows what a point and a piece of pottery look like," DeWitt told them. "She's not stupid. But do you notice that she's still working alone? No one is rushing to her aid since Paul died, are they? She's not the most popular person in the archaeology community. And some of her findings have been challenged in the past. This wouldn't be the first time."

A couple of young men brushed past the table and gave DeWitt a friendly pat on the shoulder. DeWitt was not without friends here.

JC and Robin caught each other's eye. Maybe they had been giving Cindy Pfister a free pass, up to now.

"I don't know how to deflect something like this," DeWitt told them, when the three of them were alone again. "I can't say that I found something that I didn't find. We're scientists.

A discovery isn't any good if it's just plausible. It's got to be perfect."

DeWitt rose from the table. He said that he had to go. He worked up a smile as he told them that it was nice bumping into them.

"We'll work it out," he said. JC and Robin thanked him for the beer and he was gone. That left them at the table alone.

"So, it's going to rain and all the snow is going to be gone?" Robin asked.

"There's a lot of snow out there," JC told her. "Most of it will still be there when the rain is over. We'll just stay off of it until then."

"Well, I guess we could work," she said, deliberately looking disappointed.

"I had a neighbor when I was growing up who would spray paint his grass green in the spring," JC told her. "We could never figure out how his grass got so green so early. Then, my mom jumped out of the car and ran up on his lawn. She dashed back to the car and said, 'He spray paints it!'"

"So, when the snow melts," Robin said with growing enthusiasm, "We can spray paint the dirt white?"

"That seems to be the moral of the story," JC laughed.

"So, what do you want to do now?" Robin asked and then took a sip of her beer.

That was followed by another look. This time, he didn't harbor misgivings.

22

"The Mohawks fought alongside the British, hence alongside Simon Fraser," JC told her.

"You are really a master at pillow talk," she told JC as she laid close to him in her bed.

The morning sky was gray outside of their bedroom window. It was beginning to rain. JC laid in bed with a history book balanced on his chest. It was one of the three they had that belonged to Paul Campbell.

"General Simon Fraser led British troops through the countryside, which I presume would include present-day Joseph County, to sweep out American scouts. The British didn't want the rebels to see their troop movements as they moved down from Canada toward Saratoga and Albany," JC paraphrased.

"So," he said as he stroked her arm, "Fraser was in Canada, was in Joseph County and was aligned with the Mohawks who were in Joseph County."

Despite her teasing, Robin was absorbing this. She was as fascinated by the mystery as JC was.

JC climbed from bed, saying, "I'm going to make us some coffee."

He disappeared in a closet and emerged wearing one of the hotel's white terry cloth robes and a pair of matching white slippers. The slippers were immediately noted by Robin.

"So, that's what you're going to look like when you're eighty," she quipped.

"I'm not particularly fond of my toes," JC told her. "They embarrass me a little."

"Your toes?" she asked. "Of all the things you have to be embarrassed about, you choose your toes?"

He looked up at her from the coffee pot he was preparing. They were both wearing smiles.

"They're a little smashed," he told her. "It started when I was playing sports in high school and they just keep getting smashed again. I think I wore my athletic equipment too tight. It didn't seem to matter if they were tennis shoes or ski boots, I seemed to like them tight."

"Then," she said with a grin, "you really have no one to blame but yourself."

"That," he declared as he brought her a cup of coffee, "is the story of my life."

He settled back into bed next to her and they enjoyed the morning's first cup of coffee.

"I like that robe," Robin said.

"It makes me look like Hugh Hefner," he told her.

"It makes you look like a rabbit," she replied with a smirk.

"If you're going to be mean, we can just go back to work," he said, faking injury to his male pride.

"Said the man in bed with me, reading a book."

"What did Campbell find?" JC wondered aloud.

"And was it something that got him killed?" Robin added. "And was he killed by Felix, Cornheiser or DeWitt?"

"You know," JC told her, "I hear that the old landowner next to Tomahawk is kind of a nut. I was watching the news out of Plattsburgh. They had a story about the sheriff taking away all of this guy's guns after he pointed one at a snowplow driver."

"So, Campbell could have been shot because he was poking around on that guy's land?" Robin asked.

"I guess this guy has pointed his gun at people before," JC stated. "Maybe we've been overthinking it. Campbell was found in the water bordered on both sides by this old guy's land. He points guns at people. Maybe he's the only suspect that makes sense."

"Maybe," Robin said.

"And there's Cindy Pfister," JC added.

"Seriously?" Robin said, sitting up. "I like her!"

"I like her, too," JC defended himself. "But maybe she wanted to own her business without a partner. Or maybe she wanted a piece of that bribe and Campbell wouldn't go along with it."

Robin hadn't changed her look of protest. Pfister might be on JC's list of suspects, but Robin wasn't going to allow Pfister on *her* list of suspects.

"Hey, can you get me photographs of those people?" JC asked. "Pictures that I can carry in my pocket and show witnesses?"

"Felix, Cornheiser, DeWitt and the old landowner?" she confirmed. "I'll get on it today."

"And Cindy Pfister," JC told her.

"Seriously?" she raised her head to give him a look, "You think Cindy Pfister could have shot her partner? Wow, who aren't you suspicious of? Am I a suspect?"

"I looked into it," JC told her. "You have a pretty good alibi."

"Yeah," she smiled. "I was in Colorado."

"Yep," he smiled back. "But when you have a moment, maybe you could supply me with some credit card receipts that would back that up. Gas purchase, milk at the grocery store, don't go to a lot of trouble."

She was still smiling as she relaxed back in bed. They laid under the warmth of the sheets a while longer and sipped their coffee.

"Rain in the winter sucks," Robin pouted. She could see the rain through the window. It was coming down harder, making popping sounds when it hit the glass panes.

"It happens in the East every year, usually in January," JC told her. "Then it gets cold again and the ski resorts add a new layer of man-made snow, and it's like the rain never happened. No one makes snow like the Northeast. No one in the world," JC said.

"We should probably get up," she said.

"Yep, we've got less than twenty-four hours before the hatchet drops," he said, referring to the end of the two days he'd been given by his newsroom to come up with compelling developments in their two stories.

Robin still didn't budge. She was holding a cup of coffee, so he figured that she hadn't fallen asleep. She was deep in thought.

"Would you have been a rebel or a loyalist in the Revolutionary War?" she finally asked.

"My family was in Scotland then," he told her. "So, I probably would have been fighting on the British side."

"I would have been a rebel," she said. "I think that being an archaeologist for ten years was a rebellion of my own. I was always smart, so things were expected of me. I didn't like to do what was expected of me."

"What's the worst dare you ever accepted?" he asked.

"Sleeping with you," she said and laughed. Then she kissed him as she said, "No, I'm kidding." Then, she pointed at him.

"My dare?" he asked. "I ate food out of a dumpster. It was disgusting. I mean, I looked for the cleanest food in the cleanest dumpster I could find. But it was gross." Robin had a look of horror on her face.

"I hope you bathed before you hopped into bed with me!" she laughed.

"It was a long time ago," he said with a smile. "A long, stupid time ago."

"You know what I find weird?" she then asked.

"Weirder than eating out of a dumpster?" he grimaced.

"Kinda," she said. "It's weird to me that Harold DeWitt still has an office at the Tomahawk site and he's there every day. He had to have submitted his report, or all that building wouldn't be going on. He should have moved on to his next project by now."

"I can ask Felix why DeWitt is still there," JC offered.

"If they're in it together, he'll lie," she said.

"True," said JC. "But sometimes, lies tell more truth than the truth."

"Wow," Robin said in mock marvel. "Did you get that out of a fortune cookie?"

"Can't you accept that I'm simply profound?" he said, smiling at her. She sat up and kissed him.

"We need food!" she said. "Let's order room service!"

"Oh, you're a Room Service Rebel," he smiled.

"Better than being a Dumpster Diver," she smiled back.

"I still have until the end of the day," JC protested as soon as he answered the phone. He had recognized the phone number. It was the newsroom back in Denver.

"We're actually close to something," JC told the assignment editor. "I think it would be a mistake to pull the plug."

So far, JC hadn't allowed Rocky Baumann to say a word since picking up the phone.

"You're not going to believe this," Baumann finally was able to interrupt. JC ended his filibuster. Baumann's proclamation intrigued him.

"The investigators here who leaked the Cornheiser case to us, complete with paperwork and urgency, remember them?" Baumann asked.

"I never met them," JC reminded him. "This all came from our news director. But I do have the paperwork, so I remember that."

"Well, it's off," Bauman said. "They had a big meeting of the Braintrust. Lawyers and investigators and all, and decided they didn't have the evidence to indict Cornheiser."

"Oh, brother," JC said in frustration. "Do you think they fed us this tip hoping that *we* would find the evidence that *they* couldn't find?"

"It wouldn't be the first time we've been used in exactly that way," Rocky acknowledged.

"So, why did they tell us that they did have a case?" JC asked.

"It puts egg on our face," the assignment editor said.

"No, it puts egg on *my* face," JC answered. "I'm the face that told television viewers that this guy was about to get indicted. No offense, but TV viewers don't know who *you* are. They know who I am. I'm the guy who told them an innocent man was going to be arrested for murder."

JC could hear Rocky Baumann sigh into the phone. That was the sound of capitulation.

"So, what are we going to do about it?" JC asked.

"We've got to run a story," Rocky told him. "More than one story."

That evening, JC broadcast from downtown Joseph in front of the county offices. The rain had stopped and the temperature was beginning to drop.

JC told viewers that the investigation had run aground. The evidence of Colin Cornheiser's guilt didn't float. That also meant that the disappearance of Winston Reddish remained adrift.

JC's report from Joseph included a statement on video from investigators back in Colorado saying that the case against Cornheiser was closed.

To JC's surprise, Cornheiser agreed to an interview in his office. He was gracious, saying law enforcement did their job and cleared his name.

"It will end a whispering campaign that I've endured since poor Winston disappeared, all those years ago," Cornheiser said into the camera.

After the last of three live shots, JC re-entered the county offices. Patty Macintyre's eyes launched daggers at the reporter as he walked into Cornheiser's office.

"You have every right to be angry with me," JC told the county executive. "I just want to apologize."

"I'm not angry with you," a tired Cornheiser replied.

"You knew why we were here," JC told him. "To cover a story that ended with you being led out of here in handcuffs."

"They don't throw innocent people in jail," Cornheiser said with a slight smile. He pulled off his wire-rimmed glasses and rubbed his tired eyes. "Besides, I'm not so innocent. I'm just not guilty of *that*."

JC left the office thinking about that last statement. Who wouldn't wonder about it? The reporter still had a feeling that the county executive was hiding something that he was ashamed of.

Cornheiser, JC thought, was just handed the supreme victory: a declaration of innocence from a pack of bloodthirsty cops and prosecutors. But where was the celebration? JC thought that the *vindicated* Cornheiser looked as guilty as when he was *accused*.

Emerging back out on the sidewalk, JC's phone rang.

"You did a good job, JC." It was the news director, Pat Perilla. "I'm sorry for putting you in that situation. You did a good job tonight."

"He hasn't been treated fairly," JC said. "You can't unring the bell."

"It's very embarrassing. We're a little worried about a lawsuit, too," the news director disclosed.

"He's a public figure," JC reminded him. "Not that we deserve it, but we're probably safe. Law enforcers told us they were going to arrest him. As a public figure, he can't really win a slander suit."

"Well, that makes me feel a little better," the news director said.

"It shouldn't," JC answered.

23

"Ready?"

"I am," said Deputy Liz Grant to the sheriff. "I brought these for you."

"What are those?" the sheriff asked.

"They're crampons," the deputy told him. "I'll put them in my backpack. If the mud or snow gets slick or if we run into ice, we'll fit them to our boots rather than slide down a ravine and break a hip."

"Are you looking at me?" the sheriff asked as Liz looked at him. "Do you seriously think I'm old enough to worry about breaking a hip?"

"Maybe I'll break *my* hip," the deputy said, trying to hide her amusement.

"Maybe," the sheriff said with some satisfaction.

He was wearing his waist-length winter jacket with a badge over the left breast and "Sheriff" printed on the back. He had his regulation black pants on.

Liz Grant was wearing the latest outdoor weather gear, both to repel water and keep her warm. Beneath, she had long tops and bottoms designed to wick sweat and keep her dry. They both wore ballcaps.

The rain and the fog brought by the warm temperatures had melted a lot of snow. The sheriff and his deputies had begun their day early. Black ice had triggered a number of traffic accidents in the county, but none that was life-threatening.

Sheriff Williams told Liz Grant that conditions would not be ideal on LaChute Brook Fork Trail, but it might be their best chance to look further upstream from where Paul Campbell's body was found.

"Why didn't you ask Deputy Pattern?" Liz asked, as Pattern was senior to her in rank.

"He's got his own honey-do list," the sheriff told her.

The sheriff and Deputy Pattern had walked along the brook on Stormy's land the day after Campbell's body was found in the water. They had walked until they reached the LaChute Brook Fork Trail.

There was too much snow on the trail to go any further that day. Now, much of the snow was gone.

Sheriff Williams still wanted to find where the shooting occurred. There could be valuable evidence. It might be somewhere on the trail.

He and Deputy Grant began hiking on a narrow track through marshland. Up ahead, the path would join LaChute Brook and the two would follow each other. About a quarter mile into the trail, a portion of a very old stone fence had been cleared so hikers could pass.

"Look at the size of those stones," Smudge observed. "Those were strong people who built that fence."

"So, this was farmland once?" Liz asked.

"Most likely," Smudge responded. "They didn't move those rocks because they were spoiling the view."

The trail began to ascend up the mountain. The footing, as they expected, was a mixture of mud, snow and ice.

"Lemme see those things," the sheriff said as they reached three logs stretched across the brook. Hikers had to cross over the water there.

Deputy Grant handed Smudge a pair of crampons. They both fit them over their boots and survived walking across slippery birch logs to reach the other side.

They were in dense forest now. They passed an old outlaw camp.

"People build those camps with no more title to the land than you or I have," Smudge told Liz. "They call them Outlaw Camps."

"They were illegal?" she asked.

"They still are," he said. "And there's probably a few hundred of them in the Adirondacks. People build them for hunting and fishing cabins. Some of them are pretty elaborate, with wood stoves and bunk beds. They use them until the state finds 'em and knocks them over. It's been going on for a long time."

"It's still going on?" Liz asked.

"It's still going on," Smudge told her.

The trail leveled for a while and then took another steep climb. The sheriff and his deputy were about a mile and a half up the trail when the wind picked up. They had arrived at a rock clearing with a steep drop down to LaChute Brook.

And they were no longer alone.

"You could be trampling on a crime scene," the sheriff said.

"It wasn't a crime scene when we got here," JC said. "It was a hiking trail." Smudge knew this to be true.

"I hear that you were wrong about Colin Cornheiser," Smudge said.

"That was not one of my favorite days," JC responded. "We apologized, but that isn't enough."

"It might be for him," the sheriff said. "He's a pretty nice fella."

The sheriff didn't like having an audience while he conducted a criminal investigation, especially the news media. But he also had First Amendment rights to contend with. He waited.

JC and Bip were standing on the rock clearing. Bip was shooting some video. Smudge didn't like that, either. But it didn't stop him from walking to the edge of the rock and peering over at the drop into the brook.

"Find anything?" the sheriff asked JC.

"Like shell casings or a wallet?" JC asked. "We started walking from Bonnieview Road. We didn't find anything." The sheriff looked at him. It annoyed him that the reporter knew as much as he knew about their case.

"I'd tell you if we did," the reporter assured the law officer. Smudge didn't know whether he was being told the truth.

"How'd you get around Stormy?" the sheriff asked.

"Yeah, we heard that old man can get a little crazy," JC said.

"He's not *that* old," the sheriff insisted. Deputy Grant noted the sheriff's sensitivity to age this morning.

"Anyway," JC continued, "we followed the tracks of an Amish skier across some land that can't be seen from the cabin."

"Inus?" the sheriff responded. "Yeah, he's a good kid."

"Did you cross the brook walking across those logs?" the sheriff asked, changing the subject. JC and Bip exchanged a smile.

"Yep," JC answered. "Nearly fell in. Kinda slippery."

The sheriff and his deputy exchanged a smile. But he was getting impatient with the journalists' presence.

"You about done?" the sheriff asked.

"Is this where you think it happened?" JC asked, not ready to be shooed off.

"It would be nice to find a shell casing or a wallet," the sheriff admitted. "You gonna tell me if you find something?"

"How's this? Cornheiser told me that he went hiking with Paul Campbell," JC said.

"Did he?" Sheriff Williams responded. "Did he say where they went hiking?"

"No," JC said. He watched that new data register with the sheriff.

"Are you waiting for Inus Miller to walk down this path?" the sheriff asked.

"He won't come down, he'll walk up," JC said. "He'll ski down. But probably not today. He knows good snow from bad snow, and after it rains, it's not very good snow."

"You about wrapped up here?" the sheriff asked again, impatiently. He was rubbing his face. Deputy Grant disguised her amusement.

"I think so," JC said after looking at Bip to see if he was done shooting video. JC didn't like being told by a sheriff when and where he could stand. But the reporter also knew that they had probably accomplished everything they could hope for.

"Have a good day, Sheriff, Deputy," said JC. He and Bip headed down the trail.

Finally free from the snooping eyes of the news media, Smudge looked at the terrain in all directions. It was covered in snow, other than the rock clearing where the snow had melted. He looked over the cliff again, and the brook below.

"He could have tossed the wallet twenty yards in any direction," Smudge told Liz Grant. "We'll come back in the spring and might find it."

Smudge stared at the rock at his feet, as though he could see Campbell's body lying there.

"We should probably test this," the sheriff said, pointing at a stain on the rock that might be blood. Deputy Grant took a photograph of the stain and then scratched off a sample with a pen knife and put it in a plastic bag.

"The killer didn't carry him up here," the sheriff said and looked at his deputy. "Could you imagine carrying someone up that ascent to get here?"

"No," the deputy told him. "I can't imagine that."

"So, if he was shot here," the sheriff stated, "he didn't immediately fall into the brook when he was shot. The killer removed certain things from his pocket, like his wallet and maybe anything incriminating, and then pitched him over the cliff or rolled him down the bank into the brook."

Deputy Grant liked to watch the sheriff think. He tried to envision how things happened, and he usually turned out to be right.

"Did the killer trail Campbell up to this point?" the sheriff asked out loud. "Or did they come up together, like they trusted each other?"

JC and Bip had looked for the wallet and shell casings, without luck. Bip had videotaped the rock clearing, just in case it turned out to be the spot where Campbell was murdered. Bip shot a lot of the trail. The murder could have been anywhere.

The two journalists exited from the LaChute Brook Fork Trail, after another nervous crossing over the slippery log bridge, and climbed into their rental SUV.

"We're going to stop by to see Cindy Pfister, and then we'll see you back at The T," JC told Robin on the phone.

"Are you going to arrest her?" Robin teased.

"No," JC said. He was amused. "Right now, she's just a 'person of interest.' Any luck with those photos?" he asked.

"I'm getting there," she told him. "You'll probably have them after lunch. Which brings up an interesting question. Will you be bringing lunch?"

"We could do that," JC told her and solicited her eating preferences.

Bip pulled the 4x4 up to the convenience store lot. JC noted that Harold DeWitt's car was parked next to the dig site in a Tomahawk parking lot.

They found Pfister inside a tent.

"I have a theory to run past you," JC said, and proceeded to share it with her. JC had briefed Pfister on their visit to Saratoga Battlefield and what he'd learned reading Campbell's history books.

"I see where you're going," she told JC. "I just don't know if you're right."

"Does that mean I'm wrong?" he asked.

"I haven't found anything here that could be linked to Saratoga or Simon Fraser," Pfister said as she waved at a table with small pieces of artifacts sealed inside plastic bags.

"You said you had 'Other matters to attend to' when Paul was working on the dig during the last two days that he was alive?" JC asked.

"Yes, I did," Pfister confirmed.

"Would you mind sharing with us," JC asked, "where you were?"

"If you promise not to blab it all over the place," Cindy Pfister said. "This is a competitive business. I've got to hire some new people and get some money flowing again."

"Scout's honor," JC told her.

"I was pursuing our next contract," she told him. "I was in Lake George. There's a store that's going to be built there and they always expect to find signs of the French and Indian War or the Revolutionary War when they start digging in Lake George."

"They've got to set aside time to do a dig, catalogue it and decide what to do with any remains that are unearthed," she told him. "Fort William Henry was at the southern tip of the lake. There were some big battles fought there. There was smallpox, too."

"Did you get the contract?" JC asked.

"If I can remove myself from this place," she said. "They know I can work a site in the winter; not everyone has experience doing that."

Pfister looked worried. JC guessed that she had just spelled out her concerns. She needed cash and she needed a crew. But a crew would cost cash. And if DeWitt was right, no one was lining up to work with Cindy Pfister.

"Harold DeWitt has even offered to finish up for me here and let me have most of the money," Pfister disclosed as she looked down at her dirty hands. "He's certain that I've only found a small campsite."

"So, you've spoken to him," JC asked.

"Yeah, he swears that he didn't find anything on his site," she said. "I was probably too hard on him. Maybe I jumped to conclusions. Sometimes, I let my temper get the better of me.

"Anyway, he said that he'd include the things that I showed you. He'd put them in the final report and even look around some more. If he didn't find anything additional, he'd use his report to show that it isn't a significant site."

"Are you going to accept his offer?" the reporter inquired.

"I need money, JC." She looked tired, maybe a bit confused. "That would allow me to move to the Lake George project. I might take him up on it."

In addition to tired, she looked like she felt guilty for even considering DeWitt's offer. She added with a weak laugh, "They're in a hurry. Who isn't?"

JC and Bip left Pfister inside her tent. Despite the lack of ideal conditions, they could make out skiers on the slopes of Battle Ax as they climbed into their 4x4. In some spots, dirt was mixed in with the thin snow. The skiers called it "Smud" or "Snirt."

When the sheriff and his deputy emerged from the LaChute Brook Fork Trail, they headed for the medical examiner's office in Saranac Lake.

"Could the bruising be caused by a significant drop into water?" Medical Examiner David Ryan was repeating the sheriff's question. "I suppose so."

The sheriff explained that he was talking about a roughly thirty-foot drop into a body of water that was probably four feet deep.

"Water can be a highly resistant surface," Dr. Ryan said.

"And it's even possible that the victim plunged into the water deep enough to strike some rocks," Smudge added.

"That could also explain some of the bruising," the doctor told him. "There are no defensive injuries or bruises on the hands, other than post-mortem. Sometimes, when someone is shot, they put their hand up in a defensive posture, and the bullet goes through the hand. There's none of that."

"Well, thanks, Doc," Smudge said as he headed for the door outside.

"But the bruises didn't kill him," the medical examiner reminded the sheriff. "The bullet hole to the heart did."

"Understood," the sheriff said without turning around as he headed out the door.

24

"This is going to look a lot different in five years," JC said as he drove down the wooded stretch of Bonnieview Road.

Presently, the pavement was heavily wooded on each side. Some of the breaks in the woods revealed a modern house with a price tag approaching a million dollars.

"That's a lot of money in this neck of the woods," he told Robin. "But a quarter of the housing stock is mobile homes or shacks. *Those* are owned by *locals*. And as taxes and land prices go up, they'll be chased out."

"The locals won't be able to afford to live on the road they grew up on," Robin added. She'd seen it happen before.

JC and Robin had chosen to go pick up lunch when Bip got a call from the television station's accounting department. The accountants wanted to discuss concerns about Bip's overtime.

JC was salaried. He would be paid the same even if he worked twenty-four hours in a day. Bip was paid hourly. The TV station thought this assignment was getting expensive. The screws were being turned.

JC and Robin told Bip that they'd get lunch and bring it back. They both gave him a happy wave as they left him in the room, on the phone with the accountant. Bip gave them the international sign for hanging himself.

"Got any ghost stories?" Robin asked JC as they proceeded in the car toward Joseph.

"The most famous ghost story in Lake Placid is 'The Lady in the Lake.'"

"Do tell," Robin said with excitement in her voice.

"It's a true story," JC advised her. "A college dean from New Jersey disappeared in the 1930s. She had a camp on Lake Placid. She went for a row out in the lake and was never seen again."

"This is a good ghost story. Can we build a campfire?" Robin asked.

"No, this is a rental car," JC said.

"Not in the car," she laughed.

"Anyway," JC proceeded, "thirty years later, some scuba divers were swimming off Pulpit Rock. They were over one hundred feet deep. They saw what they thought was a mannequin with a rope tied around it. The rope had been tied to an anchor or something.

"The divers realized the mannequin was human. It had been preserved, floating at that depth in such cold water. It was the college dean. And as she was brought to the surface, the thirty-year-old corpse mostly disintegrated.

"They aren't sure if she was murdered or if she committed suicide," JC told her.

"Suicide," Robin said.

"How do you know that?" he asked.

"A woman just knows," Robin smiled.

Before reaching Joseph, their car passed an Amish buggy. On the way back with lunch, they passed Patrick, who was out on his daily walk. They waved and he waved back.

Returning to her hotel room, where Bip was waiting, JC and Robin laid lunch down on the table.

Robin checked her laptop while she ate. She began to send something to the printer.

"I have all of those pictures for you," she told JC.

"All of them?" he asked, impressed.

"All of them but one with a big asterisk," she replied as she got up to retrieve the newly printed pictures. "The picture of Stormy, whose real name is Robert Jordan, is from high school."

"How old is he now?" JC asked.

"He's in his fifties," she told him.

"Has he changed?" Bip asked sarcastically.

"Totally," Robin said with a laugh. "But it gets better! I got Mr. Jordan's picture from his high school yearbook at the library. And guess who else is in it?" She produced the yearbook she'd obtained from the library.

The book was open to Jordan's picture. She flipped to another page and placed the book down in front of the two men. They looked over the two pages of pictures and then began to laugh.

"Sheriff Williams?" JC said. Bip could barely contain himself, "The sheriff and the crazy old man went to high school together?"

"I saw the old guy on that news broadcast when they took his guns away," JC told them. "He looks like he's eighty!"

JC swept up the photos and put them in his jacket pocket.

"Thanks, Robin," he said. "Nice work." She liked hearing that.

JC's phone rang. Upon answering, he was told by a secretary that Averill Felix was returning his call.

"Please hold," the voice advised.

"What may I do for you?" Averill Felix asked JC after a few minutes of waiting.

"I was wondering, Mr. Felix," JC began, "why Harold DeWitt still had an office at Tomahawk. His work was done, wasn't it?"

"As far as I'm concerned, it was," Felix said on the other end of the line. "Maybe he has some loose ends to tie up. He asked if he could have the office for a little while longer. I don't need it yet, so I didn't object. Maybe he's just looking for some free office space."

"Any other reason?" JC asked.

"No," said Felix. "Can you think of one? He did a good job for us. He can have the space until we're ready to rent it. Say, did you go up and see those homes that we're building?"

"We did, very impressive," JC told the multi-millionaire. Rich men liked showing off their work, JC thought to himself, especially when it was going to make them richer.

The call ended and JC looked at Bip, who was finishing his sandwich.

"It's time we stop avoiding the inevitable," JC told him.

"You mean, this was my last meal?" Bip said, still chewing. "Isn't it protocol to inform the prisoner before he's going to be executed?"

"I didn't want to ruin your last meal," JC retorted.

"He says we have to go talk to the guy who wanted to shoot the snowplow driver," Bip said to Robin.

"We don't know that he actually *wanted* to shoot the snowplow driver," JC protested. "He just pointed a loaded gun at him."

"Do you know the difference?" Bip asked. "About an inch on his trigger finger."

JC also had trepidations about talking to Robert Jordan. There seemed to be a general feeling in the community that he was unstable. Robin had misgivings, as well. But she kept them to herself. She knew JC would do whatever he thought it was his job to do.

As they turned off Bonnieview Road, the tires of the rented SUV pushed through the unplowed snow on the driveway leading up to Stormy's cabin. It was a bit slippery.

They'd not yet reached the cabin when the door opened. A grizzled man with an uneven gray beard emerged. He had a dirty gray jacket and a red knit hat on with uneven gray hair protruding from under it. He was cradling a shotgun.

Bip stopped the car an uncustomary distance from the cabin.

"We're close enough," the photographer said. JC didn't argue. But he climbed out of the passenger side of the car and prepared to address the property owner.

JC thought that he'd address the man as *Mister* Jordan. He thought that he'd introduce himself and remark about what a nice piece of property he had.

"Turn around and go back!" the old man said, not giving JC a chance to deliver his introductory remarks.

"Mr. Jordan, I'm JC Snow. I'm with the news," JC said. He was projecting his voice, as Bip had stopped the car about thirty yards from the front door.

"Turn around and go back!" Stormy repeated.

"I'd like to ask you a few questions," JC continued. He had to admit. He felt a little safer with the thirty-yard buffer between him and the man with the gun. It didn't matter that the firearm's slug would travel further than thirty yards.

"You deaf?" Stormy shouted. "Turn around and go back!" He uncradled the shotgun and pointed it in the direction of his uninvited guest.

"Did you know Paul Campbell?" JC asked, projecting his voice.

"You *are* deaf," Stormy shouted. "So, the sound of this shotgun won't bother you." And Stormy raised the weapon to his shoulder.

"Time to go," Bip said in a nervous voice. He had never slipped out from behind the steering wheel. JC now realized Bip had never turned the car off. It was still idling and ready to make a fast getaway.

"Time to go, JC," Bip repeated, a little louder. Stormy was now walking toward the car, the shotgun still pointed in their direction.

"Nice talking with you, Mr. Jordan," JC shouted. "Sorry if we caught you at a bad time."

JC had not quite closed the car door as Bip shifted into reverse and slammed the accelerator to the floor, backing all the way out of the driveway onto Bonnieview Road.

"You're out of your mind!" Harold DeWitt insisted.

He was inside a tent with Cindy Pfister on her dig site. This debate had been going on for a while. It was escalating into an argument.

"There was nothing on my dig site!" DeWitt protested. "You apparently don't even know what you're looking at." He waved at the artifacts on her table.

"These things were probably tossed from the window of a passing car," he sneered. There were some arrowheads, small shards of pottery and wampum beads.

"That's ludicrous," she told him.

"I hate to say this, but Paul was the brains of this outfit," DeWitt told her. "He could tell the difference between a prehistoric tool and rubbish blown across the road."

"Why are you being so defensive about this?" Pfister asked him in a calm voice. "You know what these are. We all make mistakes sometimes. You even said this might be a small campsite."

"I didn't make a mistake," DeWitt snarled. "You did. And you'd better keep your mouth shut if you don't want to embarrass yourself."

"I have to put it in my report," she told him.

"If you put it in your report," he growled, "you'll never be done in time to take that Lake George job. They'll pay good money for a professional outfit that brings credibility to their findings. You might not survive more discredited findings, Cindy. So, you'll still be here, making pauper's wages. You don't even have a crew! You're all by yourself!"

"How do you know so much about the Lake George job?" she asked. "You sure know more than I told you."

DeWitt was quiet for a moment, as though he'd said something he regretted.

"I got it for you," DeWitt finally said, lowering his voice. "Well, I got it for Paul. You were just along for the ride. And now you're going to blow that."

"You got us that job to get us off this site, didn't you?" Pfister said. "We were being rushed to get to that Lake George site and leave this one behind. Was that at your insistence?"

"Don't be absurd," DeWitt pleaded. "It's a good job. I'm busy and like usual, I was pushing business Paul's way."

"You looked in on our site every day to make sure we hadn't found anything," Pfister stated. "You offered to wrap things up for me. You wanted to whitewash *your* misdeeds! I thought you just felt sorry for me. You even parked next to our lot so you'd have an excuse to examine things here every day!"

"Cindy, you're mistaken. Don't let your temper get the best of you," DeWitt told her.

"You don't want me for an enemy," Pfister warned him. There was venom when she said it.

25

CCThat's a blurry flurry!" Bip said to JC as he watched the snow fall outside the window.

"Let's go find him," JC responded.

They pushed away from the table where they had eaten breakfast at The Gill Grill. Only two days after it rained, there was a heavy snow coming down. The snowfall had begun overnight. Snowplows were out, but they were having a hard time keeping up with the storm.

It was difficult finding a spot to pull over on Bonnieview Road. Once that was accomplished, JC and Bip sipped coffee from to-go cups and kept an eye on the pasture and the snow-covered pavement.

A half hour passed before they saw him. He was pushing through the snow on his bike. JC couldn't think of anyone else who would even attempt that.

Inus Miller carried his bike off the road and leaned it against the fence post. JC and Bip emerged from their car and crossed the road to greet him.

"It's a blurry flurry," Bip loudly declared. Inus seemed to like the ring of it and smiled.

"Chores are done?" JC asked.

Inus informed them that he had gotten up long before sunrise to complete his morning chores, planning to climb Le Trou Au Coeur outside the boundary of Battle Ax and do some skiing.

The Amish skier had an extra sweater on, poking out between the buttons on his ski jacket. He had a knit cap pulled down over his ears.

"Did you ever consider wearing a helmet?" JC asked him.

"A helmet would keep me safer," Inus responded. "But this hat will do."

"May we ask you a couple of questions?" JC asked.

"Of course," the Amish man said graciously. He looked at them both, wondering what this was about.

"Have you seen anything on that LaChute Brook Fork Trail?" JC asked him.

"I always see things. God has created a beautiful world," Inus responded.

"Beautiful world, weird cast," JC answered.

Inus' eyes smiled at that description. He thought that it was apt.

The journalist pulled five photos out of his pocket. They were all in plastic sandwich bags. JC had done that to protect them from the snowfall.

"Have you ever seen any of these people on the trail when you're hiking up?" JC asked him.

Inus carefully inspected each photograph.

"The Amish don't like their picture taken, do you?" JC asked.

"We guard against vanity," Inus said. "We do not pose for pictures."

He continued to study the pictures. Finally, he handed two back.

"I have seen those two," Inus said as he looked into JC's eyes. "They were together." JC looked at the photos.

"Are you sure?" the reporter asked.

"I saw them," Inus repeated with certainty.

"When?" JC asked.

"A week ago, perhaps longer," the Amish man responded.

"Did you overhear what they were talking about? Were they talking?" JC asked.

"They looked like they were friends, resting from the hike," Inus stated. "They were standing on that rock clearing." JC looked down on the pictures Inus had picked out.

"One had an accent," Inus recalled, "like someone from England, maybe?"

"Scotland?" JC asked.

"Perhaps," Inus agreed.

"Any chance you'd go on camera and say that?" JC asked. Inus gave him a respectful smile and shake of his head. No.

"Sheriff Williams may want to ask you the same question, about seeing them together," JC informed him.

"I like Sheriff Williams," Inus told him.

"Have fun today," the reporter and his photographer said, as Inus Miller began his trek across the pasture. His skis and a pack were hanging from his broad back.

The phone rang but wasn't picked up. Finally, voicemail asked the caller to leave a message.

"Hi Cindy, this is Smudge Williams," the sheriff said into the phone. "I thought that maybe I could graduate from lunch and we might have dinner. Think about it and I'll call you back."

Smudge disconnected the call and stared at nothing in particular. He was sitting at his desk in his office. He'd been nervous to place the call. Getting voicemail was better than getting rejected, he figured. So, all in all, the call was not a failure.

The snow was letting up. The plows were gaining an advantage.

A car pulled into the trailhead of LaChute Brook Fork Trail. The driver was glad to see a plowed lot and multiple cars left there. Nordic skiers had parked to use the trail in the fresh powder. It would mean that tire tracks would be walked over, driven over and blend in with the rest.

The driver carefully looked up the trail and in all directions. There wasn't a soul or a moving automobile in view. The driver carried a brush across the lot and cleared off the windows of a truck. The headlights got wiped off. Everything was done to prepare for taking the truck onto the road, except getting in and taking the truck onto the road.

Walking back to the other vehicle and tossing the brush into the back, the driver looked up and saw a man smiling as he walked past. He had a knit cap pulled down over his ears. He had buttons on his ski jacket instead of a zipper.

The driver wondered where he had come from? He couldn't have seen anything. But the driver wondered if that was a chance worth taking.

"Knowing what we know," Robin said, "something else is weird to me."

JC looked up from another history book he was reading, about Simon Fraser and the Battle of Saratoga. He was lying on one of the beds in her room after they'd shared lunch with Bip.

Robin was boiling water on a hot plate provided by the front desk. She had researched how to make tea out of the needles from an Eastern White Pine. Her plastic bag of pine needles sat open on the counter.

"If you boil the needles, you'll reduce the vitamin C, the antioxidants, everything useful," she explained to the two men in her audience. They were paying only minimum attention. "So, you boil the water and then add the needles in a homemade tea bag."

"Needles, little bag, hot water," Bip was murmuring to himself. JC gave him a look. "I'm taking notes," Bip said and started laughing. That started JC laughing.

Robin gave them both a disapproving stare.

She dropped the tea bags into three coffee mugs, poured the hot water over them and came to the table to deliver her steaming creations.

"Didn't you say that a truck driver told you that he carried away a lot of dirt during the archaeological survey of the Tomahawk site?" she asked.

"Yep," JC said. "I can think of his name, if you give me a chance. It reminded me of a hockey player. It was French, only the guy said that his family pronounced it like they were English." A look of recognition came across his face.

"It was Roy," JC said. "Frank Roy."

"So," Robin proceeded, "the dirt that's removed from an archaeological dig, if it's clean, normally is used again to fill in the holes. That's back dirt."

"So, you wonder why it was taken away," JC said.

"It's not how things are normally done," she told him. "I'm going to call Cindy Pfister."

"Good idea," JC said. He went back to his reading.

"No answer," Robin said after putting down her phone. "The voicemail is full. I'll try her again in a little bit."

"OK, listen to this," JC said to her. "Joseph County is believed to be named after a Mohawk chief named Joseph Brant. He was a heroic ally of the British and the Colonists during the French and Indian War.

"In the Revolutionary War," JC continued paraphrasing the words in the book, "he still fights alongside the British, but against the rebels. This says that many of the Indian tribes saw *their* stake in the Revolution as a way to protect their land. The British told the Indians that if they won, the tribes could keep their traditional lands."

"Does this get us any closer to why Paul Campbell was killed?" Robin asked.

"Only if it tells us what Paul Campbell might have found," JC answered. "Joseph Brant wasn't believed to have been at Saratoga, but he was in the area because he fought in other battles."

Robin tried to call Cindy Pfister again. Again, she was sent to voicemail and then told that voicemail was full.

"Maybe we should go find the dump truck driver," JC suggested.

"At the bar?" she asked.

"Yeah, it didn't look like it was the first time Frank Roy had been there," he said.

"So, we have a few hours before he might show up," Robin suggested.

JC agreed and stretched out on the bed with his book lying on his chest.

"Are you going to do a book report when you're done?" Robin teased.

"I could use some extra credit with the newsroom management," he smiled.

JC flipped the page in his book and something fell onto his chest. He picked it up.

"What's that?" Robin asked.

"Three pictures of dirt," JC told her after looking at them. "Archaeologists have a special relationship with dirt, don't they?"

He studied the photographs, trying to see what an archaeologist would think is important. He stared at the first photo, finally giving up and going on to the second picture. To him, it was another picture of dirt.

After thorough study, he slipped that picture to the back of the three and looked at the final snapshot. He blinked his eyes and rubbed them with his fingers.

"These images are so small," he complained. "Archaeologists are never going to be hired as wedding photographers."

He moved his face closer to the third picture, staring at an image that was as brown as the dirt it sat in. But it was different.

"Take a look at this and tell me what you see," JC said to Robin, holding the picture out for her to grab.

Robin also squinted to find anything besides dirt in the picture. She held it under a light on the bedside table.

"In the right third of the photograph, near the ruler stuck in the dirt," JC said. "What does that look like to you?"

"A '24?'" she said somewhat reluctantly. "Yeah, it's a '24.' That's odd."

"That's not odd," he said, smiling. "That's fantastic!"

A phone began to ring. They both looked away from each other to search for the ringing phone. JC realized it was his, still sitting on the table where they had eaten lunch.

He looked at the phone number and answered. It was the voice of their assignment editor, Rocky Baumann.

"JC, it's time we talked about wrapping up your coverage in New York," he said.

"Not when you hear what we just found," JC burst forth.

26

"And where is the '24?'"

"No clue," JC had to admit to his assignment editor, Rocky Baumann. It was a little deflating.

"But look," JC implored, "Simon Fraser's body has never been found. Shovels were discovered at The Great Redoubt where his body had been unearthed.

"That's a fact?" Rocky asked.

"Well, it's a two-hundred-and-fifty-year-old witness account," JC told him. "You can always go two ways with witness accounts. They're either accurate or they're not."

"I wanted to make sure you remembered that," Rocky said.

"Anyway," JC resumed, "there is no evidence that Fraser's body ever made it back to Britain. But he commanded the 24th Regiment of the British Infantry in this stage of the Revolutionary War.

"I looked up the 24th," JC continued. "As you can imagine, artifacts are rare. But their cartridge box plate had a big '24' on it. It also had a crown on top and a fleur de lis."

"So, this photograph of the '24' you found," Rocky asked. "Did it say, 'This is the property of Simon Fraser?'"

"Granted, the image is so small that I can barely make out the '24,' let alone anything inscribed on it or even if a crown was broken off the top," JC affirmed. "There was also an image I found online of a belt buckle with a '24' on it. It could be a belt buckle in Campbell's picture. The belt buckle didn't have a crown on it."

"And where is this '24' again?" Rocky repeated.

"You're killing me, Rocky," JC said. "I don't know exactly where it is located. But if Paul Campbell found this thing at his site, then he would have wanted to have the same discussion that we're having about the possibility. He had three books about the Battle of Saratoga and Simon Fraser for some reason!"

Rocky was silent on the other end of the phone.

"It's a heck of a story, JC," the assignment editor said. "You'd have tremendous interest across this country, and Britain and Canada. Let me talk to Pat and I'll get back to you."

Pat was the news director, and JC thought that this was the best possible outcome of this conversation. He'd have to wait for the news director's thumbs up or thumbs down. Until then, he'd keep working on it.

"How did it go?" Robin asked. "I couldn't quite tell, only listening to your end of the conversation."

"As well as could be expected," JC told her. "At least he didn't press me on the question that I couldn't answer."

"What question would that be?" Bip asked.

"Where that picture of the '24' was taken," JC said.

"Well, we'd better figure that out before he asks," Robin suggested.

Robin picked up the phone and called Cindy Pfister. There was no answer. Her voicemail told the caller that it was full. Robin stared at the phone.

"She could be back in Lake George," JC supposed.

A phone rang and JC picked his up. There was no one there. A phone rang again and Robin realized it was her phone ringing.

"It's Rocky," the voice on the other end informed her. "Tell JC, no offense, but you *are* the producer, so I'm calling you. Anyway, this story is worth pursuing. We realize that you'll need a couple of days. Keep us informed."

"OK," Robin said, and the phone call ended.

"That was Rocky," she told her two co-conspirators. "He says we can pursue the story."

"I hope we're not going to make complete fools of ourselves," JC said. But all three had smiles on their faces.

"What's next?" Bip asked.

"I think that we need to find that dump truck driver," said JC. "The snow probably got him a day off, so he's either at home with the missus or he moved up cocktail hour."

"Let's hope he's had a spat with the missus," Robin said, "and he needs a stiff drink."

Bip asked if he could go shoot some fresh footage of skiing at Battle Ax, if he wasn't needed immediately. He said fresh powder is always a nice touch.

"Frank already told me he didn't want to be identified as our source," JC told Bip. "So, I doubt he'll do an on-camera interview. Keep an eye on your phone. If he changes his mind, I'll give you a call."

Bip grabbed his snowboard and headed for the chairlift. JC and Robin climbed the stairs to the Poo Ice Bar and scanned the room. At one end of the bar, there was a man with a camo ball cap and blaze-orange, down jacket. Frank Roy.

"Buy you a beer?" JC asked as they slid into the seat beside Frank Roy and ordered another Genesee for the truck driver. A couple of craft beers from the Blue Line Brewery in Saranac Lake were added to the order for JC and Robin.

"Hey!" the dump truck driver greeted JC, recognizing him. "That would be mighty neighborly of you."

"You have the day off?" JC asked.

"Yeah, it's a mess when there's fresh snow. The guys can work inside, but everything they want me to haul is under a layer of snow."

They sipped from their beers.

"You see those twigs over the bar?" Frank asked. "Those are mine. They're white cedar. I pick 'em up when I'm scouting for deer and I give 'em to a friend of mine who built half of this bar."

"That's really cool," Robin told him.

"What are you guys working on?" Frank asked them. "You're reporters from Colorado, right?"

"Good memory," said JC. "We're working on the murder of that archaeologist from Colorado, Paul Campbell."

"That's his name. I'd forgot," Frank conceded. "But I saw him a lot, over on the site next to Tomahawk. What are they going to build, a gas station there?"

"Yep, a convenience store and some pumps," JC said. "You'd see him over there working?"

"I guess so," Frank answered. "Usually, I'd just see him standing there talking to Mr. Felix and the guy who did the archaeology for *our* site."

"For Tomahawk," JC asked.

"Yeah," said Frank. "Oh, and sometimes the county executive would be with them."

"Colin Cornheiser?" Robin asked.

"Yeah," Frank told them. "Not always. Sometimes it was just Mr. Felix and the archaeologist. Sometimes, Mr. Cornheiser would join them."

"*Your* archaeologist's name is Harold DeWitt?" JC asked him.

"Yeah," Frank said. "Nice enough guy. I did a hike with him once. A group of us was sent up into the woods to gather more twigs for furniture and fixtures and stuff. That's the only time I talked to him. Otherwise, I just saw him with Mr. Felix."

"You saw Mr. Felix standing over on the convenience store site talking to Paul Campbell?" JC asked.

"Yeah," Frank said. "Five or six times, at least."

"How long were these talks?" JC asked.

"I don't know," Frank said with a smile. "I didn't time them."

"But were they just long enough to say 'Hi, it's a nice day,'" JC asked, "or were they longer than that?"

"Oh, they were real conversations. They'd last a long time," Frank answered. "Sometimes I have my truck parked, waiting for instructions, and I can see that lot. I wasn't spying or anything, but I'd watch them talk for ten or twenty minutes."

"Five or six times," JC confirmed.

"Yeah," said the truck driver, "at least that."

JC looked at Robin. They knew that meant Averill Felix had lied to them when he said he didn't know Paul Campbell.

"Did you ever get an idea of what they were talking about?" JC asked Frank.

"No, I did not," Frank replied and swallowed more Genesee. "They'd point in the general direction of the Tomahawk site or the little site where the store is going to be built. But I couldn't tell you what they were talking about."

JC bought another round for the three of them.

"Where do you hike to get the best twigs?" Robin asked, sipping her Saranac.

"You can get them most anywhere," Frank said. "The carpenter for Tomahawk gave us directions to a good place up LaChute Brook. He said we'd find a bunch of good branches. It was nearby. That's why I think he chose it."

"So, Harold DeWitt came on this hike with you?" JC asked.

"Yeah," Frank said, but he started laughing. "He's not an outdoorsman, by nature."

"What do you mean?" the reporter asked.

"Well, he was sent with us by management to be sort of the group leader," Frank grinned. "I guess they figure that anyone who jumps in holes and gets dirty looking for old skeletons must be a woodsman, right?"

"But I get the feeling that DeWitt fell short of that mark?" JC asked with a smile.

"He is scared to death in the woods!" Frank laughed. "First of all, he's carrying a firearm in a holster on his belt. I don't know what he thinks he's going to shoot. We were just hoping it wasn't going to be one of us.

"And if you heard a twig snap," Frank was giggling, "you'd see him reach for his holster. One of the guys would say, 'Easy, Trigger,' and we'd all start howling."

"What was he afraid of?" JC asked.

"He said bear, moose, coyote," Frank smiled.

JC remembered asking DeWitt about the handgun in a holster on the shelf in his office.

"We came up on an outlaw camp," Frank told them. "It was probably still being used in hunting season. It had a chimney and an old stove. We thought we'd check it out. DeWitt opened the door and a chipmunk blasted out of there. I thought DeWitt was going to empty his magazine shooting at that poor little thing. I laughed so hard I pissed myself."

"Do I remember you telling me that you hauled dirt from the Tomahawk site?" JC asked. "That came from the archaeology dig?"

"Yeah, from the first day I got the job," Frank agreed, after taking another hit of his beer.

"It was near the archaeology site?" Robin asked.

"There was nothing being built yet," Frank said. "The only thing going on *was* the archaeology site."

"Back dirt?" Robin asked. Frank gave her a puzzled look. Robin waited.

"I do think that's what they called it a couple of times," Frank told them. "It's a funny name, but I think that's what they called it."

"Do you remember where you took it?" JC asked.

"I grew up around here," Frank said proudly. "This whole place is my backyard."

"And?" JC asked, trying not to be impatient.

"Out on Silver Lake Road," Frank said. "About eleven miles from here. Don't get me in trouble, now. I can't swear that's a legal place to dump. But he told me that it would be fine. Mr. Felix would take care of it."

"Averill Felix?" JC asked.

"Yeah," Frank confirmed. "Listen, I'm still paying for my truck. I don't want to get in any trouble."

"I'm sure that you're fine," JC assured the man. "You were following orders."

"Yeah," Frank said. "I was. Dewitt said the orders were from Mr. Felix."

"Does that road get much traffic?" JC asked.

"Not that part of it," Frank responded. "I backed my truck in where he told me to and I dumped it."

"How would I find that spot?" JC asked.

"Eleven miles," Frank said. "From here to the spot on Silver Lake Road where there's an old sign for a fruit stand that's not there anymore."

"Will I see the dirt from the road?" JC asked.

"You would," Frank told him. "But it's covered with snow. But the spot can be seen from the road. Look for something that looks like piles of dirt that's covered with snow, near that old sign."

"Would you take us there?" Robin asked.

"Like I said," Frank told her, "I'm still paying for my truck. I don't want any trouble."

"You won't get any from us," JC told him as he and Robin slid from their bar stools.

"Have another," JC told the truck driver as he tossed enough money on the bar to pay for their tab, a tip and another Genesee for Frank.

"To Simon Fraser," JC said, as they all held their beers aloft for a toast.

27

Robin's call to Cindy Pfister went to voicemail again. Then she called Harold DeWitt. Again, no one picked up the phone.

Robin was sitting at a breakfast table in The Gill Grill with JC, Bip and Patty MacIntyre. Patty's arrival with Bip was a surprise. Robin found her to be delightful, but the county executive's administrative assistant rarely spoke to or even looked at JC.

"Where's Patrick?" Robin asked, scanning the diner. "We usually see him here."

"Someone said he was at home in bed with a cold," JC told her.

"Should we stop by and see if he needs anything?" she asked.

"Maybe later today?" JC answered. He recognized a nurturing element in Robin. He liked it. It hadn't occurred to him to check in on Patrick.

After breakfast, they parted company with Patty MacIntyre, who walked down the street to work. Merchants were already out on the sidewalk, preparing for the Chowder Fest to take place that afternoon.

JC, Robin and Bip climbed into their rented 4x4 and drove to a hardware store. Inside, Robin supervised them on the purchase of three brooms, three medium-sized paintbrushes, some thin plastic gloves and some small garden tools.

"I love these," Robin said, after they made a quick stop at a pharmacy to buy small toothbrushes. "You can scrub the final layer of dirt away and get a first good look at your discovery. It's like a little magic wand."

Back in the car, they drove north from Joseph. The county became even less populated. They passed the occasional hunting or fishing cabin, but there were not many communities remaining between them and Canada.

Bip turned their car left on Silver Lake Road. By now, there were no vehicles ahead and none in the rearview mirror.

They saw a beaten wooden board with the word "Fruit" painted in fading red letters. It was accompanied by a small, faded wooden building that probably used to be the fruit stand.

Bip slowed down the car and they scanned the woods for an opening. It wasn't far. They drove off the road and down a path over the snow as far as they could. They parked where there were three mounds of snow in front of them.

Presumably, there was dirt under the snow. It would be dirt removed from the Tomahawk Resort site.

The snow-dirt mounds were surrounded on three sides by what locals sometimes called "junk trees." The fourth side was where the dump truck backed up from the road and delivered its payload. The forest stretched as far as they could see.

Robin supervised. It wasn't a perfect dig site, she thought to herself. The dirt had already been compromised. It was unearthed eleven miles from where it now sat.

But she urged them to be tender. They would start by brushing the snow off the dirt using the brooms. That took some time.

"Gently," she told them. "Don't be a man for the next couple of hours. Don't scrape the ground harder if enough of it doesn't move to your liking, and don't punch anything. Treat the dirt gently, like you're afraid you'll bruise it."

"Let me see that little shovel," Bip asked.

"It's a hand trowel," Robin told him. "And no. You have to be gentle, remember? Use the paint brush."

"Did we forget to buy paint?" JC asked. Bip thought that was pretty funny.

"You brush the loose dirt away, rather than dig through it, to make sure you don't disturb anything valuable," Robin told him. "Then you can use the trowel. This dirt is going to be hard because it's cold, so you'll probably use the trowel more than usual. But be careful."

JC and Bip exchanged a look. Bip went back to using the broom.

"Sorry, am I being bossy?" she asked.

"Yes," said JC. "And I don't think you're that sorry." They all giggled a little.

"I also like to run my hand over a new surface," Robin told them, pulling off her warm mittens to expose a thin plastic glove, "to see if my glove snags on something I can't see. A lot of things in the dirt take on the color of the dirt. But, that's just me."

She saw Bip raising his hand and looking at her.

"Yes Bip? Did you find something?" she asked.

"No ma'am," he responded. "I need to go to the bathroom. And I should probably videotape you guys digging, in case someone wants us to do a television news story later."

"Ha-ha," she said sarcastically. "I'm not your boss. Don't get any on your shoe."

Bip pulled his camera out of the backseat, where it had shared the space with Robin during the drive. The photographer opened a plastic pack about the size of his palm.

He pulled out a hand warmer that he normally placed in his gloves during a cold day of snowboarding. He shook it to activate the ingredients. The pack was adhesive on one side. He adhered it to the side of the battery on his camera. Keeping a battery warm in cold weather would extend the life of the battery.

"That's clever," Robin said.

"I'm a clever boy," Bip told her, and commenced documenting the work being done by his two colleagues.

"We're lucky it's fresh snow," JC said. Their job of removing the snow from the piles of dirt had been easier than if the snow and dirt had a chance to bond.

From time to time, they retreated to their car to turn up the heat and regain the feeling in their fingers.

Outside again, JC kneeled in the snow and stared at the mounds. It was a little overwhelming.

"What exactly are we looking for?" Bip asked as one eye peered through the viewfinder of his camera.

"We'll know, if we see it," JC told him.

After careful inspection of the exposed surface, and failure to move much of it with a broom or paintbrush, they leveraged small portions of dirt with the trowel.

"Careful," Robin reminded him. "You don't want to destroy the very thing you're looking for."

"What's this?" JC asked, extending his hand. Robin looked into his outstretched palm.

"Oh cool!" she said. "It's a shell, probably wampum! See? This is fun!"

Picking through pieces of dirt, they also found an arrowhead.

"More wampum?" JC asked as he held out his palm, holding another small cylindrical piece that was hollowed out in the middle. Robin picked it up to give it a closer study.

"I don't think so," she said. "I think it's part of a stem from a clay pipe." She looked up at JC, her look suggesting it could be significant.

"The English smoked clay pipes," JC suggested.

"So did some Indians," Robin told him. "But white men gave the pipes to them."

Bip approached and they held their treasures in their open palms while he took tight shots.

"How did he miss this?" Robin asked of DeWitt, the archaeologist of the Tomahawk site. "How did he not find this?"

Robin expressed her belief that this dirt, when on the Tomahawk site, probably extended to the convenience store site where Cindy Pfister was finding so many artifacts.

"It was probably a village," Robin said. "But this screws everything up. These artifacts have been removed from the place they've rested for two hundred and fifty years or longer. They belong back where they came from." She looked despondent.

JC was brushing his hand over the dirt he had exposed with the trowel. His glove caught on something for a moment. He pulled his hand back and looked at the dirt. He saw nothing.

He brushed his hand across that spot of cold soil again and he felt the same small projection. He leaned in for a closer look and began digging at it with his index finger.

"Look at this," JC said cautiously to Robin. She moved over to see what he was doing. He scratched at the dirt some more, exposing a surface that could be metal.

"Go ahead and use the toothbrush to scrub the soil away. Then pull it out with your fingers, if you can," she said. "Gentle."

There was a small loop of metal protruding from the dirt surface, appearing to be attached to the larger metal surface.

"I snagged my glove on that," JC told her as he ran the toothbrush across the surface.

"Poke with your finger to see if you can find where it ends," she said. "Is it a circle? Is it a square?"

His finger traced out to the end of the object imbedded in the dirt. Then, following the edge, he made a circle.

"I think I know what it is," JC said quietly, but with excitement, "We're looking at the back of it."

He traced the circle in the dirt again, only deeper. He did it again. And then he tried to pry his finger under the object. It popped into his hand.

He brushed more dirt off with the toothbrush and turned it over in his palm. It was discolored. It could have been brass or copper.

"It's a button," Robin said. The raised impression said "24."

28

"I'm tingling," Robin said.

JC didn't admit it, but he was, too. He held a button in his palm with the raised impression of a "24."

"Fraser commanded the 24th, right?" Bip said.

"Yeah. And I've been reading Paul Campbell's history books for a week. OK, I admit that I've also looked up more stuff on the internet. I've become something of a geek about Simon Fraser."

"It's brave of you to admit you're a geek," Robin said. "But, we already knew."

"If this is an officer's button of the 24th, it's probably copper," JC said, dismissing her quip with a grin. "It would have been plated in gold or silver. Fraser also probably wore a red coat with gold trim and braiding."

"Geez," she said, "you *are* a geek."

"I concede that point," JC said. "But there's something else. We would call the 24th an infantry regiment today. But back then, it was called the 24th British Regiment of Foot."

"Foot," Robin said, after giving it thought. "It has two Os." JC gave her a knowing look.

"It means," JC added, "that Paul Campbell knew what he had stumbled upon."

"Let's face it," JC said to his colleagues. "This doesn't mean this is Fraser's button. But maybe it is, or it could belong to someone under his command. Maybe someone who was escorting the body."

"Or it could have been worn by a Mohawk," Robin suggested. "They were known to pick things up off battlefields. They were souvenir hunters."

"Yep," JC agreed. "But it might mean there was a British military presence or influence at the Tomahawk site's Indian camp. How could DeWitt have missed this?"

"Come on, Cindy, pick up." Robin had her ear to her phone again. But again, her call to Cindy Pfister went to voicemail.

"We should leave the rest of this alone," Robin said. "We have our evidence. A real archaeologist needs to see this, even though the feature has been compromised by an eleven-mile trip in a dump truck."

"Is it time to talk with the sheriff?" JC asked. He already knew the answer.

"I think so," Robin agreed.

Bip drove them back into Joseph. He turned up the heat in the car to thaw their bones after spending hours in the cold.

It was early afternoon as they drove back downtown. There was a crowd on the sidewalks. People were roaming in different directions and giving the central business district a bustling feeling that it did not normally have. It was Chowder Fest.

The three journalists found Sheriff Williams in his office behind his desk. JC knocked this time.

"I guess I should be out there making sure Chowder Fest doesn't become a dangerous food fight," he said.

JC took a seat in the office after offering one to Robin. Bip sat, too.

"Have a seat," the sheriff offered belatedly. "Make yourselves at home."

"Sheriff," JC said, "we may have found a motive for the murder of Paul Campbell. I told you we'd share anything we found."

The sheriff leaned forward at his desk. His face had a skeptical expression. He wouldn't allow the news media to waste much of his time with nonsense.

JC laid out the progression of discoveries leading them to the dirt mounds on Silver Lake Road. The sheriff jotted some things on a notepad, including the whereabouts of the dirt mounds.

The reporter informed the sheriff of the small artifacts they found, including the button, and how that fit into a scenario described to them by Cindy Pfister.

JC did not show the button to the sheriff. It remained inside a plastic sandwich bag in JC's pocket. He didn't want to risk it being taken from him and stashed inside an evidence locker.

The sheriff was attentive but did not seem entirely impressed.

"Do you have an archaeologist who says that what you are supposing is actually fact?" the sheriff asked.

"I've been trying to reach Cindy Pfister for two days," Robin told him. "I can't reach her." That raised the attention level of the sheriff.

"I've tried to reach her also," Smudge acknowledged. He rubbed his hand over his face, thinking.

"Have you tried Harold DeWitt?" the sheriff asked. "He's an archaeologist, isn't he?"

"We did," Robin replied, "but he didn't answer, either."

The sheriff hadn't shaved that morning. He rubbed his whiskers, thinking again.

"My deputies are making sure the Chowder Fest remains lawful," Smudge smirked. "I'll go try to find Cindy."

JC, Robin and Bip departed from the rear of the county courthouse, thinking about what their next move was.

"Can we go check in on Patrick?" Robin asked. "I'm worried about him."

"Sure," JC said. "That won't take long."

"It's only a block from here," Robin told them. "Do you want to walk?"

They agreed. The air was cold, but walking would warm them up.

JC was quiet as they walked. He was thinking that he hadn't told Sheriff Williams about having a gun pointed at them when he and Bip had attempted to speak with Stormy Jordan. It could wait, JC decided.

Patrick's house was a two-story, wood-frame on the corner of the block. It was unremarkable but it looked like the ninety-five-year-old paid someone to maintain it. The walk was shoveled.

They rang the doorbell. No one came to the door. They knocked, but that also failed to get a response.

"He lives alone, right?" JC asked.

"He does," Robin said. She had learned particulars about Patrick's private life while they talked at the Burns Supper. "His wife died, years ago."

"If he's in bed, maybe he just doesn't want company," Bip suggested. "You said he was sick, right?"

"He's ninety-five," Robin said and gave Bip a look.

JC tried to turn the doorknob. The door opened.

"In towns like these," JC remarked, "no one locks their doors."

"Patrick?" Robin called out as they walked into the foyer. It caused a bit of an echo.

There was a living room on the left and a dining room on the right. The stairs were ahead of them.

"Patrick?" Robin called again.

"I'm going to check upstairs," JC said.

"I hope we don't get arrested for breaking and entering," Bip said. Robin gave him a disapproving look.

At the top of the stairs, JC had a choice of three rooms. The hallway was short and too narrow to hang any pictures. His shoulder would have knocked them to the floor as he passed.

JC turned in one direction and looked into an empty guest room. It was decorated in a style that probably dated back to the 1960s, but it was neat and clean.

Another bedroom looked like office space. A desk and shelves were cluttered with stacked books, photos and papers.

JC looked down the hall in the other direction. That had to be the master bedroom. Only a tall dresser made from dark wood was visible. There were family photos on top.

"Patrick?" JC called. No answer.

JC entered the master bedroom and peered over to the bed. There, Patrick laid as if he was sleeping. His skin had more pallor than even his old Irish skin normally had. But he looked like he was enjoying a good nap.

"Oh, no."

JC turned his head and found Robin looking over his shoulder. Her hand was held over her mouth and she was beginning to cry. JC turned to embrace her, her moist eyes still watching over JC's shoulder at Patrick.

"It looks like he died in his sleep," JC told Bip as the reporter came down the stairs. "It's too bad. He was a nice man."

Robin stayed upstairs for a few more minutes. She sat on Patrick's bed, wiped her tears and spoke with him.

"A woman just knows," she said to him as she leaned in to kiss his forehead. "We wanted to come sooner."

The news crew remained at the house until Deputy Peter Colden arrived. He asked them routine questions.

"He has some children?" Robin asked, knowing the answer. She had looked at the family photographs.

"Yeah," the deputy told her. "They're nice kids. They live out of the area. We'll be in touch with them. You can all go now. Thank you for the call."

"We have work to do," JC said. "We should get something on the news tonight about what we found. Not Patrick, but the artifacts. The sheriff might not be happy about it, but we found it. We can report on it."

They agreed to remain vague about the location of the dirt mounds they found. They didn't want scavengers finding it and removing more artifacts before Cindy Pfister could get a look.

Robin called the TV station in Denver and told them the story. JC wouldn't report their growing suspicions that Tomahawk may have deliberately ignored the finding of a significant archaeological site. That was a certain lawsuit until they had certain proof. They would just report on what Campbell seemed to find and say it might finally offer a motive for his murder.

Deputies Tim Pattern and Liz Grant were strolling through the crowd at Chowder Fest. Their presence would maintain the peace and project a positive image for the sheriff's office.

They greeted County Executive Colin Cornheiser as they passed him. He was doing what politicians do in a crowd, shaking as many hands as he could.

Some people stopped to tell Cornheiser how terribly he had been treated by the news media.

Deputy Pattern's phone rang. He picked it up and said, "Hello, Sheriff."

He listened to his instructions. At some point, he turned toward Deputy Grant, while still listening to the sheriff.

"We've got to go," Pattern said when he got off the phone. "They found a truck at the LaChute Brook trailhead and the sheriff thinks something doesn't look right."

29

Sheriff Williams looked a little more concerned than he usually looked at a crime scene, Deputy Pattern thought. Deputy Grant thought he looked a little angrier.

"Whose truck is it?" Pattern had asked when he rolled up to the sheriff in the parking lot of the LaChute Brook Fork Trail. Deputy Grant was right behind him in her silver patrol car.

"Cindy Pfister, the archaeologist," the sheriff told them with a grim face. He was searching the landscape, as though he'd see her walking down the trail or out of the woods.

Smudge Williams looked at the snowpack covering the gravel parking lot and walked toward the trail. He was scratching his face.

"Liz!" he called out. She dashed to catch up with him.

"Find somebody who has been using this trail since the last snowstorm," he ordered. "There must be tracks of two dozen cars and cross-country skiers here. Check with the locals and see if we can figure out how long this truck has been here."

"Its windows are cleared, Sheriff," Deputy Pattern offered. "She may have come here after the storm to do some Nordic skiing."

The sheriff looked at Pattern and nodded.

"Do you cross-country ski?" the sheriff asked Tim Pattern.

"No, Sheriff, I'm sorry."

"Liz," the sheriff bellowed. She was climbing inside her patrol car to carry out his orders when she heard him. She jumped back out of the vehicle and quickly made her way back to him.

"Do you cross-country ski?" Smudge asked.

"I do," Liz said.

"Good, go get your skis and I want you to mount a search up that trail," the sheriff ordered. "Call in a part-time deputy and take them with you."

"I know one of them snowshoes," Liz offered. The sheriff nodded his approval.

"Tim," the sheriff turned his attention again to Deputy Pattern. "I want you to find some cross-country skiers who were here who can tell us how long this truck has been here."

"I'll check at the ski shop, Sheriff," Deputy Pattern told him. "They'll have as good an idea as anyone about who comes here."

"That's good thinking," the sheriff said. He was still searching the woods for something he wasn't going to find.

"Two days ago, Sheriff. We told you that at the office," JC reminded the sheriff over the phone. Sheriff Williams had just asked when the last time was that JC and his news crew had seen Cindy Pfister.

"What's up, Sheriff?" JC asked. The sheriff paused. This was the news media he had on the phone, after all. Did he want Pfister's disappearance blabbed all over Tarnation?

But the sheriff also weighed their usefulness in trying to find Pfister. They were the news media. They could reach a lot of people in a short amount of time. And they were her friends.

"Cindy Pfister is missing," the sheriff told JC. "Her truck has been found at the trailhead of the LaChute Brook Fork Trail."

"If you want the public to be on the lookout," JC said, "I can call our sister station in Plattsburgh and get the word out."

"Yeah, do that, will you?" the sheriff asked.

"As soon as they run a crawl across TV screens and put it on their website," JC told the law officer, "the newspapers, radio and all the other news outlets will pick it up, too."

"Thank you," the sheriff said, preparing to hang up.

"Sheriff!" JC caught Williams before their call was disconnected. "Have you spoken with Inus Miller, the Amish skier?"

"Not lately," Smudge said.

"I showed him photographs of five people, including Cindy Pfister," JC said. "And Inus picked out the two pictures of DeWitt and Campbell, saying he'd seen them together."

Sheriff Williams thought this was interesting but not necessarily telling.

"They were old friends," the sheriff stated. "You would expect to see them together."

"I guess it's not that they were seen together," JC explained. "It's *where* they were seen together."

"And where is that?" Sheriff Williams asked.

"Inus said that he saw them together on the LaChute Brook Fork Trail. It was around the time Campbell's body was found," JC responded. "On that same rock feature where we saw you."

"Campbell and DeWitt?" the sheriff asked for confirmation.

"That's right, Sheriff," JC confirmed.

"The partner of murder victim Paul Campbell has now disappeared," JC told viewers in Denver that evening. He was live at the parking lot of the trailhead, using a satellite truck borrowed from Plattsburgh.

"Cindy Pfister, an archaeologist, was working on the same dig with Paul Campbell until Campbell's murder here in the North Country of New York," JC told his audience. "Campbell went to college in Colorado and lived there for some time after ..."

JC's report also showed viewers the British military button and other artifacts they'd uncovered off Silver Lake Road, saying they all somehow might be tied to the murder of Campbell and now the disappearance of Cindy Pfister.

Robin tried to keep busy, to keep her mind off the disappearance of her friend, Cindy Pfister, as well as the death of Patrick Ross.

She called Pfister's phone again, and again it went to voicemail. She called DeWitt's phone again, and again there was no answer.

It was dark now. As JC approached the sheriff, Deputy Colden attempted to block his path.

"It's OK, Peter," the sheriff said. "He's been pretty useful."

"Can you figure out which way this is going?" JC asked the sheriff.

"What do you mean?" the sheriff asked.

"Cindy is our friend," JC approached gently. "But two people are missing. We can't find DeWitt, either. It can't all be a coincidence."

"No," the sheriff agreed, "it probably is not."

"Here's two scenarios," JC offered. "DeWitt is responsible for the disappearance of Cindy and the murder of Campbell because they caught him covering up the discovery of historic relics at the Tomahawk site."

"OK," the sheriff said, waiting for the other.

"Another scenario could be that Campbell and DeWitt, who were old friends, caught Cindy doing something wrong and she's covering her tracks," JC said.

"You're saying," the sheriff asked with doubt in his voice, "that Cindy Pfister killed Campbell and now she's taken off after killing DeWitt?"

"We can't rule out the possibility," JC told the sheriff. "We know she has a reputation for a short fuse. And she owns a 9mm handgun."

"You should see it," the sheriff said, recalling the gun's poor condition.

"They're scenarios," JC told him. "It doesn't mean that I believe any one of them."

Smudge hoped that Cindy Pfister was not guilty of anything. But if she wasn't guilty, was she still alive?

Deputy Pattern pulled up in his patrol car and got out, walking toward the sheriff.

"Is that all, JC?" the sheriff asked.

"Not quite, Sheriff," JC said.

"Well then, give me a minute. Go inside the tent and get some coffee," the sheriff said as he walked away from the reporter and toward Tim Pattern.

A tent had been set up for the growing search party. The Red Cross had come with a truck to set up the tent and provide food and warm drinks.

"I found a few people who were Nordic skiing here the morning after the big snow, Sheriff," Deputy Pattern reported.

"And what did you find?" Smudge asked.

"There was a couple who came here to ski," Tim Pattern said. "They saw the truck. And then there was a solo skier, and he said something interesting. He said he got up real early to make sure he was the first one on the trail, so he'd have 'first tracks.'

"He saw the truck when he got here, but he says he is positive that the windows were all covered with snow," reported the deputy. "And when he skied back down the trail about four hours later, the truck was still there but the windows had all been cleared."

"I guess Cindy could have returned to her truck," the sheriff theorized. "Maybe she forgot something. Maybe she drove to breakfast or somewhere and then came back. It's possible."

"Yeah," Deputy Pattern said. "But there was still all that snow on the hood of the car. If anyone had driven it, the engine would have heated up and the snow would have fallen off the hood. Some of it, at least."

Smudge just looked at his deputy. It was a smart observation. It meant that someone cleared the windows on that truck but didn't move it.

"Now, why would someone do that?" the sheriff asked.

Deputy Pattern was advised to get on the radio and call the search crews back in. The night was so dark, it was unlikely they'd find anything unless they tripped over it.

It was an order he should have given two hours ago. The terrain they were searching was dangerous. There were cliffs and steep ravines, and it was only getting colder.

"Let's do this. Tell them we'll start again at sunrise," Smudge told him. "We'll have coffee and donuts waiting for them."

He knew what his order meant, that if Cindy Pfister was somewhere up that trail, she probably wasn't still alive. If she was badly injured, she'd die overnight. But he couldn't further risk the lives of his search team.

"Come on, Punch. Where are you?" the sheriff said to himself.

After the sheriff spent a few minutes by himself, he got a cup of coffee out of the tent and walked back toward JC Snow.

"So," the sheriff said, "you have something else?"

"A third scenario," JC told him. "I'm just thinking out loud, Sheriff. But there is at least one person who will sleep in his own bed tonight." The sheriff looked at him for an answer.

"Colin Cornheiser," JC told him. "I saw him downtown today. And there are two Os in Colorado. That's scenario three."

"There's two Os in Ohio," Smudge answered with some obstinance.

"You suspect Stormy Jordan?" JC asked.

"No," the sheriff answered. He displayed exhaustion. "No, I don't."

30

"Oh, hell," the sheriff muttered to himself.

"We found something," a voice had just said on the radio over the static.

The call came from a search team. Sheriff Williams recognized the voice as Liz Grant's. He also recognized the tone. It was the tone everyone used when they had to say something they did not want to say.

Smudge's phone rang. He saw that it was the phone assigned to Deputy Grant.

"We found her, Sheriff," Grant said in a subdued voice. "She looks like she's been dead for a couple of days."

"Did she freeze to death?" the sheriff asked.

"I'm not so sure about that, sir," was Grant's reply.

In not much time, and with the arrival of the coroner, the trail was packed down by all the foot traffic heading for the spot where Cindy Pfister was found.

Photographs were being taken, the medical examiner had paid a visit and deputies were searching the surrounding area for clues.

Her body was not far into the woods at all. Smudge Williams thought that, had she been alive, Cindy could have called out to him last night and he would have heard her in the trailhead parking lot. He wished that she had.

Instead, they had spent the night near each other at that trailhead and neither of them had been aware of it.

Smudge thought of his wife, of his responding to a boating accident and seeing the faces on his deputies when they realized the victim was Mrs. Williams. His heart sank.

He had taken a walk out to the spot where Cindy Pfister was found. It was only about fifty yards from the parking lot.

When more of the snow was brushed off of her by the medical examiner, there was visible blood pooled and dried in her red knit hat. Removing the hat, the medical examiner found clotted blood dried in her hair.

"A blow to the head, Sheriff," Dr. Ryan said solemnly. "I'll take a full look back at my lab, of course, but it looks like that gash to the head was enough to kill her."

"Killed here?" Smudge asked.

"Doubt it," the M.E. told him. "There would be a lot more blood. Blood really lights up the snow. There's no blood here that isn't in her hair or her hat."

"So, this happened somewhere else," the sheriff said with a stern face. "This is a murder."

Smudge Williams walked back toward his patrol car. He'd slept in it last night. Deputies Colden, Pattern and Grant all fell in step with the sheriff to await orders.

"I want to take a look at Cindy Pfister's dig site and I want to take a look at Harold DeWitt's office at Tomahawk," the sheriff said. "All three of you come with me. Liz, you call DeWitt. If he doesn't answer, call Averill Felix and ask him if he knows where DeWitt is."

The deputies all turned for their patrol cars. Liz Grant was already on her phone.

"Son of a bitch!"

The deputies heard the sheriff's bellow behind them. They kept walking for their cars without turning around. They knew the voice. It was ferocious. Smudge Williams was transforming into a predator.

Their first stop was the convenience store lot. The sheriff and deputies quickly separated to check each tent and any other feature on the site.

"Sheriff?" It was Deputy Colden's voice coming from one of the tents. Smudge and the others soon joined him.

"It looks like someone tried to dig it up, scrape it to remove the soil," Colden said to the sheriff as he looked at the dirt floor. "But there's still blood."

The tables were clean. There were only a few boxes in the tent and a rectangular hole dug in the middle of the space. It was about two feet deep.

Deputy Pattern crouched and used a pen to turn over a large stone. It had blood on it. He looked up to see if Sheriff Williams was watching. He was.

"The killer gave up trying to clean," Deputy Colden said. "He was probably freaking out. He probably turned his attention to hiding the body so he could get on the road."

"Maybe it was dark," the sheriff said. "He thought it was clean, but he missed spots. That would put it at night, just before or at the start of the snowfall. He wanted it to look like she fell while going for a walk on the LaChute Brook Trail and got covered with snow."

"He put her in her own truck and drove her to the trail," the sheriff continued. "But the snow covered up the truck. Maybe he even came back in the morning to wipe the snow off the windows of the truck, so he could change the timeline."

"If he drove her truck to the trailhead and parked it there, how did he get back to his own vehicle?" Deputy Pattern asked.

"Good question, Tim," the sheriff said, taking a last look around the tent.

"We'll figure it out, Sheriff," Colden said. "Someone must have given him a ride or someone must have seen him walking."

"Right," Smudge said, distracted. He walked out of the tent and his deputies followed. They climbed into their patrol cars. The sheriff drove off the convenience store site and onto the Tomahawk Resort lot, his deputies in tow.

"Liz?" the sheriff commanded as he climbed out of his vehicle. Liz Grant hurried up to walk alongside the sheriff.

"Harold DeWitt doesn't answer his phone, Sheriff," she reported. "Averill Felix says he doesn't know where DeWitt is and hasn't seen him for days."

The sheriff looked at Liz with a hard face, "He never knows nothin', does he?"

"I'm learning that, sir," Deputy Grant responded.

"Tim?" the sheriff bellowed. "Push through those plastic drapes and ask the construction workers where Harold DeWitt's office is."

"Yes, sir," Deputy Pattern said, heading for the plastic strips hanging in the doors of the buildings to keep the cold out.

"Never mind," the sheriff hollered, turning left and walking toward a door across the freshly laid cobblestone walk.

Smudge Williams walked past a rental car he recognized as belonging to JC Snow. It was parked in front of some office space that looked like it was being used.

Bip Peters was shooting video of DeWitt's office when the sheriff walked in.

"Knock that shit off," the sheriff barked at the news photographer. JC gave Bip a look advising him to comply. They could always resume gathering video after this very pissed-off sheriff was gone.

JC watched as the sheriff and his deputies studied the office. The sheriff walked over to DeWitt's desk and thumbed through the paperwork.

He picked up a piece of paper and a map. He looked them over before handing them to Senior Deputy Colden.

"What does that suggest to you, Peter?" the sheriff asked. Colden studied the piece of paper and then looked at a circle on the map.

"That he's headed to Nippletop Mountain in Keene Valley," the deputy responded. "To an outlaw camp he's circled there."

"Then you and Tim go there and get him," the sheriff said with determination. "And don't stop to piss in a dead zone. I want you on your radio at all times."

"Sheriff?" JC spoke, not unaware that Sheriff Williams might be easily provoked.

The sheriff spun his head toward the reporter, like someone had just spilled hot coffee on his clean pants. Williams' gaze at the reporter was seventy-five percent fury.

"He had a gun there," JC said, trying not to show the law officer how intimidated he was. The sheriff slowly turned his head in the direction JC was pointing.

"He had a holstered handgun on that shelf," JC continued. "We talked about it. He said he carried it to shoot bear and moose."

"The bear are hibernating," the sheriff told the reporter as he turned to face him again.

"I know, Sheriff," JC said. "But that's what he told me. And the gun isn't here, now. I looked for it."

The sheriff stood there and thought about it.

"Liz," the sheriff ordered, "you go with Tim and Peter to Nippletop. I want all of you to look out for each other. If he shoots at you, shoot back. I want all of you to keep an eye out for each other, you understand?"

"Yes, sir," all three deputies responded.

This guy is going to war, JC thought to himself.

The three deputies departed for Nippletop, as ordered. That left Sheriff Smudge Williams in the room, staring at JC.

"What else do you know?" Sheriff Williams snapped as he pointed a finger at JC. He was not smiling.

"He's afraid of the woods," JC responded. Smudge gave him a curious look

"The dump truck driver I told you about, who told us where he unloaded that back dirt with the artifacts. He says that he went up into the woods with DeWitt last spring. He said DeWitt brought that handgun, hanging from that holster on his belt, because he was afraid of being attacked by a bear or a moose."

"Did he shoot anyone?" the sheriff asked, showing a small smile and the ridiculousness of it all.

"He shot at a chipmunk, I understand," JC said. "I don't know if he hit him."

"Yeah," Smudge said. "Chipmunks can be dangerous." The sheriff looked around the room. His booming voice then found Bip.

"You done? I've got to seal this room off," the sheriff told the news photographer. But it sounded like an order to get out.

"Sure, Sheriff," Bip said.

"What kind of gun did you say that was?" the sheriff asked JC as he and Bip were preparing to leave.

"I don't know, Sheriff," JC said. "Sometimes I notice, but I'm not really a gun guy."

31

Smudge Williams' impatience grew as the day wore on. He spoke to the medical examiner, who confirmed that Cindy Pfister died from a single blow to the head.

The sheriff notified the New York State Police, asking them for assistance looking for a car belonging to Harold DeWitt. The sheriff also called the Black Pool Border Crossing into Canada. He put them on notice to look for DeWitt and asked them to spread the word to all the nearby border crossings between the U.S. and Canada.

He returned to DeWitt's office to make a more complete search through his things. He didn't find the gun, either.

The sheriff thought about Cornheiser. Smudge had a collection of good eyewitness reports saying that maybe all of those meetings the county executive had with Averill Felix dealt with building plans and zoning issues. The county was trying to accommodate the developer.

Smudge was trying to envision Cornheiser as the murderer. The sheriff thought that there were too many times Cornheiser was not in the right place at the right time to be the killer. It was DeWitt. The sheriff knew it.

At about three o'clock, with about ninety minutes of daylight left, Deputy Colden called the sheriff on his phone.

"Sheriff," reported the senior deputy, "we have been marching up and down the trail to Nippletop. We have driven up and down the road to see if he might have taken another way into the woods, and there's just no sign that he's been here. There's no sign of his car."

"Have you asked around?" the sheriff asked.

"We have, sir," Colden answered. "We have found some people who were snowshoeing and they say they were breaking fresh tracks all day. There wasn't a sign of anyone being in those woods since the last snow."

The sheriff was sitting at his desk in his office. He was the only one there. He rubbed his face with his hand while he thought.

"Alright, Peter," the sheriff began. "You stay there in your patrol car. Follow your instincts. Send Tim and Liz back."

"Roger, Sheriff," Colden replied. Sheriff Williams was reviewing all of the accounts of the day. He phoned JC Snow.

JC had decided not to chase the deputies to Nippletop in Keene Valley. He wasn't certain that he was making the right call, but he thought it was better to stay near the sheriff. Smudge Williams was still the center of the storm.

If DeWitt was captured at Nippletop, Bip would be at the courthouse, his camera rolling, when the murder suspect arrived there in handcuffs.

On the other hand, JC had told his crew that if they went to Nippletop and something unfolded in Joseph, they were over an hour away.

JC's phone rang.

"Where did you say DeWitt went hiking with that dump truck driver?" the sheriff asked.

"I didn't," JC answered.

"Where he shot the chipmunk," the sheriff pursued. "Where was it?"

"Up LaChute Brook Fork Trail," JC told him. "The chipmunk bolted out of an outlaw camp up there."

"OK," the sheriff said and ended the call. He thought about the conversation. His jaws clenched.

"Son of a bitch!" he bellowed. He grabbed his body armor and stormed out of his office.

Smudge Williams pulled into the driveway of Stormy Jordan's land and parked his patrol car at the side of Stormy's cabin. The sheriff didn't ask permission to park there or even knock on the door.

He began to march up the bank of LaChute Brook, never taking his eye off the mountain, Le Trou Au Coeur.

Stormy watched the sheriff through the grimy window of his cabin. Stormy thought he looked pissed off, better to be avoided.

The sheriff figured that he had about an hour of light. It didn't seem like enough time to reach the outlaw camp. It didn't concern him.

He had pulled his body armor over his head and attached the Velcro strips near his waist. The vest said "Sheriff" across the front and back. His Glock 22 was in a holster at his side.

There was a cold breeze that was picking up. It was coming over the mountain. He saw that he was following footprints now. They had come from somewhere else. They were heading up the mountain, too.

They could belong to the Amish skier, the sheriff thought. They could also belong to Harold DeWitt.

He had not reached the trailhead yet, when he saw a figure ahead. The man was walking in the same footprints that the sheriff was following, only the man was walking in the direction of Smudge Williams.

It did not take Smudge long to recognize the man as Harold DeWitt. It also looked like DeWitt was struggling to maneuver over the snow. He was staggering, like he was cold and tired.

The sheriff stopped walking, pulled off his gloves and pulled out his gun. DeWitt looked like he was going to make it a lot easier, by stumbling right up to Smudge.

DeWitt stopped about ten feet from the sheriff. The suspect was having difficulty standing. His feet were wet.

"How did you do, crossing that log bridge?" the sheriff asked.

"I fell in the water," DeWitt answered in a weak voice. That was how he got wet.

"You spent the night up there?" Smudge asked.

"In that cabin. I nearly died. It was freezing," DeWitt told him. "And there were predators prowling around all night."

Smudge assessed that this man was spent. Whatever threat he had posed was frozen out of him. The sheriff noticed that DeWitt's holster was empty. Smudge holstered his own gun.

"What happened to your gun?" the sheriff asked. DeWitt shrugged his shoulders as though he didn't know.

"What kind was it?" the sheriff asked, more than curious.

"A Glock 19," the defeated man told him, after thinking to remember.

"Figures," Smudge said.

"I really did like him," DeWitt offered. "Paul was my friend."

"Then what happened?" the sheriff inquired.

"He asked me to go on a hike up there," DeWitt said, nodding his head in the direction of the LaChute Brook Fork Trail.

"What did you talk about?" the sheriff asked.

"Old times, at first," DeWitt told him. "Then, he pulled artifacts out of his backpack. He said he'd found them in some of the back dirt from my site. He said he wanted to talk to me first, so we could make it right. He was actually giving me a chance. But I denied it."

"He began accusing me of turning my head when I found artifacts," DeWitt tried to explain. "He said they indicated there had been a large Mohawk village on the Tomahawk site, and maybe something even bigger."

"Had you?" Smudge asked.

"Not at first," DeWitt told him. "When I found some artifacts, I brought my discovery to Mr. Felix. He didn't want construction held up. He offered me a considerable bonus if I'd just keep working and write a clean report."

"A report making no mention of what you had found," Smudge suggested.

"Right," DeWitt said quietly. "It was a lot of money. And it would be a big deal if someone like Averill Felix owed me a favor, you know?"

"And you killed Paul with that Glock 19," the sheriff surmised.

"I panicked," DeWitt told him, looking the sheriff in his eyes. "He was my friend. I don't even remember pulling the trigger. I panicked. For just an instant, I thought money was more valuable than friendship, than a human life. But a gun makes it so quick."

"You shot him twice," the sheriff noted without sympathy.

"I wasn't myself," DeWitt said, trembling. "I was only worried about myself."

"And then Cindy Pfister figured you out," the sheriff added. DeWitt just looked away. He looked like he was going to be sick.

The sheriff pulled his handcuffs from his belt, stepped forward and reached for DeWitt's left arm.

But DeWitt reached behind his back, where he'd stuffed his Glock 19. His hand swung from behind him and he pressed the gun under the chin of the surprised sheriff.

Smudge reached for his own gun in its holster, but found DeWitt's other hand already gripping the handle of the service weapon.

DeWitt's pistol was pointed up. After the chin, the bullet would pass through Smudge's brain.

"Don't do something stupid, son," the sheriff told the archaeologist.

DeWitt quickly pulled the sheriff's Glock 22 from his holster and backed away, out of the bigger man's reach.

"I don't need blood splatter on me," DeWitt told him, "when you're shot with your own gun. Put your hands up."

Looking at the barrel of the Glock pointed at him, Williams couldn't help but think that it would be handy to have a vicious dog with him at this moment.

"Are you sure you want to do this?" Smudge asked calmly as he raised his hands. The sheriff had a slow fuse. He didn't generally react emotionally to things for the first few minutes.

"I didn't think I did," DeWitt told him as he pointed his gun at the sheriff's head. "But sometimes I'm impulsive. I think we both know that by now. And here we are."

"You faked the map, and the notes about Nippletop?" Smudge asked.

"I needed some time to think," DeWitt told him. "I didn't know if you would fall for it. Good for me. I may pull this off." DeWitt smiled at his improving prospects.

He appeared to lower his head an inch to place the sheriff's head in the gun's sights. The sheriff watched DeWitt's hand tighten around the grip.

The blast of gunfire wrenched the sheriff's head back. His eyes closed and his body flinched.

When he opened his eyes, all he saw was the backdrop of Le Trou Au Coeur in the fading daylight.

At his feet, he saw the astonished look on the face of Harold DeWitt. The suspect was laying in the snow on his back, his head crooked to the side. Bright red blood was seeping into the snow and pooling.

It registered with the sheriff now that he heard the bullet from his own gun, in DeWitt's hand, whistle over his left shoulder. An equally shocked Smudge Williams began to scan the landscape.

His eyes fixed on Stormy Jordan, about twenty feet away, holding a Remington Wingmaster shotgun.

Stormy's eyes were on the sheriff, who thought he had taken all of Stormy's guns away. Stormy didn't utter a word. He had a worried expression on his face.

"It was my favorite," he then croaked in a weak voice. "I buried it a little."

32

"Turn out the light!"

Bip Peters was squinting into the sky.

"What is that?" he whined.

"It's the sun," JC told him. They hadn't seen it during quite a stretch of gray overcast days.

"It is going to be my favorite day," JC declared. "Twenty-seven and sunny!"

The morning rays of the low sun made Battle Ax look like something painted by Thomas Cole, when the landscape artist introduced the world to the Hudson River School of Art.

JC, Bip and Robin Smith's night had ended late, and their day had begun early. They'd reported live to viewers in

Denver, last night, about the death of the former Colorado resident who had killed another former Colorado resident, Paul Campbell.

The national media was fascinated by the story because it tied to an archaeological find, and perhaps resolved the mystery of Simon Fraser's whereabouts. Granted, JC thought, few Americans outside Saratoga County ever knew that Simon Fraser's remains were missing.

But it was a great story. JC was interviewed before sunrise on a couple of national morning news programs.

"You hit another home run, JC," his news director in Denver had told him last night. They both knew that their trip to Upstate New York was standing on very thin ice until DeWitt's dramatic demise.

JC was expected to be on the air for the noon news in Denver, too, and then again in the evening.

But for two hours, they were at the Battle Ax Ski Resort and had planks on their feet.

"What kind of snow is this going to be?" Robin inquired as they rode up the chairlift.

"Vanilla Ice," JC told her with a smile. "We don't ski on ice a lot anymore in the East. They just call a lot of it ice. Vanilla Ice looks hard but it's soft. You can carve it like butter."

Bip licked his lips at the thought of snowboarding on butter. Robin looked at JC.

"You put a sticker on your boring helmet," she said.

"Now," he smiled at her, "it's not so boring." The expanse of black that was JC's helmet now had a sticker on the forehead. It was a green ram with horns curled at the side. It was a Colorado State University logo.

From the top of the chairlift, they could see mountains all the way to the horizon. Beyond that, unseen but there all the same, were East Coast ski mountains like Tuckerman's Ravine in New Hampshire.

JC told them that Tuckerman's was the Mecca for Eastern skiing. It was stunningly steep and without any lifts. You had to climb up its sheer walls to take a run. A hard-core skier had to do it at least once.

Beyond that, there was Sunday River in Maine where they tell you they have "All the Pow Mein You Can Eat."

There was Killington, "The Beast of the East." And there was Bousquet in Massachusetts that began as a mink farm a century ago.

"What do you think that piece of paper meant, with the two letter Os?" Bip asked as they rode the chairlift.

"I'm not sure we'll ever know," JC responded. "I don't think it was Ohio or Colorado. I think it was 'Foot.' Campbell knew what DeWitt had done. The whole line said '24th Foot,' Fraser's fighting unit."

The runs at Battle Ax were dotted by skiers. Some were wearing the latest ski fashions, and some were wearing hunting jackets and camo or their favorite football team's jersey.

One run was closed by yellow tape. Racers were training on a slalom course. They could have been young skiers from the Northwood Ski Academy in Lake Placid. They aspired to earn scholarships and race in college. At least one racer from the school, Andrew Weibrecht, had won silver and bronze for the U.S. Ski Team.

JC and Robin were on skis and Bip was on his snowboard. They carved down a ski run called Arcane, connected to one called Really Dru.

Robin showed her moves on mogul runs called Be Patience and Ty'd Up.

A cruiser called L-E-S had Bip scraping his rib cage on the snow during devastating carves, with JC torquing racing turns behind him.

On their next trip to the top, JC spied a figure at the side of the trail, just outside the boundary of the Battle Ax ski area. The man stood next to a jagged rock feature jutting up from the snow.

JC skied to a stop next to the skier. He wore a knit hat and had buttons on his ski jacket instead of a zipper.

Robin and Bip had skied ahead and were waiting for JC where the trail divided.

"You taking the chairlift up today?" JC asked. The man shook his head.

"I can go down their slopes," Inus said with a smile, "as long as I walk up."

"You want to take a run with us?" JC asked.

"At the bottom of your run," Inus gestured toward the base lodge, "it is a longer walk to my bike."

"We can give you a ride," JC said. He knew that some Amish accepted car rides from Mennonites.

"I could," Inus told him, "but I will not."

"You know those photographs I showed you?" JC asked. And the reporter explained to Inus why two of those men and the only woman among the five pictures were now dead.

"Someone took a life for this?" Inus asked and shook his head at the waste.

JC told his friend that they had to get going. They had work to do, expected for a live shot on the noon news.

"Let me see you ski," Inus requested.

JC felt a little self-conscious, but he arced some racing turns down the steep hill and disappeared from Inus Miller's view.

JC caught up with Robin and Bip at the half-pipe. Bip was the next one in.

"I'll bet he tries a flip again," Robin said. "You didn't see it last time."

Bip was getting more height each time he rose above the half-pipe's wall. He executed the back flip and drew cheers from everyone watching. As he landed, his weight shifted and he slipped off the tail of his board, landing on his back.

"Back dirt!" the other boarders screamed as they laughed. Bip rose with a good-humored smile on his face and brushed himself off.

"Back dirt!" screamed JC and Robin.

As promised, they left Battle Ax after a couple of hours and did their live shot for the noon news.

Following that, a licensed archaeologist, a woman named Topel LeFebvre, stood at the three mounds of dirt off Silver Lake Road with JC, Robin and Bip.

"It's quite a find, quite a story," she said. "It's a mess, but it will be fun to sift through. I think I'll wait until the weather warms up, though."

"The sheriff said that he'd keep it roped off," JC told her.

LeFebvre had dark hair and sharp features. She smiled a lot. She said that she grew up in Quebec, Canada, and still spent much time up there visiting family. She was dressed in a thick red jacket and a knit hat with a Canadian flag.

"It's been pretty severely compromised," she added. "But the story will interest everyone." The small Joseph County

Museum said they would obtain a grant to pay LeFebvre for her work.

The button that JC found, and anything else the licensed archaeologist would discover, would go on display at the little museum. It was on a street facing a side of the courthouse.

"You know," Topel LeFebvre told them, "the developers at Tomahawk Resort deny any of this came from their site. That's an Averill Felix? That makes it more difficult to verify where your button for the 24th Foot actually came from, even though we know."

"So," LeFebvre asked, "you believe that Mr. Campbell's theory suggested the Mohawk Indians disinterred General Fraser at the battlefield and moved him north, hoping to rebury him in Canada?"

"That's what I believe Campbell was thinking," JC agreed. "His discovery could have told us that General Fraser's remains made it this far, if no further. It's even possible that we've brushed up with Fraser's final resting place."

"Well, I did some research after you called. There is absolutely no evidence that General Fraser's remains made it to Canada. But he certainly would have been among friends there," LeFebvre told them. "Lots of Canadians in the East are descendants of British loyalists. They had to flee America when the Revolution was won."

"It's funny," Robin said. "If DeWitt had just disclosed his find instead of covering it up, he would have discovered the button and the box plate and who knows what else. He would have enjoyed a lot of acclaim. It would have opened a lot of doors for him, the right way."

"That is certainly true," LeFebvre agreed. "But no sign of the belt buckle or cartridge box plate with the '24' on it?" she asked.

"No," Robin told her. "We've looked. Maybe *you'll* find it. We put Paul Campbell's picture of it in the envelope with all our research that we're turning over to you."

"Well, as I said," LeFebvre told them apologetically, "the evidence chain is well-damaged. It will be hard to prove it came from the feature at Tomahawk. But we might yet get a more interesting story from the back dirt."

33

"Give Back Our Land," one sign said.

About a half-dozen protesters, some holding signs, stood across from the entrance to the Tomahawk Resort development. They identified themselves as descendants of the Mohawks who once lived on the land.

They were incensed at the news disclosing that the archaeological dig at Tomahawk may have ignored the presence of a historic Mohawk village within its footprint.

JC, Robin and Bip saw the protesters while driving back from breakfast. JC and Bip had already interviewed the demonstrators and their story had aired on Denver TV, as well as the stories picked up by national news.

The day before had been a busy one for the three journalists, editing new stories for their TV station in Denver, doing live shots and accommodating interest in their story from as far away as Britain.

Now driving back to The T, Bip chose a safe place on Bonnieview Road to pass an Amish buggy.

They would have time to return to their rooms, do some preparation for this evening's live report and then change into clothing suitable for a funeral.

Services for Patrick Ross were held that day. His children flew in for the Mass. Actual burial would wait until the ground thawed.

During the wake, Robin approached Patrick's casket.

"I'm sorry that I couldn't get to you sooner, Patrick," she whispered. "I tried." Then, she looked at his kind face and said, "A woman just knows."

Smudge Williams was at the funeral. After the service, JC sought him out to tell him they would be leaving in the morning.

"I think I'm going to get that dog," the sheriff told the reporter. "There's a girl dog who just had a litter. She's a bomb sniffer for the state police. You had a girl, right?"

"Yep," JC said. "I usually get along better with females."

"Maybe it will help *me* do that," Smudge said, thoughtfully.

"What are you going to name her?" JC asked.

"I think I'll call her 'Punch,'" Williams told him.

As the sheriff left the church, a woman who was unfamiliar to him approached.

"Sheriff Williams?" she asked, "I'm Celeste Jordan, Robert Jordan's daughter."

Smudge was caught with a surprised look on his face.

"You're surprised," Ms. Jordan said. "You didn't know that Mr. Jordan had a daughter?"

"You're from Ohio?" the sheriff asked.

"Yes," Celeste Jordan answered.

"I'm sorry, and you're right. I didn't know Stormy had a daughter," the sheriff told her. The girl in the pink hat in the picture, the sheriff thought to himself.

"No harm done," she smiled a professional smile. "We aren't close. I really don't know him well, myself. But I am here to represent him."

"You're a lawyer?" the sheriff asked.

"Yes," she replied. "My mother asked me to come and look after his well-being in the latest charges against him."

Smudge thought about that statement. The woman was probably in her mid-thirties. That meant she was an infant when Stormy was sent to prison in Ohio.

After being released from prison, Stormy moved back to his hometown, Joseph. Smudge surmised that meant that Stormy and his bride did not agree on the direction of their future together with a young daughter.

But Stormy and his wife, or ex-wife, must have been in touch if the woman thought enough of Stormy to send their daughter to help him avoid going back to prison.

The sheriff and the daughter of Stormy Jordan stood outside the church, facing each other.

"I am aware that my father can be a little difficult," Celeste Jordan said as she handed the sheriff her business card. It said "Attorney at Law."

"Do you remember much of your father, when you were a little girl?" Smudge asked.

"I'm not sure what business that is of yours," she said. "But, no."

"When did you arrive in Joseph?" the sheriff asked.

"Really, just an hour ago," she told him. "I was told that I could catch you here. I'll go say hello to my father after this."

"Well, you're in for a treat," Smudge muttered.

The sheriff began to walk toward the back of the courthouse, to his office.

Celeste Jordan was left wondering what the sheriff meant by that last remark.

"Bring your father around to my office this afternoon," the sheriff said as he stopped and turned to face her. "We'll talk this out. Do you need directions to your father's cabin?"

"That won't be necessary," Ms. Jordan replied. It actually *was* necessary, but she felt that asking the sheriff for directions would show weakness. She hoped that GPS would lead her there.

"Part of the investigation is going to continue," JC told Rocky Baumann. The assignment editor at the Denver television station wanted to know what was left of the story when JC, Bip and Robin flew home in the morning.

"It will be spelled out in my live shots tonight," JC told the assignment editor. "Someone paid Harold DeWitt enough money to file a fraudulent archaeology report with the state. He'd face quite a scandal and some jail time, if he weren't dead."

"Who do we suspect?" Rocky asked.

"The first one the sheriff will look at is the owner and developer of Battle Ax and Tomahawk, a very wealthy man named Averill Felix. The state police are going to get involved, too, as well as the state attorney general. There's a lot of fraud against the state involved in this, filing a false report."

"Do they have a case against him?" Rocky asked.

"Not right now," JC responded.

Sheriff Williams had not shared with the news media that Harold DeWitt told him Averill Felix promised a significant bribe. That admission came only moments before DeWitt was shot to death.

But even without that knowledge, JC had a sound understanding of the hierarchy at Tomahawk, by now. Cindy Pfister made it clear that a *child* playing with a toy shovel wouldn't have missed the artifacts buried at the site.

"It's clear that someone bribed DeWitt, probably Felix," JC told his assignment editor. "But so far there is no money trail. If he was paid in cash or if the payment hadn't actually been delivered yet, how will they ever find a money trail?"

"Could Colin Cornheiser be involved?" JC was asked.

"He doesn't have that kind of money and he really didn't have that much to gain. Not compared to Felix," JC told him. "It's unlikely."

There were still pieces to fit together, JC thought. DeWitt killed Campbell. But was he ordered to kill the archaeologist or did DeWitt improvise? Was DeWitt being honest with Sheriff Williams when telling him that he just snapped?

"Who do you think did it?" Rocky inquired. "Not that we can say it on the air, but your hunches have been pretty accurate."

"Well, DeWitt killed Campbell. But my gut tells me that Felix played a role, at least by bribing DeWitt," JC said. "Felix lied to us. When I asked him if he knew Paul Campbell, he said that he didn't. And yet, a witness tells me that he saw

Felix having long conversations with Campbell on a number of occasions. Mr. Felix lied."

"But you don't have enough to say that in your broadcast?" Rocky asked.

"I have one uncorroborated witness," JC explained. "And *he* might even deny he told us that. He works for Felix and says he's still paying off his dump truck."

"What are you going to do with that information, then?" the assignment editor asked.

"I'll tell the sheriff," JC disclosed. "And if Felix is ever arrested, we'll know that will be part of the evidence against him. We'll report it then. If the truck driver is subpoenaed to testify in court, he'll have to tell the truth."

"We just don't have enough proof, right now, that Felix bribed DeWitt," JC told Rocky. "It's not worth getting sued for. We might not win, even if we're right."

Celeste Jordan entered the sheriff's office with her father, Robert "Stormy" Jordan. She was dressed in a business suit. Stormy was dressed in a worn, plaid work shirt and jeans with only thin denim remaining over the knees. His hair and his unruly gray beard had been combed.

"Ms. Jordan, Robert," the sheriff ushered them into his office. Two chairs had already been placed at the sheriff's desk, opposite where Smudge would sit.

"Coffee?" the sheriff offered.

"No thank you," Celeste Jordan responded. Smudge thought that Stormy looked like he was about to say, "Yes, please" or at least "Yes," but was cut off by his lawyer-daughter.

"The charge of illegal possession of a firearm," attorney Jordan began, "is based on a felony in Ohio that is over thirty years old. My client ... my father voluntarily surrendered all of his firearms upon your request."

No small talk, Smudge noted, just down to brass tacks. He rubbed his hand over his clean chin. He'd shaved that morning for the funeral.

"All but one," the sheriff corrected.

"Yes," the lawyer acknowledged. "All but one old firearm that he'd forgotten he'd buried."

"He forgot he buried his favorite gun?" Smudge responded. He was deliberately directing his questions to the attorney, not Stormy. He was not interested in Stormy incriminating himself, which Stormy would surely do if given the opportunity to open his mouth.

"He forgot," the lawyer-daughter repeated.

"I might add," attorney Jordan indeed did add, "if not for my client, that funeral this morning might well have been yours."

"That is not lost on me, Ms. Jordan," Smudge said to her.

"How much discretion do you have?" Celeste Jordan asked after taking a moment to search for the right words.

"Discretion?" Smudge asked. "Not a lot. That's why we're here. Influence? I've got some. Sort of like you."

"Me? I have the power of the laws of New York behind me," Ms. Jordan declared.

"Not quite. You're an attorney," Smudge acknowledged, "but you're not a licensed attorney in New York. And you only arrived here this morning, so you haven't made any arrangements. So, while I believe you're acquainted with the law, we're really just three friends talking here. Only, I really am the sheriff."

This opened the eyes of the lawyer. She now understood that she was not dealing with a hayseed who got to wear a badge because he wasn't very good at ranching.

"Getting back to the point," the attorney from Ohio said, her tone a little more respectful, "You, as sheriff of Joseph County, might have influence with the judge?"

"Now, you're catching up," Smudge smiled as he leaned back in his chair. He looked toward Stormy.

"Stormy," the sheriff said, "you have anything to say?"

Stormy just gave the sheriff a blank stare. Smudge realized that Stormy had been skillfully advised by his lawyer-daughter not to say a word.

"Well, someone once said," the sheriff began, "'learn the rules, so you can break them properly.' Stormy, I'm not convinced that you understand all of the rules, but I think you broke them properly."

The lawyer-daughter understood, even if she would have to explain it to her client-father later.

"So, we're done here?" she asked as she began to slide from her chair.

"Except for the formalities," the sheriff told her. "I'll speak with the judge."

"Stormy," the sheriff turned his eyes toward his old high school classmate. "I don't think I properly thanked you for saving my life. Thank you. But I'm afraid that I'm going to have to keep that Remington Bird Slayer, the one you forgot you buried. I remind you: You're not allowed to possess a weapon. Have a good day, you two."

JC locked the door to his room at The T and walked down the hall lined by walls made from rough round logs. He passed the large stone fireplace where the clerk was relaxing with his feet up on a coffee table, rather than sitting behind the desk.

"See you in a bit," JC said as he walked out into the cold air and slipped into their rental SUV. The sun was starting to set.

He drove toward Joseph, down the heavily forested corridor that was going to be thinned in coming years to make way for a building boom of luxury homes and condominiums. They would house more skiers, snowboarders and people who were now allowed to work from home anywhere in the country.

JC and his team would fly out in the morning and he was a bit sorry to leave. He'd come to feel at home again in the Adirondacks. They were good people, he felt, and they had good mountains and forests. He thought about coming back in the summer.

He slowed the 4x4 and performed a U-turn in the road. He pulled over onto the snow-covered shoulder and got out. He approached a fence post. In the snow, there were depressions of day-old footprints and bicycle tires.

JC took one last look at his black ski helmet and perched it atop the post. There was a note on it saying, "For you, Inus."

When JC returned to The T, he knocked on Robin's door. She pulled the door open and gave him a smile.

We won't be seeing Bip tonight," she said. "He told me that Patty is cooking him a going-away dinner."

JC nodded and gave the thought a smile.

"Are you cooking *me* dinner?" Robin asked JC, curling her arms around his neck and glancing toward the small kitchenette in her room.

"Hmm, I'm without doubt the worst cook you've ever met," he told her. "But I cook a great omelet. How about an omelet for dinner?"

"You can cook me one of *those,* Jean Claude, for breakfast," she said, pulling him closer.

The last rays of light made LaChute Brook sparkle. The cold water rippled when it hit rocks large enough to break the surface, a mile and a half from the trailhead.

At the bottom of a thirty-foot drop from a rock clearing above, the last light of the day reflected off an object sitting in about eight inches of water: A flat copper rectangle framing a "24."

34

"I've gotta clean up a mess I made," JC told Robin.

"Can I come?" she asked.

"I was hoping you'd ask," he said to her with a smile.

Officially, along with Bip, they were given the rest of the week off, in return for their work in New York that had stretched the boundaries of permissible work hours.

"I'm always up for a good adventure," Robin said.

On the plane home to Denver, JC and Robin had shared with Bip their desire to keep the new relationship between JC and Robin a secret for a while.

The new couple wanted to figure out what kind of couple they were, first off. JC liked being with Robin. She was smart,

279

funny and giving. She looked out for him, which was something he could use.

But he didn't want their relationship to be one like he'd seen so many times before. JC and Robin had fallen in together while on a shared assignment in New York. They shared solving a compelling mystery and being strangers in a strange land.

He recognized that the path was similar terrain to one taken by a friend of his. That led to a massive broken heart.

His friend fell in love while he was in the military. The woman he fell for was someone he served with. They had so much in common while they were together in the armed forces. But when they left for civilian life, there was a different world waiting for them and they became different people.

JC and Robin agreed to explore the possibilities. But they would do it in private, until they were sure of what they were doing.

So, on one of their official days off, JC and Robin drove north on I-25 to Fort Collins, Colorado.

"It's not really your mess, you know," Robin told him.

"I feel like it is. I've got to clean it up as best I can," he said.

"You went to college in Fort Collins?" she asked.

"I did," he acknowledged.

"Well, you skipped a class that a lot of people really like," she told him.

"Which one?" he asked.

"The one that teaches you to pawn off all the problems you cause on the next guy," she smiled.

"Yeah," said JC. "That would have been a useful one. But, not for me."

"I think you flunked it," Robin told him with a smile.

"I think that's a compliment?" he told her.

"It is," she said, sort of beaming.

JC steered his red FJ Cruiser down College Avenue in Fort Collins. They passed the campus of Colorado State University. Robin pointed at a logo on a CSU sign, green with a ram's head on it.

"That reminds me," JC said, "I've got to get a new ski helmet."

He steered his SUV left and headed for the mountains until taking a right on Overland Trail Road. He pulled into the driveway of a home built out of concrete blocks, painted yellow.

He had arranged to meet Louise Aarons there.

When they had departed the New York of twig furniture and Adirondack fixtures and their plane landed in Denver, JC and Robin had taken the train from the airport to Union Station, downtown.

They walked to his apartment in Larimer Square and retrieved his car with the license plates spelling LEME SKI. He dropped Robin off at her apartment and then he drove to the TV station. He was off the clock, but he had something on his mind.

He had asked Bip for the interviews shot with Cornheiser in New York. For two hours, JC sat in an editing bay and watched the interviews, looking for something he might have missed. And he found it. Cornheiser mentioned that Winston Reddish had a girlfriend.

JC and Robin climbed from their car in the driveway of a home on Overland Trail in Fort Collins. A lovely woman with a head of long thick gray hair emerged from a yellow house built from concrete blocks.

JC thought that she was about the same age as Colin Cornheiser. She had a shawl over her shoulders, to keep her warm until they went back inside.

JC thanked her for seeing him and introduced Robin. JC noticed, not for the first time, Robin had a way of smoothing arrivals and introductions. She was instantly likeable and had great intuitions.

Louise Aarons led them back into the house. It was sparsely furnished. A worn rug covered most of a concrete floor. There was a table in the middle of the room near a large electric space heater. It was the only source of heat in the four-room house. The only door in the interior was the one opening to the bathroom.

"It's not much," the woman said, "But I lived here for seven years, during college and after. It's where I lived with Winston."

Louise Aarons produced a photo and handed it to JC. It was the picture of a couple sitting on the ground in the woods. The young woman in it was clearly Louise, with a thick mane of dark hair. The young man had long blond hair and a ready smile. He was wearing shorts. His arms were wrapped around muscular legs. He was leaning on Louise in an affectionate manner.

"What a wonderful picture," Robin cooed softly as she returned it to Louise. The older woman gave it one more glance and smiled to herself.

"I say that we lived here," she said looking up from the picture but maintaining the smile. "He went to school in

Denver, of course, but he was here every minute he could be. Corny was here a lot, too."

"Colin Cornheiser?" JC asked, smiling at the nickname the young Cornheiser was called.

"Yes," Louise said. "I haven't lived here for decades, but when it came on the market for such a low price, I bought it. Maybe it was for nostalgic reasons."

Louise Aarons explained that she never moved away from Fort Collins. She became a college psychology professor. She got married and had children. She said that she had lived a happy life.

"But poor Winston," she said. "He never got to enjoy all those things that the rest of us have enjoyed. He deserved better."

"Do you know what happened to him?" JC asked.

"Not really," she said. "But maybe I do."

"What do you think happened?" JC carefully inquired.

"It's a complicated answer," Louise said. "It was a complicated time, I guess. At least, it might seem like that to those who didn't live during those times."

Louise looked to the west, through three large panes of glass in the next room. It was separated from the rest of the house only by a low wall of concrete blocks. The windows offered an unobstructed view of the foothills.

"That was our bedroom," she said serenely of the room with the large windows. "We had tie-dyed curtains when we wanted privacy. Otherwise, we loved the view."

JC and Robin sat silently. Louise was transporting herself back into the 1970s.

"Corny and Winston shared a small house they rented in Denver, while they were in college," Louise told them. "I guess I spent a lot of time down there, too. We had a wonderful time together."

"Corny had come to school from the Plains, Burlington maybe. He had a full scholarship. He was smart," Louise explained. "But he lost the scholarship his sophomore year, through no fault of his own. There were budget cuts."

"He didn't want to drop out of school, but he didn't know what to do," she said. "Then, everything was suddenly paid for. He could afford college and he could share the rent with Winston. And he could afford it when we all went out to a bar or whatever."

"I asked Winston if he was giving Corny money," she told them. "Winston's family had quite a bit of money, you see. And it would be just like Winston to do that. He and Corny were such good friends. But I was surprised, because I didn't think Corny was the kind that would accept that much charity. I mean, college tuition and rent and eating and what have you? That was a lot of money.

"That's when Winston told me that Corny was selling drugs," Louise said in a slightly quieter voice. "Not the horrid drugs like heroin or cocaine. He sold a lot of pot, and LSD and mushrooms."

"They were the toys of our generation. Turn on, tune in," she said. JC knew that she was trying to explain a different time in the human experience, one identified with the 1960s and '70s.

"We certainly did our share," she said with a coy smile.

"Well, Corny turned out to be a good salesman. People liked him," Louise said. "And he made enough money to stay in school and pay his expenses. And there was always some inventory left to take care of *our* needs." She smiled a naughty smile again to JC and Robin.

"Did he ever get arrested?" Robin asked.

"No," Louise said, dismissing the possibility. "He wasn't greedy. He was good to his customers and they were loyal to him. They were his friends and he treated them like friends."

"Just before graduation," she continued, "Winston and Corny threw a big bash for a big group of friends. I was there. They just wanted to thank everyone for being their friends. It was one of the last occasions they'd have to be together before they all graduated and went their separate ways to save the world."

"Winston and Corny both put down a lot of cash," she smiled at the memory. "They bought lobster and shrimp and oysters and wine and lots of grass! It was lavish," she laughed.

"That had something to do with why police think Corny was involved in Winston's disappearance," the woman told them. "Because Winston had all that money and they couldn't figure out how Corny had any money at all, unless he stole it from Winston!"

"Which you're sure he hadn't?" JC asked.

"I knew what Corny was doing. He didn't keep any secrets from me," she said, waving her hand to shoo away the notion that Cornheiser would steal from his friend.

"And mind you," Louise cautioned, "Winston had Corny's permission to reach into his box of tricks, drugs I mean, and take anything he wanted to *anytime* he wanted to." She began to look out the large windows.

"The drugs?" JC asked, interrupting whatever thoughts she was having. Louise nodded.

"One day," Louise began, "I was at class. I was a year behind Winston and Corny. I was a college junior. Winston had stayed here the night before and said he might go up into the hills and drop some acid or something, just enjoy the day."

Her mood had become somber. She put her hand to her mouth and paused. She was on the verge of tears.

"He wasn't here when I came back from class, and he didn't come home that night," she said sadly. "I never saw Winston again."

"Did they ever find his car?" JC asked.

"His car was here. He didn't take it. I knew what had happened," she said. "But I called Corny. I asked if he knew where Winston was, of course. He said he didn't. I asked him if he knew what Winston would have been dropping that day. He said it might have been LSD or he might have added something to it. A little of this, a little of that." She smiled a weak smile. "It was a different time. People today wouldn't understand."

"You looked for him?" JC suggested.

"Forever," Louise said. "Or at least, it felt like forever. Corny rushed up from Denver and we walked across the street," she waved at the foothills in full view out her window. "It doesn't look very big, but it is. I'm sure that we didn't cover half of that hillside."

"Did you call the police?" JC asked.

"Yes," she said. "But we didn't tell them the whole truth. We just wanted them to help find him. We wouldn't believe that he was dead, so we didn't want to tell the police that my boyfriend took a massive amount of drugs and probably overdosed, you know? If they found him alive, they'd have arrested him and put him in prison. That's how times were, then."

"This may sound random, but what was he wearing that morning?" JC asked her.

"The uniform, what we all wore back then," she said, again thinking of a sweet memory. "Blue jeans, a tee shirt. He got the tee shirt as a giveaway at a concert at Hughes Stadium. A radio station was throwing them into the crowd. It was yellow and had a silhouette of a guy playing a guitar. The silhouette had a huge Afro."

"And you never saw Winston or heard from him again?" JC asked.

"Oh, I saw him hundreds of times," she told JC, looking into his eyes. "But it was never him. I'd see him on the street, I'd see him at concerts, I'd see him on TV, but it was never him. I loved him. I'd see him everywhere."

Her head bowed, exhausted from reliving that pain. JC turned his eyes subtly to Robin. It was time for them to go.

JC thanked Louise for baring her soul to them. Robin gave her a long hug.

"I just hope that it helps Corny," Louise told them. "He didn't do anything. He was devastated by losing Winston, and blaming himself, being the drug dealer, you know?"

"What happened to Cornheiser after that?" JC asked.

"He wandered," she said. "He couldn't stay here. I'd get a postcard from Santa Fe, then I'd get a postcard from San Francisco. Eventually, I didn't get any more postcards."

Driving away from the yellow house of concrete blocks, JC and Robin were silent. They were both thinking about the three lives of Louise, Winston and Corny.

Until now, JC and Robin never knew that those lives were lived. Most of the world would never know. Driving away in JC's car, they both thought about the crushing loss those friends had suffered.

"And yet, the world keeps turning," Robin said.

"How did you know what I was thinking?" JC asked as he swung his head in her direction.

"A woman just knows," she said with a tired face.

35

They spent the night at the Armstrong Hotel, in downtown Fort Collins. Louise had told them that it used to be a flophouse, where those losing life's struggles could find a cheap place to sleep.

Now, it was a boutique hotel with architecture, stairwells, molding on the ceiling and a lobby from another era.

They had breakfast at Vern's, a diner north of town serving food since the end of World War ll. They ate by a window with a view of the mountains and under the watchful eyes of taxidermy mounts of elk and buffalo.

JC had suggested to Robin, before they left Denver, that she pack a small bag. He also suggested *what* she might want to pack. She loved Fort Collins. So did he. Without saying it, they both wondered what a future there would be like.

After breakfast, JC drove them back to Overland Trail Road. They parked in the driveway to Louise's yellow concrete block house. They knew she wouldn't be there. She'd be at her real home with her real family.

JC and Robin crossed the road, hopped a fence and walked west. Much of the long grass was uncovered, thought matted by the snow that had buried it until melting. It was a typical Colorado winter day. The sun made the air feel warmer than the temperature.

They began to exert themselves as they hiked up the foothills.

"This was all the real Overland Trail," JC said as they rested and turned back toward the road where they parked. "The pioneers walked or rode along here searching for a pass that would take them west. I think they found the best one further north, in Wyoming."

"Who owns this land?" Robin asked.

"Colorado State University bought it for their Foothills Campus," JC told her.

"There used to be three mountain lion cubs in a small building down there," he pointed toward the road. "I think their mother had been killed. So, the cubs were raised in the little building with a stockade fence in the back. It allowed them to go outside. I used to go peek between the fence posts and sometimes I'd have a curious mountain lion eye peeking back at me."

"What would you be doing here?" Robin asked.

"I lived on Overland Trail Road, too," he said. "I used to walk my dog on the foothills campus. Sometimes, we'd come see the mountain lion cubs. They were growing up by then. Anyway, they'd play."

"Your dog would play with mountain lions?" Robin asked.

"Well, the lions were on one side of a very sturdy fence and my dog and I were on the other side. It was fun," JC told her. "The dog and the cats would catch each other's scents first, then they'd peer through the cracks between the stockade fence posts and they'd chase each other back and forth along the fence. Like I said, it was fun."

"There are a few more structures here now?" she suggested.

"Yeah," he said. "There's an equine center for horses. And that's a center where they study natural gas." He was pointing to a facility to their south.

"Louise says this all used to be a pretty quiet place. There weren't any buildings at all. Just long grass blowing in the wind," JC said. "The school probably purchased it knowing that they'd need the space, decades from then. Louise said that she and Winston used to come up here for romantic picnics. That's why we're here."

"Oooo," Robin teased. "We're here for romance?"

"We're here to find Winston," JC told her.

They walked further up the hill. On the other side would be Horsetooth Reservoir, a popular recreation area. But JC and Robin were walking as far away from any development as possible.

"Following the force," JC said. "Put yourself in his shoes. Where would you want to be if you were looking for a good view to drop some acid?"

They walked horizontally for long stretches of time, then they climbed higher on the hillside. They stopped and shared a lunch they had brought. They admired an enormous letter "A" to their south. It was outlined by rocks on the hillside and painted white. It could be seen for miles.

"That's from when CSU was known as the 'Aggies,' primarily an agricultural school," JC told her. "We won't go any closer. That direction gets its fair share of foot traffic. He would have been found by now if that's where he was."

They continued to walk in a direction chosen to remain as far as they could from any man-made development. They walked with about twenty yards spread between them.

"Having fun?" JC asked, not knowing what to expect for an answer.

"I like hiking," Robin said. "And this is our day off!"

"I've got to like your enthusiasm," JC told her as he laughed. "You could have been the social director for the invasion of Omaha Beach. You would have said, 'We're going to the beach? Yay.'"

They both laughed at that.

"There's nothing wrong with having a good attitude," Robin protested.

"Nope," JC confirmed. "Nothing like a good attitude at altitude."

Robin didn't respond. That registered with JC. It wasn't a common occurrence for Robin. He turned around and saw that she'd stopped. She was looking at a collection of short brush.

"What's up," JC asked her as he hiked the steep decline back down to her. She continued to look at the brush, and then looked at him.

JC searched the brush with his eyes and saw a hiking boot. Not far from it was a faded pant leg.

"Stay here," he advised her, and he walked forward to investigate.

"That's him, isn't it?" she said next to his shoulder. JC looked at her and then at the spot where he had told her to wait. I guess I should get used to this, he thought.

"Don't touch anything," JC said. "This will be treated as a potential crime scene as soon as we call police."

Closer to the brush, they could see the boot, a pair of faded jeans and some bones. The bones had been scattered, probably by animals scavenging.

There was also what may have been a tee shirt. It had been in the weather for so long, it was dirty and its color had faded to white. But there was still a faint figure on it of a man playing a guitar.

Police told JC that modern science would probably be able to identify him, especially because they knew who they were looking for.

"Hair might do it," an investigator from the Larimer County Sheriff's Office told him. "It's nothing but bones, but it looks like there's some hair. Hair is a great source of DNA. We'll check with his family and get a hair sample from them. Where can you be found?"

JC gave the investigator a card. The law officer then put JC's name together with his face. He recognized him from television.

"You're one of the good ones," the investigator said, smiling. "What were you doing up here?"

"Looking for him," JC said. That elicited a surprised look from the law enforcer.

"Why would you be looking for him up here?" the investigator inquired. "I'd be suspicious, but if it's who you think it is, he may have died before you were born."

"I think you're right," JC told him. "We're working on a story, tying up loose ends."

"Any idea what he would be doing up here?" the investigator asked.

"No idea," JC told him. The same hair sample they would use to identify him would also find what killed him, if they looked for it.

People today would not understand, he remembered Louise saying.

JC and Robin stayed in Fort Collins that night to report live on the discovery of human remains in the foothills overlooking Fort Collins. JC also told the audience that there was reason to believe the remains belonged to Winston Reddish who had been missing for forty-five years.

It didn't turn out to be a day off for JC and Robin, after all. And there would probably be more to do tomorrow.

JC called Louise, telling her what they had found. There was both gratitude in her voice and sorrow.

"All that time," she said. "He was so close by."

The journalist also called Colin Cornheiser in New York. The news was first met with silence.

"Winston," Cornheiser whispered. "I'm glad you found him. And I'm glad the truth is out. I should thank you," the county executive said. "I know what's going to come. I'm going to have some explaining to do, about my past."

"They seem to think of you as family in Joseph," JC told him. "Family tries to understand."

"I'll have to reach out to Winston's family too," Cornheiser said. He almost sounded like he was talking to himself. "I'll have to say I'm sorry. I'm going to have to tell so many people I'm sorry."

The reporter had covered many politicians during their falls from grace. Cornheiser would have to explain his background as a drug dealer. Louise might be right, people today would not understand.

JC gave Louise's contact information to Cornheiser. She had asked JC to do that.

"I blamed myself for Winston's death," Cornheiser told JC over the phone. "I went through a pretty dark period. I got strung out on my own stuff. I went to Santa Fe for a while and then I drifted to San Francisco and got lost in the lifestyle there."

"Those are the missing years I was asking about?" JC asked.

"Yes," Cornheiser responded. "I guess I'm glad it's all going to come out. I won't have any more secrets."

So, Cornheiser was innocent, JC thought, at least of murder. And at least according to the mores of the "Love and Drugs Generation." Maybe not according to today's standards.

And because Winston had helped himself to Corny's stash, Colin Cornheiser probably would not be guilty of anything the statute of limitations hadn't expired on a long time ago.

Voters in America rarely elected former drug dealers to lead their government. But forgiveness was a common American trait. Colin Cornheiser would have to live with the voters' verdict, come the next election. He would have to live with himself for the rest of his life.

"They're not always guilty, you know," JC told his assignment editor over the phone. "And sometimes they're guilty, just not what you thought they were guilty of."

JC was alone in his apartment in Larimer Square. He wanted a good night's rest and to catch up on things at home. Robin had agreed and kissed him good night when he dropped her off at her apartment in the trendy RiNo District in Denver. The kiss nearly changed his mind about where he wanted to spend the night.

With his feet up on the coffee table and sipping a wee dram of Dalmore, he had little interest in flipping through social media, even as he did exactly that.

One post, though, caught his attention. A friend informed JC that Shara had called off her engagement.

As he slowly began to fold the top down on his laptop, another message caught his eye. It was from Shara. It said, "Thinking of you."

"Now what?"

Acknowledgements

My education in archaeology was a welcome crash course while I was working as a journalist. Dedicated professionals like the late David Starbuck at Plymouth State University in New Hampshire and Bill Bouchard, Tricia Barbagallo and everyone at Karen Hartgen Archaeological Associates in Rensselaer, N.Y., took time to explain things to me.

Darrel Pinckney, an archaeologist now with Caretakers of History, as well as an adjunct professor at Schenectady County Community College, did the fact-checking on my work for this novel.

Dean Snow, in his fascinating book titled *1777: Tipping Point at Saratoga*, wrote one of the best explanations regarding the mystery surrounding the whereabouts of General Simon Fraser's remains.

The late David Pitkin, author of *Haunted Saratoga County*, described to me some of the ghostly apparitions at the battlefield.

Saratoga National Historic Park, the site of the battlefield, is a treasure of stories and artifacts regarding the combat and the combatants there.

The late Patrick Glavin, of Albany, was an Irish gentleman. He is the true owner of his childhood tale about running guns for the IRA.

Lake Placid Lodge was a wonderful host while we conducted research. Ernie Rice provided some valuable background of the region.

And I want to thank the good people of northern Essex County who allowed me to annex some of them into my fictional county of Joseph.

Thank you to my editor, Deirdre Stoelzle, who can see what I cannot.

Thanks, also, to Debbi Wraga, the Morrows, and Clark and Lu French at Shires Press for helping get this book to readers.

About the Author

Phil Bayly was a television and radio journalist for over four decades. He was a reporter and anchor for WNYT-TV in New York's state capital, Albany. He anchored the top-rated morning news for fifteen years.

He attended the University of Denver and is a graduate of Colorado State University.

He's been a ski racer and a ski bum. It's too late to stop.

He was born and raised in Evanston, Illinois. He lived and worked in Colorado, Wyoming, Pennsylvania and New York. He now resides in Saratoga County, New York.

Visit Phil at murderonskis.com.

CPSIA information can be obtained
at www.ICGtesting.com
Printed in the USA
BVHW031308201121
621900BV00005B/20